# THE MEMORIES WE PAINTED

## CAITLIN MILLER

Printed in the United States of America

Cover by Hannah Linder
Edited by Ellen McGinty

ISBN 978-1-955057-02-8 (paperback)
ISBN 978-1-955057-03-5 (e-book)

To Grace—
Without your story, I never
would have written mine.
Thank you for being brave,
and for showing me
what courage looks like.

# CHAPTER 1

I was six years old that night—the night I learned what the words *handicap* and *limitations* meant, felt like.

Words that went right over my head a year ago now plunged into my heart and hurt it so bad. Why couldn't I do the one thing I desperately wanted to, the one desire that bled into my thoughts during the day and dreams at night? Why couldn't I show everyone that they were wrong about me—that I could be okay and walk to school and run around the schoolyard with my friends during lunch break again?

But all of them—the doctors, the specialists, even my parents—told me that I couldn't. Not now, and maybe never. Something had changed with a cup of water—a handful of infected liquid I downed as a young kid, not knowing what the difference between clean water and infected water could do to my body. How it could make my legs and feet go to sleep forever . . . never wake up again. Paralyzed. And I could never un-drink that cup of water, could never undo what had been done.

And as I sat there in my bed, desperation clung to me like a too-heavy blanket, and I wanted to throw it off and watch it burn. I wanted to stand on my own two feet—and I knew I had to try.

Twenty minutes later, after hallway lights dimmed from bulb-yellow to dark and my parents came in, said goodnight, kissed my cheek, and made promises none of us could believe then—I'd be okay, and someday things would get better—and the house was sleep-quiet, I knew it was now or never.

*Never* was the deck of cards this illness handed me. *Now* was what I chose, and I threw away that set of cards—spades of impossibilities, clovers of limitations, hearts of disappointment, and diamonds of cutting loss—and picked up my own stack.

My heart swelled beyond recognition in my little chest. I think that's what fear and wondering and daring felt like on the inside.

Then somehow—I don't really know how—I swung my legs over the side of the bed, and they dangled there: inches from the floorboards and yet a million miles away. That's what my limitation, my handicap, had reduced me to: always leaving me so close to what I desperately wanted but never allowing me to quite reach it. It was always dangling up above or down below . . . unreachable.

The earthquake-shaky breath that got past my throat, out my lips, shouldn't have been something I was so acquainted with. It was too heavy, too burdened, too *everything.*

But I knew it all the same.

I wanted to know something different. Like floorboards beneath my feet. Like green blades of grass between my toes. Like pockets of leftover rain in the cracks on the sidewalk tickling my ankles.

Enough *be-careful's.* Enough *you-can't-walk's.* Enough *you-have-polio's.* Enough things limiting me. Enough. This was my Lazarus moment: *wake up . . . come out. Live again.*

I squeezed my eyes shut and willed my legs down another three inches, painfully slow. I mouthed *one, two, three, four, five* on my lips, giving myself five seconds to have the soles of my feet on the floor. When those five seconds were over, my eyes shot open, and I looked down at my feet. Warm air left my mouth, a breath I didn't even know was dammed in my chest.

My eyes opened a little wider, rapid-blinking wonder and fear: I'd done it. My feet were on the ground, the December-cold floorboards my bare and feeling-less toes were numb to.

I grabbed onto the metal bed frame, gripped it tightly with all ten of my fingers, and slowly, slowly, pushed myself up. My fingers and knuckles lost color and feeling. But I'd never felt more at that moment—more alive, more real, more me ... more *Josie.*

My shaking and swaying *back-forth-back-forth* legs would have registered a 6.0 on the Richter scale. Maybe it was because I was actually scaring away all the odds that told me I could never do what I was doing right then: holding on and standing up. Maybe it was because my legs weren't the same anymore, and they couldn't help but tumble about like granules in a saltshaker when I tried to do what my bones and nerves had deemed impossible. Maybe it was a hundred things.

But those things didn't matter.

What mattered was this moment that I wanted to freeze in time —my waking-up-and-coming-out-Lazarus-moment.

My eyes brimmed with the kind of tears that burned but wouldn't leak out from my eyelids. They just stayed there, making my eyes look like watery glass. I felt like that—like glass. Like I might shatter at any second. Like this moment was so fragile, I would either stay together or break apart. And I didn't know which one I'd be in five seconds or five minutes from now.

But I knew one thing for sure: this little victory—me taking the first step, defying the *no's* and the impossible odds—lifted my heart a little higher. And my heart hammered in my chest, loud and aching. I could see it falling and rising against the cotton nightgown that clung to my chest with sweat.

I wanted this. Needed this.

I closed my eyes, but the moment was briefer than the five seconds I'd closed them just a minute ago. I felt a breath of air come out my mouth, and instinctively my hands shot out in front of me. A protective instinct that every one of us has inside when we're about to hit something. When we're about to crash and fall, break skin or bones.

My eyes were still closed, and I didn't have time to open them before my palms slammed hard into something and stung. The pain made my eyes open as I gasped, gulped in air like a thirsty person devoured water.

But something was different—my perspective was different. Not me seeing this moment on my feet differently . . . me seeing my *bedroom* differently. Not right-side-up and me looking at the bedroom door five feet ahead of where I stood and at the walls covered in purple and pink artwork of unicorns and rainbows on either side of the door frame.

No.

Now I saw the room sideways, like a tilted movie screen, floorboards inches from my eyes, pressing against my nose, my face, the left side of my body. Any part of me it could touch, it did.

*What happened?*

A feeling, a crashing. A noise, a thudding. A sound, a screaming.

My body giving out, tumbling to the ground, leaving me a tangled mess of limbs on the floor. A scream that followed a gasp, leaving my mouth wide open, a horribly perfect *O*-shape.

I fell. I broke. Shattered into sharp fragments of glass on the floor. And when I attempted to move, to get up and try again, I couldn't. Every part of me hurt. No part of me worked.

It hit me like a ton of bricks as I laid there, crying: I wasn't just shattered—I was broken. I couldn't hold myself up. How could I possibly hold the weight of all this brokenness?

I hit rock bottom, the lowest place I could be there on the ground, palms stinging like a swarm of bees plunging their stinger into one's flesh. The bottom fell through—and I was free-falling in the lonely dark.

A sliver of yellow light—the hallway light—filtered in from under my door, and then two feet and two legs came running towards me, bent beside me. Two legs and feet that could do everything that mine couldn't: walk, run, carry me wherever I wanted to go. Down the cobblestone street, around the windy block, across the ocean-water-and-green-earth world.

*Mom.*

"Jo!" The aftermath of Mom's scream echoed in the room, in my ears, in my head and heart.

Mom's eyes found mine as she lifted me up, cradled her soon-to-be first grader in her arms. She held me so close, like she was afraid I'd disappear if she let go. I was afraid, too.

Her eyes mirrored mine: blue irises full of tears, disappointment, pain. I felt mine close, and all I could see was thick and heavy blackness. All I wanted was to stand for five minutes while others could stand for a lifetime. Was that asking too much? My limp form on the ground, legs still on the floor and the upper half of me on Mom's lap, said it all: yes, it was—it was asking too much.

And right there on the cold floor, as strong arms that had carried me almost all of my young life, always warm and safe and comforting—Dad's arms—lifted me up, I left my dreams down there and picked up my reality:

*Limitations. Handicaps. Polio. No's.*

It hurt worse than anything.

# CHAPTER 2

**JUNE 21, 1951**
**(Present Day)**

"What do you think?"

What should have taken me three minutes to show, say, and ask, took me thirteen minutes to get the courage to do—and an additional twelve seconds before I lifted my hands from their hiding place under the table. I pulled out an envelope, cleared my throat, told my parents I'd gotten a letter yesterday, and gave voice to the words my aunt had written to me on two sheets of rosebud paper.

An invitation to do something new. An opportunity to grow—to stretch my wings a little wider. A gentle whisper to go and a strong urge to answer that voice, to say *yes,* no matter how wild or impossible that rosebud-stationary-calling sounded.

My fingers held three things in two hands: a letter, anxiety, and hope. Reading that letter did something to me—awakened me somehow. A stirring, a desire, a rebirthing of dreams and longings I thought my medical condition had slammed the door shut on, locked tight. But maybe now I could pick the lock, unhinge the rusty hinges, knock the door down flat on its back.

Mom and Dad watched each other, their eyes meeting in silent communion, wordlessly expressing all their questions and *I-don't-knows*. Mom and Dad didn't always need words. They heard the other through the sighs or the deep breaths they took, read their thoughts through the furrowed brows that dug trenches in their foreheads when worried, or the way their eyes lit up like fireflies when excited.

"I don't know, Josie." Mom started half-shaking her head *no*, her words directed to me, but her eyes still glued on Dad. I looked over at Dad, too. I tried to find an anchor there: something to hold on to; a sign of hope that I wasn't crazy for wanting to accept my aunt's invitation to stay at her home while she and my cousin Sophie—my best friend—traveled abroad for the next few months.

Dad looked at me, torn by the fear in Mom's eyes and the longing in mine. He was still holding Aunt Carol's crinkled letter in his hands along with the envelope I'd ripped open earlier and the words I'd read faster than I could even process them.

"How long would you be gone?" Dad was giving me a chance, being the anchor that I needed to stay afloat . . . and I wasn't going to miss it.

"Over the summer until Aunt Carol and Sophie get back from their trip, so for the next few months. Or just a month—whatever you and Mom think is best. I just—"

"But what would you do there?" Dad sank back into his chair and his thoughts.

I'd thought about that, too. The mental list of things I could do and the ways I could spend my summer days at my aunt's home was incredibly short. But I could do the one thing I truly believed I was born to do. Oh, not like destiny or fate or anything like that. But something I was given the moment I was born and blinked in the world full of colors and sights and sounds through my infant eyes for the first time—a love for art.

"Work on my paintings, mostly."

Dad's eyes softened a little around the edges. Mom's, too. Dad saw that desire to paint when I was a little kid, and Mom bought me my first paint set, and how I lived and breathed the same air under the same sky that the whole world did, but I saw things differently. I didn't just see existence; I saw stories and memories and things that needed to be remembered. Not with words, but with colors. Not with sounds, but with shapes and strokes and texture. Not with perfection, but with detailed simplicity.

"I've never been to New York before, and there will be so many new places and things for me to paint," I went on. I'd used my Pennsylvania-home landscape as the backdrop or center of a hundred paintings I'd done over the years. I wanted new sights, new things, new people to paint.

"But you'll be all alone, Jo." I think that world—*alone*—scared Mom. Not because she was afraid that I'd do something wrong or she didn't trust me, or that I wasn't old enough to be on my own. But because of what that word meant—*alone*: without anyone right there to help me if I needed it. Being hundreds of miles away instead of just a bedroom apart.

"I can do this, Mom."

Somehow, I knew I was ready for this chapter in my life, even though I felt so unprepared for it. Somehow, beneath all the *what-ifs* and *buts* and *how's* and every other insurmountable thing running marathons in my mind . . . I could do this. And I silently prayed Mom could see that conviction. *I'm ready.*

Mom searched my eyes, and I knew—knew she was looking at me and through me, needing to know that if I did this, I would be okay . . . that her letting me go for however long—weeks or months— wasn't a mistake that would devastate us like my health diagnosis did. Our reeling from that broke us so badly . . . and the only way we made it through was because our broken pieces put together were *holding* us together. Sharp, hurting edges of our three hearts glued into one kept us whole when my diagnosis came, and for every one of the thousands of days we lived the hellish aftermath of it.

We'd never been apart for more than a few days at a time—when Dad had to go on business trips for his work—and now, out of the blue, the June sky-blue, I was asking to leave for longer than the sum of Dad's work trips put together.

"I just have this feeling I'm supposed to go. I don't know why . . . but I have this feeling deep down that something's out there for me. And I want to find it. I don't want to miss it." Maybe it sounded cliche—me having this *feeling* that I couldn't rightly put into words that I needed to go to New York—but it was honest: and it wasn't a feeling that would be there today and fade away tomorrow. It was deep-rooted—and those roots were begging to be given a chance to grow.

My eyes dropped down to the table, focused on the cotton napkin folded across my lap. My neck ached, but I couldn't lift it. It was as if the burden of this moment was so heavy and weighed me down so hard, I couldn't lift myself back up—and it just held me there, arrested me in that neck-aching position like a prisoner locked behind bars.

"Well" —Dad's voice— "before your mom and I decide, let's talk about some of the details." There was the lawyer in Dad—asking questions, seeking answers, figuring out solutions to problems, finding perspective in a hazy mess.

An hour later, they were decided. I'd stay until September—the full length of Aunt Carol and Sophie's trip. I'd go by train because it was cheaper than flying, and Mom had always been wary of airplanes. She wanted our feet planted on the ground and not dangling in the sky. Dad had saved up enough money over the years that he could give me enough to tide me over the next few months to cover my expenses.

It seemed too perfect, like the pieces had fit together too easily, and I was afraid this couldn't be real.

Dad's chair scraped against the floor, screeching in protest as he pushed it out and stood up. "I'm going to drive by the station and see if I can get you a ticket for next week. We can work through the rest of the details and call Carol in the morning."

That was his *yes,* the answering to prayers I'd sent under my breath up to heaven a hundred times around this old dinner table.

Mom looked at him and nodded her *yes,* too.

Before I could stretch out my arms across the table and grab onto Dad's hand and squeeze it tight and hope my touch expressed everything I couldn't find words to say, Dad was out the door. With a set of jangling keys in his hands, one of them the keys to the car, he stepped into the barely-summer-but-already-warm night.

Everything felt out of sync, like time was slow-ticking; the seconds going *tick-tock-tick-tock* on the clock hand were slow-crawling to the sixty-second mark. And I was still sitting there, hands open, fingers reaching for the ones that had anchored me tonight. But mine were left holding empty air in Dad's absence.

A minute later, a minute that stretched infinitely long, something jolted me out of my mental coma: flesh on flesh, hand on hand. Those fingers, that warm touch, had helped keep my stone-cold heart that was broken from pain and devastated from loss from becoming too cold, freezing to death from the emotional hypothermia that ate away at my chest.

"Mom?" I sounded like a little girl again, my voice fragile as I whispered for her under my breath, needing her.

Mom knelt beside me, held my hand, looked at me with eyes veiled in misty almost-tears. My saying her name with a question mark at the end wasn't me asking if it was she who was right here with me. It was *me*—me needing to know that Mom wasn't angry with me. That she wasn't hurt by my decision and Dad's confirmation of it. That she wasn't disappointed in me for wanting to chase after something I had no idea what I was looking for.

I needed to know that we—her and me—would be okay *when* I left . . . just like Mom needed to know I would be okay *if* I did.

Mom nodded her head so soft I would have missed it if I wasn't looking for it. But I was: I was wading chest-deep through murky waters, searching more intently for what I needed to see down there in the ocean depths than ever before. A sign, a word, a reaction—anything to tell me we'd be okay. And her nod, the slightest bobbing of her head that made her shoulder-length brown strands of hair tickle her collar bone, helped me more than she could ever know.

I could tell Mom was searching for words—she got this look on her face when her mind wandered, combined letters into words, and put those words together and formulated sentences.

In the end, Mom chose eight letters, three words, one sentence: *I love you.*

I think three word-sentences are some of the most powerful and life-giving ones we can ever speak.

They hold forgiveness: *I forgive you.*

They hold reminders: *It'll be okay.*

They hold promises: *Never letting go.*

They hold presence: *I'm always here.*

They hold pride: *Proud of you.*

But the one I needed to hear the most, the one that wrecked me right there in the silence of our near-empty home, was the one that held love.

"I love you, Jo."

I could see it so clearly—the love in Mom's eyes. But I saw the fear, too. It was still there, overshadowed by love but still present. But wasn't that what love looked like—loving and being afraid?

Wanting the best for someone but afraid of what that meant, of letting go when everything in you still wanted to hold on?

Mom's hand slowly left mine—and it was like both of us were understanding this, beholding an epiphany: Mom's fingers releasing mine was her letting go of me.

Because she loved me.

*No*—I realized. My head was like a clock pendulum, swaying left, right. Mom's love would *never* let go of me. It would hold me, always. Even if holding on looked more like letting go in that moment . . . in the end, it wasn't. It was still holding on. Different, yes. Harder, yes. Impossible? Never.

Love knows no limitations, no boundaries, no time. It lasts through the holding on and the letting go. Lasts through every today and tomorrow and eternity.

I looked at Mom's hand now resting at her side, and then mine. Our fingers weren't woven together, but our hearts were still knit together. Because love is ever close.

"I love you too, Mom."

And I knew then: in a world where not a lot of things were okay, *we* would be okay.

# CHAPTER 3

JUNE 26, 1951
(Present Day)

*Union Pacific System*
*Passenger: Josie L. Carter*
*From: Philadelphia, Pennsylvania*
*To: Adams, New York*
*Issued: June 21, 1951*

The window I sat beside and looked out of from the back seat of the car was a tear-streaked mess of rain. And up beyond that, a mass of angry clouds raised shouts of thunder across the grey sky. That was the only noise that invaded the heavy silence in the car.

I held my train ticket in my hands. If lines could fade away from being reread over and over again, the black ink on my ticket would have disappeared by now. The information on it—my name, where I was going, when I was leaving—was a confirmation to me, my rainbow in the sky, followed with a promise that I'd be okay. That if I took the next step in front of me without knowing where the next one would lead or if I'd end up at a dead-end, I'd made it through whatever these summer months held for me.

Dad positioned behind the wheel, and Mom, in the passanger seat beside him, were as quiet and unmoving and breathless as the mannequins I stopped and stared at when going to *Macy's* department store on shopping trips with Mom.

*What are they thinking?*

I couldn't even keep a mental tab of my thoughts. My mind jumped from one thought to the next before I'd even formulated it, answered the set of mental questions staring me down.

The car dipped a little, thinning tires going over a pothole in the road.

I closed my eyes and listened: to the rain, to my thoughts, to the rhythmic *thump-thump* of my heart that beat in sync with the *tick-tick* of the car blinker as Dad signaled a left turn on the street ahead. The heartbeat in my chest was a reminder to me that my life had purpose and that my story wasn't over, but only beginning—and driving to the train station was like a tangible promise of that purpose, something I could hold in my hands as I did my ticket.

But that reminder didn't make the fear dissipate like smoke plumes. It was still there, crowding my thoughts with its claustrophobia-like presence. My head was like a choir chanting *no, no, no,* in a deep voice and haunting melody, while my heart was gently whispering *yes, yes, yes,* in a soft and reassuring lilt. The battle between my head and heart was one I fought daily—the urge to say *no* out of fear or wisdom. I knew my thoughts. I knew when I was walking away from something because I was scared or because it was the right decision. Every doubt I felt now was based on fear . . . and that's why I was in the car, headed to the station: because it was the right decision.

"We're here." Dad's words were like a safe haven in the midst of the torrential downpour we found ourselves in. I knew he was as sad as those raindrops falling from above, knowing I was leaving, but he didn't show it. He braved a smile just for me. Panic gripped my chest at the idea of leaving him, but his smile comforted me, instilled enough bravery in me to smile back.

Dad shut off the engine. With black umbrellas in hand, he and Mom got out of the car, stood in front of its back door, and waited for me to hand them my suitcase.

The five seconds that passed between me lifting my hands off my lap and putting them on the door handle were impossibly long. I was scared—and opening this car door meant things would change. Every second I hesitated made me want to stay right where I was and not move.

My bare fingers trembled against the door handle, my fear and courage meeting the other in a head-on collision of *will she do it?* and *she will do this.*

"Okay," I whispered, and opened the door. Dad's helping hand waited for me, sheltering me from the rain with his umbrella, a refuge of black leather.

Dad's voice was close. "I've got you, Josie."

I never doubted that.

"Thanks," I whispered, so soft, so quiet. I didn't know if Dad even heard my voice before the sound of my gratitude was drowned out by the torrent of rain pelting the umbrella, merciless like hailstones.

Once my arms found my crutches, were secure there as I hobble-walked beside Dad and Mom a step behind us, I whispered it again: *Okay.*

*Okay, courage . . . you win.*

Courage—it didn't dress up in confidence and readiness, wielding a sword and shield in hand. It showed up still just as scared and unready as it was in the beginning, holding a sling and stone in two trembling hands.

"You know what courage is, Jo?" Dad asked, his breath warm on my ear, like he overheard the secret words I exchanged with myself in the silence of my mind. Dad cocked his head at me. "Courage is what you just did—opened the door, stepped out of the car. It's you walking up to the train platform right now and not backing out when you easily can. It's you holding your train ticket in those shaky hands of yours." His voice dropped, and I leaned in closer to listen, desperate to glean from his words like a farmer gleaned his harvest crop. "Courage is your sling and stone, Jo. Hang on to it, and you'll be okay."

"Thanks, Dad," I whispered.

I looked at Mom and Dad, knowing goodbyes were coming and months of separation would be a reality the moment I stepped out of their warm embraces.

All the words I'd thought, all the lines I'd rehearsed, all the things I planned to tell them and reassure them of . . . I couldn't remember any of it when I looked at their faces. Time was slipping through my fingers—I could hear the train slow-chugging over the tracks, getting close—and I wished I could slow down time, make minutes turn into hours.

"Have a good time, Jo." Dad's hand was on my shoulder. "You know the drill—be careful, stay safe, and check in when you can. We're only a few hours away. If you need us, call us, and we'll be there. Your Mom or I can come take you home at any point. Make sure to be careful and not go outside after dark by yourself."

"I will, Dad." Dad's arms wrapped around me, hugged me close, comforted me.

When I stepped out of Dad's embrace, Mom's arms found me, hugged me as tight as she did when she found me on the floor that night when I was six—hugged me like she was afraid I'd disappear if she let go. Only this time, I would.

"I'll make you proud, Mom." The words surfaced from somewhere deep in me, somewhere I didn't even know was aching and desperate to make her proud, and came out in a hushed whisper.

I hoped she heard them above the rain and the train whistle blowing loud and clusters of strangers talking nearby.

"You already have. You have nothing to prove to me." Mom squeezed tight one more time before letting go.

I knew I needed to go. I heard the train conductor yell *All board!* for the final time. Dad took my suitcase and boarded the train as I stood on the platform with Mom. He found my seat, set my suitcase on the floor beside the seat in the compartment he'd reserved for me last week—*Car A, Compartment E.*

Dad returned, squeezed my shoulder as he walked by—his last goodbye to me—and headed back to the car to get that stubborn engine of fuel to start.

"There's a whole world out there that needs to be painted," Mom said, tears filling her eyes but not spilling over onto her face. "Go do it, Josie Girl."

*Josie Girl*—Mom was the only one who called me that. And in spite of all the sadness and second thoughts and wonderings, that made me smile a little.

The sound of the rain and the car motor running and Mom's whispered *goodbye* all faded away, cut out abruptly when I stepped into the train, and the doors closed minutes later.

I traced Mom and Dad—both their faces barely visible through the rain-streaked glass window I pressed my nose against—and held on to that memory as the train left. Because I had no other choice now but to look ahead.

# CHAPTER 4

**MAY 07, 1937**
**(6 Years Old)**

Close to six months—that's how long it had been since my polio diagnosis.

Every one of those days bled into a nightmarishly long one, and they all felt the same: because they were all filled with whispers. Nearly silent exchanges between my parents and every doctor, therapist, and specialist they'd taken me to, hoping that each new appointment would be the one to resurrect hope, to give me an answer.

I pretended not to hear the hushed whispers between my parents in the car, at home, in their bedroom during the long nights, but I heard every word of it. Sometimes it was easier to pretend I couldn't hear them, to drown out the sound of their voices with my own. I was tired of whispers, of appointments, of everything. And in the tomb-like silence of the night, I cried into my pillow, soaked my pillowcase in tears and snot, whenever I couldn't make-believe these past six months hadn't been real, weren't still real, right now.

It was happening again: hushed whispers outside the door between my parents and a doctor. And as I sat in bed and waited for the news I expected to get but didn't want to hear, I clapped my hands over my ears.

*I'm sorry . . . no change.*

Their silence shouldn't have been so deafening to my muffled ears. Their desperation shouldn't have been something I recognized well enough to trace like I could circles or straight lines. The sadness on their faces shouldn't have been so seeable to me through the closed door separating us. But closed doors can't shut out pain.

A minute later, the door opened. The light cast shadows that imitated the objects in my room—my dresser filled with neatly folded clothes, my clean desk, and a bin full of toys I never played with anymore—and Mom's figure filling the floor space.

"Hi." Mom tried to smile—and she sort of did—but I knew it was a smile that couldn't pretend everything was okay when it clearly wasn't. Tears flickered in her eyes like the silhouette of city lights I watched each night from my bedroom window while falling asleep.

Mom sat on the edge of my bed, close enough to reach out and hug me. She looked out the window, but I knew nothing out there had caught her eye. No. She didn't want me to see the pain in her eyes.

I couldn't sit there and watch Mom wrestle to find words, to gently tell her six-year-old daughter news that would break her little heart. "I know nothing's changed, Mom. I know I won't walk again."

Mom still didn't look at me, didn't take her eyes off the window and the colorful landscape now a shadowland of dark structures, void of color, under the night sky. She was afraid to tell me those words I spoke just now because she didn't want to break my heart. But her heart busted in two hearing those words fall from my lips with brutal honesty—fast and detrimental like a sinking ship.

"Things might change, honey. Just . . . not right now."

I may have been young, but I wasn't naive. I knew the odds were stacked so high against me that there wasn't room for hope, and it was a wonder those odds hadn't toppled over and buried me alive, Pain had forced me to grow up more in maturity than I had inches in height—faster than I ever should have. My biggest concern at that age should have been what toys to play with or making sure I didn't miss any episodes of my favorite radio shows: *Little Orphan Annie and The Lone Ranger.*

"*Might* doesn't mean they will. *Might* doesn't mean anything—"

"*Might,*" Mom cut me off, knowing where my list of *might's* would lead to, "means that—*might.* It doesn't mean *yes* yet, but it doesn't mean *no,* either. But until then, you've got to keep living and doing things as best as you can."

I picked at the tiny fuzz balls on my cotton blanket, rolled them in circles between my index and middle finger, massaging my anger. "I can't do anything, Mom." I was a volcano about to explode, about to spew fiery lava onto everything before me, and we both knew it. "I can't stand. I can't walk. I can't go to school and play with my friends. I just . . . sit."

Mom didn't flinch. Didn't sigh. Didn't walk out of the room and try to talk some sense into me again later.

She stayed. Came closer. Looked at me.

"If your world is only as big as your abilities allow it to be, then you truly live in a small place, Josie Girl." Mom's words whispered close to my ear were like sirens blaring in my heart. Sirens that begged me to hear what Mom was telling me, that despite every dream and hope and longing in me that had died, I could still live somehow—here, now.

Mom's eyes dared me to try, to not give up. My eyes begged her to help me, to show me how to keep going. As if reading that plea that didn't need words to be heard, Mom squeezed my shoulder, said she'd be right back. And true to her word, Mom came right back, but the hands that were empty on her way out were now full. A cardboard box with its flaps peeled open was the object her hands wrapped around and carefully held.

"I bought something for you this morning." Mom set the box beside me, stepped back, gave me space to see what was inside for myself. "I thought of you when I saw it."

I leaned forward, curiosity tamping out my anger, and made a mental inventory of what was there: a sketchbook, a palette, three paintbrushes, and four tubes of paint.

I looked from Mom's gift to her, trying to understand, to piece together the puzzle before me. But it felt like half the pieces were missing, and I was left trying to figure out how to make sense of the ones I had, to make them fit together in an imperfect shape.

"Do you remember that painting you gave me when you were in preschool?"

I remembered. My preschool teacher told me and the other four-year-old's in my class to paint a picture for Mother's Day. And when that Sunday came, I ran into Mom's room before the sun had barely blinked its own heavy eyes and cracked light over the night sky. I jumped onto the bed she shared with Dad and gave her the first painting I'd ever done—a butterfly with wide-spread wings flying into an infinite blue sky above.

Mom's eyes had been as radiant as sunlight as she cupped my face into her soft hands, her voice filled with pride as she told me it was the most special gift she'd ever received. She framed it in her bedroom that same day, gave it a home on her nightstand. It was still there, now.

"Jo, when I went to pick you up the next day from preschool, I ran into your teacher, and she told me that your painting was one of the best she'd ever seen a preschooler do. She wasn't just saying that to be nice—she meant it. You have potential, Jo . . . and you should grow that talent."

"I don't know—I don't know if I can do it." Wouldn't I have known for myself if I had a talent for art? Wouldn't there have been a feeling . . . a confirmation . . . something? That butterfly had looked like an ordinary butterfly to me, not something that showcased talent and caused a teacher to take note of.

Mom knelt beside my bed, looked at me. "Rarely does any person look at something they've done and thought that they could do it. But they try anyway, regardless of whatever excuses could hold them back." Mom's eyes didn't leave my face for a second. "You have talent, Josie Girl—and just because you can't see it doesn't mean it's not there. *I* see it. You just have to be willing to trust me to be your eyes until you can see it with your own."

I stayed still for what felt like the longest time. Mom didn't move from where she was on the floor, didn't stand up and stretch out her legs even though they had to be tingling with numbness by now. I was scared to say something, to shatter the silence with words, because I knew: if I tried this—the one thing I could actually do—and I failed, it would wreck me. But if I didn't try, I'd never know, and I'd always wonder if I *could* have done it. The madness of it would send me on an eternal trek through a mental wilderness from which I would never return until I'd found the answer to my question—*could I have done it?*

Both the *yes* and the *no* held something that would hurt me—the pain of trying and maybe failing, and the pain of not trying and never knowing.

I didn't want to get cut by either of those sharp edges . . . but I had to reach out and choose one to hold all the same.

"I'm scared, Mom." My voice cracked, unexpected. Or maybe it was expected. Until I heard my voice crack like a fractured bone, I didn't know I was crying—and from the tears that had already stained my cheeks and caked onto them, I'd been crying for minutes. "What if I can't do it? There's nothing else I *can* do . . . "

"If you try and it doesn't work, try again. And if you want to try something new, try whatever it is. There's something out there that you can do, Jo. Just because your legs and feet don't work doesn't mean your arms and hands have stopped working, too. There's so much of you still that can make a difference in the world, do something incredible. Nothing can take that away from you. Nothing."

*Try.*

No one could guarantee the success of anything because, in life, nothing was certain. Today wasn't certain. Tomorrow wasn't guaranteed. The future could hold anything from the best of the best to the worst of the worst.

But no one could deny success, either, until first, they'd tried.

My small hands reached out and barely cupped the sides of Mom's face. My thumbs climbed up the skin on her face until they reached her eyes. Mom's eyes closed, and I fingered the soft skin that protected her pupils from harm.

"Please be my eyes." My voice was still shaky and scared and unsure. "Please."

And she became the set of eyes I adopted there, like how one adopted a pair of spectacles to help them see better, clearer, stronger. She was all three of those things to me—and three million more.

"I want to try."

There it was: my first attempt—my *try*.

# CHAPTER 5

*Adams, New York*—home to approximately two million fewer people than my hometown.

That was one of the first things I noticed when I got off the train —how there was still the hustle and bustle found in every train station, with people catching trains and getting off them—but that something was missing in that population of roughly 3,600 people. The chaos, the unending noise, the constant coming and going and never stopping that was always there in a city where the lights never went out, the streets were never empty, the noise never not loud.

Time seemed to slow here . . . as if the minutes ticking away on the clock didn't matter as much. People took the time to be nice to each other. To stop and say hello with New York-thick accents. To be kind and help out a stranger.

In the short ten minutes I'd waited on the train platform, one person asked if I needed any help with my bags, and another complimented my traveling outfit—a cream blouse tucked into plaid slacks.

I glanced down at my wristwatch. Seconds ticked by as I waited for Aunt Carol and Sophie to pick me up and take me to the place I'd be calling home for the next few months.

A voie, sweet and inviting like the *Caron Belldgia* perfume Mom liked to wear on special occasions, permeated the air: "Jo!"

I could barely turn around before someone pulled me into a hug, wrapped their arms so tight around me that if I were a china doll, I would have shattered on impact.

Sophie.

My older cousin by a year, three months, and twelve days.

My taller cousin by 2 ½ inches.

My forever cousin and always best friend.

"Sophie," I said, taking a breath and inhaling the scent of her air that always smelled like freshly squeezed lemons. It had been over a year since I'd last felt Sophie's hugs. I missed them more than anything. Missed the way Sophie said my name. Missed seeing the light in her eyes when she shared a secret with me. Missed her.

There's something healing about hugs, I realized, as I was held in Sophie's embrace. Maybe it's that they hold together in careful arms what would have fallen apart on its own. And throughout my twenty years of life, Sophie had been there for me, was the glue holding me together when on my own, I would have most definitely fallen apart.

"I'm so glad you're here." Only one word came to mind when hearing the sound of her voice and seeing the smile on her lips and the light in her eyes—*happy*.

"Me too, Sophie." I missed her more than I realized.

Minutes later—in the time it took to get me, my wheelchair, and luggage to my aunt's *Buick Skylark* car—the black-and-white of the train station faded away into a kaleidoscope of green meadows, blue sky, wide earth.

"Jo?" Sophie whispered beside me, her voice quiet enough for just the two of us to hear from the backseat of the all-vinyl interior car.

"What?" I whispered back.

"My flight to London doesn't leave until noon tomorrow. Can I take you somewhere in the morning?"

Sophie had this gleam in her eyes that made her look like a little kid, eyes like blinking Christmas lights.

"Where?" I asked.

She smiled wide at me and said, voice full of wonder, "You'll see."

*You'll see.*

How many times had Sophie told me that over the years? Told me *you'll see* when I wondered what my life would amount to in a wheelchair. Told me *you'll see* when I doubted my worth and felt I would never be enough. Told me *you'll see* on all the Christmases we shared together when I wanted to grab the gift Sophie put under the tree for me and ask her what was inside or rip it open when no one was looking.

Always a mystery with Sophie. Always wonder. Always magic.

I knew without a shadow that doubt could cast, whatever Sophie had planned for us tomorrow, I would see—because, with Sophie, I always saw what I would have missed on my own.

# CHAPTER 6

"Where are we going?"

I felt like a little kid being led blindfolded, arms tugged ahead on an invisible journey, going somewhere bound to hold something that was worth the secrecy. Except I wasn't blindfolded, but I still had no idea where Sophie was taking me. Everything was new to me: the street names, the people, the scenery.

Sophie gave me a smile that said she wouldn't tell me where we were going, but if I would be patient long enough to wait until we got there, I'd see for myself.

Gravel popped like popcorn kernels under my crutches with each step I took. My pits were rubbed raw from the crutches. You'd think after years of using them every day, my skin would have been calloused there by now. But the only thing that had gotten tough was everything under my skin—my heart, my mind, my soul . . . *me*.

Sophie stopped in front of a building that reminded me of the schools I passed by when I was a kid that I would have attended myself if my health hadn't forced me to learn at home with private tutors—tall and spacious with brick wall exteriors and lots of windows letting in the sun rays.

"This is the place." The way Sophie looked at me made me think there was more to it than that. Maybe it *was* just a place on the outside, but there had to be something more—something within its walls, behind its closed doors.

Sophie never dished up answers on a plate and served them to me. She wanted me to ask, to give her my pile of questions, and she'd trade them for a pile of answers, one at a time. The beauty in both the asking and the receiving was something Sophie never took for granted in all the years I'd known her, through all the chapters of our lives we shared together.

My eyes were like half-open blinds, squinting in sunlight through partially closed lids as I stared ahead. "What is it?"

"This, Josie, is an art gallery." Sophie's arms stretched out wide, animating her words with a dramatic flair of movement. "A family friend of ours, Mrs. Ridge, owns this place, and she's displaying some new paintings today." Sophie's eyes read what she didn't have to voice for me to hear: that I would love this place, and that it was worth the secrecy and the wait and the effort to get here—another fulfilled *you'll see.*

"The gallery doesn't open for another twenty-five minutes, but Mrs. Ridge said we could come in early." Sophie pulled on the doorknob, held the door open until I'd stepped inside. "She wants to meet you, too."

Positioned all across the room were pieces of art mounted on the walls with wooden frames. Sophie went ahead to the wall in front of us, and I traced her footsteps there. She nodded to the collection of paintings hanging on the wall just mere inches away from our faces. "These are the new paintings I wanted you to see."

The doorframe of my eyes couldn't open any wider as I beheld life being breathed into a world of colors. The bluest sky I'd ever seen with pregnant clouds birthing white across the sky. A garden of roses bleeding red petals and thorns, carefully painted in soft, rich soil. A child whose face looked so real I could have reached out and cupped its dimpled cheek in my hand.

The magic in these paintings rattled my bones.

I said what I couldn't stop thinking: "These are incredible."

"They are," Sophie said, her head bobbing up, down, rhythmically like a cork adrift at sea. "Some of them are done by the locals here. The others are ones Mrs. Ridge collected over the years when she traveled abroad with her husband in the early thirties— before the second world war started."

There was history here—I could feel it, see it. Stories of artists who lived their lives and loved what they did and painted with passion and wit and talent. Artists whose names might not be remembered but whose works would never be forgotten—whether known by the world in the *British Museum* or known by a few on Paris street corners.

I soaked it in like a sponge desperate for water. Sophie's fingers landed on my shoulder, tap-tapped me, snapped me out of my thoughts. And when I turned around, a set of soft brown eyes fell on mine.

"Hi, Mrs. Ridge," Sophie said with a smile. "This is my cousin, Josie Carter."

"It's so nice to meet you, Josie." Mrs. Ridge's smile landed on me, warm and inviting and kind. She tugged on a defiant strand of greying hair, willed it to stay in its resting place behind her ear. "Sophie tells me you're an artist."

"Not professionally, but yes, I do paint." I stole a glance at Sophie, wondering what she had told Mrs. Ridge about my artwork. The pieces I'd done seemed amateurish in comparison with some of the paintings on the walls.

"What do you paint?" There was a genuine interest behind her question, a kind of warm curiosity in her gaze. She wanted to know what my place in the world of art looked like.

"Stories," I blurted out and realized that answer didn't make any sense, that I needed to explain what that meant in more than one word. "I paint stories of my life—of places I've gone, things I've seen, people I've met . . . memories I've lived."

That's what I painted—stories that deserved a frame of their own on the mental wall of art in my memory.

Mrs. Ridge smiled at me again—a smile that said, *I know what you mean. I know what it is to remember stories and paint them, give them existence outside the walls of your imagination and memory.*

"I'd love to see some of your work. Maybe for tea—on Friday?"

With a nod, a smile, and a confirmation of the time and place, it was a date:

The neighbor two houses down from Sophie's home—*2:00 p.m.*

# CHAPTER 7

The sky fell asleep before Sophie and I did that night.

As it slumbered in black sleep and pale starlight, we were two wide-eyed girls, painting pictures under fluorescent lamplight.

"I need more blue paint." Sophie clawed at her right forearm, attempting to scratch off the dried paint that caked itself onto her, and remove its stain from her bare skin. The humble beginnings of a blueberry-blue sky made its way onto the canvas propped up in front of where she stood.

I couldn't help but laugh as I watched tiny blue flakes fall soft and slow like snow onto the floor, dance around Sophie's sockless feet. It felt good to laugh . . . freeing. I'd laughed more these past few weeks with Sophie than I had that entire year so far. I needed each one of those laughs. Needed to laugh at the good things and the silly ones and everything between.

"I think you used more paint on your arm than on your picture."

"Can I help it if I'm better at painting here than there?" She gestured from her arm to her picture and shrugged.

I laughed again—the fifth time I'd laughed in the past half hour we'd spent painting when we should have been asleep.

I didn't want this to end and yet . . . I knew it would. Soon—a week from today. That realization made the bellyache from laughter cease and twist my stomach into pretzel-tight knots. Good things always end sooner than we want them to.

My silence felt loud—like all the things I couldn't put into words made wordless, yet hearable, noise. Silence with a megaphone of its own. Sophie must have noticed. Her hand was on my shoulder, blue paint stuck under her fingernails from the dried chunks she'd successfully scratched off her arm, squeezing me. "Josie, what's wrong?"

I shook my head. But I couldn't shake away the truth, couldn't make it any less unreal with the *left-right-left-right* swiveling of my neck.

"Jo." Sophie's voice was soft, quiet . . . unmissable.

How could two of the five letters that spelled out my name get me to spill out of my mouth what was dammed in my head?

Because she was Sophie—she was family. And the way the ones closest to you say your name, how the syllables slip off their tongue in a way only they can accomplish, how they reach you in the place you've shut them out of and are hurting alone in, changes everything.

"I don't want you to leave." I needed Sophie here with me. I wanted to laugh with her forever and paint silly pictures late into the night every day of the year and never have to say goodbye or have things change. I wanted to see her face and not have to picture what it looked like and if she was smiling or wide-eyed with curiosity or sad at that moment over the telephone. I wanted to feel her hand in mine, not a set of cold rotary dial numbers on my fingertips.

"Aw, Jo." Sophie smiled softly at me. "Even if I'm not here, I'm always with you" —she put her hand over my heart— "in there. If you make room for me, I'll stay there forever."

If forever really did go on and on with an infinite amount of *evers,* I wanted that.

Sophie knelt beside me, wrapped her arms tight around me. And my world didn't feel as lonely, and I didn't feel as alone in it. The two of us were a mess of wild braids and blue paint, cocooned in each other's embrace.

When the end of the week did come, and I had to say goodbye to Sophie, and her eyes were gathering storm clouds, and mine were already a downpour of tears, I found a note tucked under my pillow that night. I flicked on the lamplight.

*Josie—I'll see you again soon. This isn't goodbye; it's just 'see you later.' Turn the page around and look at the ~~botom~~ bottom corner —and ~~rememmber~~ remember what I told you.*

I turned the page, and what I saw made me smile and tear up again: a heart . . . with both mine and Sophie's names in the center of it—our halves coming together and becoming one whole.

My hand found my heart, felt its steady pulse thrumming under my fingertips. Sophie, the other half of my heart, was truly in there with me—and that would be enough to last me the months it would be until I saw her again, and for every time after that followed the *see you later* until the *hello* again.

Because while good things end, their memories still go on. Memories don't have an expiration date like time does—they outlast time . . . outlast endings.

# CHAPTER 8

JUNE 27, 1951
(Present Day)

Time—it changes a lot of things.

It tears apart. It mends.

It hurts. It forgives.

It forgets. It remembers.

It cries. It laughs.

It can change anything—from the size of our shoes to the way we talk, from our dislikes to our loves, from our realities to our dreams.

Time had changed a lot for me. It had broken me beyond what I thought was repairable but showed me a glimmer of hope in a pile of rubble—a new beginning at an ending. It showed me how to live my life even when it wasn't the life I wanted to be mine. It had changed a lot for Sophie, too. It had hurt her and robbed her of one of the people who should have always been there for her, forever been part of her life, and been the hand to help her back up when her dreams and disappointments met in a head-on collision and Sophie was trapped between them.

I remembered that summer when she was thirteen, and I was a few months shy of turning twelve, and she held my hand, squeezed it so desperately tight with all the pain she was forced to feel when her dad divorced her mom, just walked away and left them behind for reasons Sophie would never understand. What should have been forever became temporary—fragile and broken. The breaking of her parent's marriage was the shattering of their daughter's heart. How do you heal from that kind of hurt? The kind that says goodbye and walks away when it should be there with every whispered goodnight, every new sunrise, and always stay? Maybe you don't. Maybe you heal *through* it every day it hurts, every moment that aching in your chest makes you hold your breath because even breathing causes pain, just as Sophie had.

Time had been a friend and a foe. But for Sophie and me together? If time had changed anything, it had brought us closer. And the halves of our hearts that we'd given each other eleven years ago still fit together and always would.

I heard footsteps coming from behind me and the *clank* of heels against the floor. Sophie set her two suitcases down by the door and came to me, where I sat in my wheelchair on the porch. She looked two feet down to meet my face, and I looked that same distance up to meet hers. I knew we didn't have a lot of time to say goodbye. That, in a moment, Aunt Carol would honk the car horn, signaling Sophie to grab her bags and head to the car. That whatever I wanted to say to Sophie, I needed to say now.

But Sophie beat me to it.

"I'll call you once I get to the hotel in London. And you can call me whenever you want to talk or if you need anything, Jo. I'll be there, just as I've always been," she said. "Are you going to be okay on your own?" Her eyes were focused on me, reading every line on my face.

"It's going to be an adjustment." I felt the weight of my confession on my shoulders. For all my life, I lived with my parents. They were always there to help. Mom cooked meals. Dad grabbed things out of kitchen cabinets or closet shelves that I couldn't reach. I did dinner dishes after I finished my school homework. But I don't think I realized how dependent I was on them for so many things, how much I needed them every single day. Now, everything I could and couldn't do was my responsibility to accomplish—and that weighed heavy on me.

"I'll make it work." I swallowed a lump so big in my throat it hurt, and I reached for Sophie's hand, felt the warmth of her fingers wrapped around mine. I didn't have any other choice but to *make* it work.

"I know you will." Her gaze was steady, confident, believing.

"Have a good time, Sophie. Make a lot of memories for me. And I'll be here when you get back—I'll see you soon."

Sophie smiled, and seeing that smile was nostalgic to me, resurfacing a hundred bittersweet memories of *hello's* and *see you soon's* we'd said to each other over the years. "See you soon."

And as if both of us sensed that time was running out, that our hourglass of sand was almost at its end, Sophie knelt down, reached for me with arms that weren't ready for goodbyes yet. I hugged her close, breathed in the lemon fragrance of her hair. Sophie felt smaller than I remembered her being the last time I saw her . . . her bones felt more fragile against mine. Or maybe I'd never squeezed her this tight before and the outline of her pencil-thin frame never pressed against mine as much as it did now. But regardless, her love for me was just as strong as it had always been.

"Don't ever let fear stop you from doing what's right, Jo," Sophie whispered close to my ear.

The arms that were wrapped around mine let go and picked up a suitcase in either hand. Sophie trudged down the few steps leading from the porch to the walkway. As her feet landed on the last step, I heard one thing and noticed another: Sophie's quiet grunt and her taut arm muscles shaking.

Under the weight of sadness, a small laugh emerged. "What, did you pack the whole world in there?" I said, cocking my head to her luggage.

"Says the queen of over-packing," she said, setting her bags down and turning back to face me so I could see the grin on her face.

"*Touché.* Well played, dear cousin." I laughed again, harder this time. "From the looks of it, though, there's enough stuff in there to last you a lifetime."

Sophie turned around, lifted her bags off the ground, and resumed her slow but steady march to the car. "I hope so."

I felt an emptiness as Sophie whispered she loved me, climbed into the car, and disappeared from sight. She may have left me at that moment—and her absence carved a hollowness in my chest—but her words hadn't—the ones about being brave and not letting fear stop me from doing what's right. Those words stayed and followed me back into the house, soaked into the paint colors I mixed and the bristles of the brushes I cleaned under lukewarm sink water.

A breeze ran with invisible legs through the house, caught my eye, had me look out the kitchen window to a backyard dotted with trees and stretched wide with green grass and kissed with pink tulips. I grabbed a pencil and started sketching what I saw with the noon sun shining down, casting shadows and light. That was the reason I came—to paint all the new things my hands could create with a brush and colors while I was here. And whatever I was supposed to capture and recreate, it started with what was in front of me. Too many moments slip by when waiting for the most beautiful kind of beauty before painting the simplest kind of beauty all around.

I lost myself in the shadows and sunlight and glimmers of hope and life.

# CHAPTER 9

(Present Day)

The sound of the doorbell vibrated my finger a little as it lifted off the button and waited.

I listened as its *bzzzzz!* hummed like a choir of bees as the sound traveled across the house, into rooms, past hallways, through walls.

"Josie." There it was again: that soft smile that framed Mrs. Ridge's eyes, looked warm and inviting as she opened the door. "Come on in."

She welcomed me into her home like I had always belonged there.

We sat on a grey couch, inches apart from each other, with steaming cups of coffee on the wood-stained coffee table in front of us. Its cushions were old, sagging with memories of conversations and smiles exchanged on its fabric over the years.

"Is this your first time in New York?" I knew Mrs. Ridge was inviting me into a conversation, wanting to get to know me and not just the pieces of artwork stacked one on top of the other in the bag resting by my feet.

"Yes, it is, actually." All the memories I had with Sophie and me—they were spent at my house on summer vacation with my parents.

I'd never been to Sophie's house before, never seen what her bedroom looked like when she was five and loved the colors pink and blue, never played with the dolls made of glass she had when she was seven, never watched Greer Garson in *Pride and Prejudice* or Errol Flynn in *Gentleman Jim* on the black-and-white screen together in the movie theater when we were both just shy of our teenage years. Why? Because health limitations and family problems kept both of our summer worlds from colliding in New York.

"I like it here, though," I went on. "My aunt's home is lovely, and this city—it's calm and beautiful and . . . inspiring, too."

She nodded at me slow, knowing. "It's why I've lived here since I was a child. My husband was raised here, too. He was an artist for as long as I can remember. He painted me a portrait and wrote me a note one day when I was seventeen, asking me out on our first date. He gave me my love for art. I can't paint myself, but I collect artwork to display at the gallery. Beautiful things are rare things— and they should always be remembered."

"I think of beauty like the tide," I said, imagining the ocean with my mind's eye. "It pushes the waves closer to the shore and drags them far out, but they never come and go the same. Always different. Similar at times. But never the same. Not even the pattern of ocean waves can be replicated. Each crashing of foamy saltwater is individual, rare, just like beauty is."

Our conversation paused as we slurped hot sips of ink-black coffee from china cups.

"Art is silent poetry," she said. "It's God's way of allowing us to hang on to memories when they fade or grow old without needing words to remember them." She smiled. "How long have you painted for, Josie?"

"Almost fifteen years. I started a few months before I turned seven. My dad always says I've been painting for even longer than that—long before I could even hold a paintbrush in my hands or recognize the names of colors. I've always seen the world as a story to be remembered—and the best way I can do that is to paint what I see."

Remembering goes on as long as we do, but so many things are forgotten. Words spoken can't be heard the same way. Smiles smiled can't be envisioned the same way. Memories made can't be remembered the same way. I didn't want to lose the memories worth remembering. I wanted to see them every day of my life, whether in a myriad of paint colors or in black-and-white pencil sketches.

"I want to remember what tears me down and builds me up," I went on. "What makes me weak and what makes me strong. What makes me doubt and makes me hope. Both of those lessons aren't found in the easy memories, but the ones that hurt to think about, too. Without the good and the bad, I wouldn't be" —I searched for the word— "*me.*"

"And that's why you paint," Mrs. Ridge said to me, the understanding of why I painted stories and memories breaking through her mental sky like the dawn.

"Yes," I said—and before I could stop myself, my fingers searched for that leather bag and started pulling out my paintings, one by one, being vulnerable enough to lay them all out on the coffee table and say, without words, *this is me on paper, this is me in paint, this is what I do and what I love and what I've poured endless hours of time into. Here I am.*

I watched as she leaned forward, and her eyes scanned each of the four paintings I'd brought with me from home from top to bottom, side to side.

Painting #1—a summer night with Sophie.

Painting #2—patients dressed in matching hospital gowns in hospital beds.

Painting #3—an attic full of an artist's supplies.

Painting #4—train stations and rainy goodbyes.

"Josie." She said my name slow, deliberate. "How long will you be in town?"

I could see the wheels in her head turning, but I had no idea what was causing them to spin round and round. "For the next few months. Why?"

"I don't know if this is something you would ever consider or be comfortable doing . . ." Her words slowed to a pause. "If I were to ask you if I could commission you to do some paintings that I could display at my art gallery, what would you say?"

I double-blinked. "I . . . I think I might say yes."

I couldn't believe that was the answer that passed through my startled lips.

"And if I were to ask you if I could hire you to teach art classes at the gallery over the summer," she went on, her next words having me hold my breath so I wouldn't miss them, "what would you say?"

I didn't know what to say, much less think. All I did was wonder —wonder how four paintings on a table took an afternoon conversation over coffee to two opportunities I'd never been given in my whole existence: a commission and a job.

My eyes searched hers, and I just wanted to know . . . *what did you see?* Because she saw something in me that no one else had.

"I'd tell you I've never had any formal training before. That I've never even attended an art class or done paid commissions. And I'm not sure what kind of a teacher I'd make."

I wasn't the artist who knew what she was doing and had all the qualifications the world said you needed to have to succeed. I was Josie Carter—the artist in the attic. The girl who didn't know how to sort through the messiness of life, so she transformed an old attic into a studio and painted on the pages of her life, tried to make something beautiful out of it despite all the scratches and dents and rips.

Mrs. Ridge listened to the bucket list of reasons I gave her, my warning signs in flashing neon lights that blinked my inexperience and disqualification. Her brows didn't raise, didn't dip, didn't reveal any emotion of surprise at my confession. And I knew each reason I gave her could mean losing the opportunity she'd placed within my grasp—but I had to be honest before I could give her my answer. My honesty wasn't a *no* . . . it was seeing if hers, despite my shortcomings and inabilities, would remain a *yes*.

It did.

"And I'd say to that—I still want you."

My head and heart were at war, and the eighteen inches that separated them felt infinitely long, stretched wide like a battlefield. My head, the logical thinker in me, demanded me to ground myself, to know what I was getting myself into before I committed. But my heart, the dreamer in me, asked me to try and do the impossible without having every detail figured out.

"Then," I said, awakening that dreamer in me, "*yes*."

# CHAPTER 10

**SEPTEMBER 21, 1940**
**(9 Years Old)**

I needed to be outside, breathe the fresh air. It helped clear away some, but not all, of the mental cobwebs of exhaustion that spun itself around my head, made it feel heavy and thick.

"How are you feeling?"

My wheelchair was positioned next to the park bench where Dad sat faithfully by my side, a newspaper clipping from September 16th in his hand. Even though it was five days old, Dad held onto it tight, couldn't seem to let go of it. The edges were creased and frayed from his thumbprint.

September 16th had changed a lot of things. Men had to kiss their wives goodbye, not knowing if they would ever see them again. Fathers had to hug their children goodbye, not knowing if they would return and ever feel the warmth of their embrace again. Brothers had to whisper farewell to their siblings and parents, not knowing if that last goodbye would truly be the final one.

President Roosevelt signed the Selective Training and Service Act into law that day—and if Dad had been two years younger, I would have been one of those kids saying goodbye to him. But Dad was forty-seven—and those who were between the ages of twenty-one and forty-five had to serve their country. Two years . . . age hadn't mattered much to me growing up. It was just a number, whether single or double-digit, indicating that someone was either young or old or somewhere between the two. But it mattered to me now. Two years saved me from saying goodbye. Two years allowed me to sit here with Dad at the park on Saturday morning, his only day off from his job as an attorney, making memories that so many kids would never be given a chance to make.

I didn't want to shatter this moment of togetherness by worrying Dad, telling him that my head felt funny and something wasn't right. Maybe I was just tired. Maybe it was nothing.

"I'm okay," I said, digging deep into my dangerously low reserve tank of energy to make my voice match my words. "Just tired."

Dad set his hand on my lap, wrapped his fingers around mine. This war, barely a year old, was taking its toll on everyone . . . and it was hitting Dad hard. So many of his friends had been drafted into the first world war, as he was, but many of them had come home not alive but as dead heroes. Maybe that's why Dad was holding on so tight to that newspaper clipping—because he wasn't ready to let go of those he'd already lost, not wanting to lose those he cared for once again in this second hellish war.

Pain and loss have a way of resurfacing themselves at the most unexpected moments with the most unexpected things—a park bench, a newspaper clipping.

I squeezed his fingers gently, even though mine ached.

"Would you like something to drink?" My skin felt like hot coals, and my mouth was desert dry. I nodded, and Dad told me he'd be right back as he walked across the street to the corner drug store.

Laughter—loud, belly laughter—made me look up. A group of kids, probably close to my own age, were playing baseball up ahead, running wild and free with nothing stopping them as my wheelchair did me. I couldn't help but wonder sometimes: what was it like . . . to run like that, jump like that, play like that?

I'd spent so long in a wheelchair I couldn't remember what it was like to be out of one.

The laughter I heard turned to shouts, and I felt my eyes scrunch up while I tried to figure out what was happening. And I realized: someone was yelling and gesturing at *me*. I couldn't figure out why. All I knew was that my head was pounding, and my vision was hazy, and the words those kids shouted at me didn't reach my ears.

Only when a boy with a freckled face in dirty farm overalls tore across the field and stopped short of me did I realize why: a baseball stained with dirt and fingerprints had somehow veered off course, crashed and landed five feet in front of me, instead of on the other side of the grassy field as it should have.

The boy's eyes were two stones, pummeling hard into me. "Why didn't you throw it back?" he demanded to know. "We lost the game because of that!"

I met his blurred silhouette and tried to tell him that I was sorry, that I hadn't seen the ball land near me, that if I could have reached it in time, I would have. But none of the words came out. They were trapped somewhere between my mouth and throat, stuck there, voiceless.

He stared at me, and I knew he was fighting back angry words. My eyes pleaded with the boy whose name I didn't know to understand what I couldn't tell him. As he bent low, picked up the baseball and a handful of grass blades and earth with it, he fingered the ball in his hands, looked from it to me. "Are you as dumb as you look in that stupid wheelchair?"

The sound of his feet tearing into the earth as he turned and ran back to the now-dispersed game, with the winning team members cheering and the losing ones just as angry as the boy had been, reverberated like claps of thunder in my ears.

"Here you go." Dad was back a minute later, and he slipped something cool into my open hands, sat beside me once again.

Funny how in five minutes, so many things could happen. Words said, actions done, looks given, emotions showed. No—not funny. Heartbreaking.

"Dad," I said, my eyes still stuck on the spot the angry boy with the angry words had stood, "why are people so mean?"

I felt Dad's eyes searching my face, trying to figure out what images my eyes had seen, what words I'd heard and the blows they'd dealt, what memories now had a place in my mind.

"I don't know, Josie." His sigh was heavy and deep. "There's never a reason that makes it—being mean—okay. But there are reasons that make it understandable. Most people hurt others when they're hurting, too."

I nodded, knowing what he said was true and knowing that that boy had hurt written in clear lines across his face. Maybe he had to hug his dad goodbye last week, not knowing if he would ever see him again. Maybe he didn't have a dad. Maybe his life was hard and unfair. Maybe a lot of things. But those maybes didn't make the hurt he'd caused me to go away. "It doesn't make it any easier to be hurt, though."

The glasses that framed Dad's eyes framed his understanding, too. "I know. It doesn't. But when others hurt you, Jo, don't hurt them back. Stay true to yourself and who you are, not letting the things that others do harden your heart."

I let that sink in.

Sometimes we think the chance encounters we have with someone—whether on a street corner, a church pew, outside of a grocery store, or at a park, like mine—will play a redemptive role in our lives. That someday, we will see that person again when we least expect to. But that's not always how it works. Some people we meet once in our lives and they hurt us. Others change for the better. Not all chance encounters turn into life-changing moments—and that's okay. The nameless boy that I knew I'd probably never see again had done the hurting. But maybe there was someone out there, another person whose name I wouldn't know and would only encounter once in my lifetime, would do the healing. But until then, what I had to do was the simplest and the hardest: to stay true to myself and who I was, not letting the things that others did to me harden my heart.

I looked at Dad, gave him a smile I knew he needed to see. And then, I felt cold liquid spill over my lap, soak my dress and my bare legs underneath—the drink Dad got for me that I hadn't even sipped yet. Dad yelled my name, but I didn't see him anymore. He was replaced by a shadowland of darkness that my head was swimming headfirst into, drowning in.

And then: nothingness.

# CHAPTER 11

(Present Day)
*Telephone conversation*

**Mom:** *"Hello?"*

**Me:** *"Hey, Mom. It's Josie."*

**Mom:** *"Josie Girl—how are you?"*

**Me:** *"I'm doing okay—a lot has happened these past few days. I met a family friend of Sophie's, Mrs. Ridge, and she owns an art gallery in town. She invited me over to her house yesterday to talk, and she also wanted to see my paintings. To make a long story short, she asked me if I'd be willing to take on art commissions for her that she could display at her gallery and . . . she asked if I'd teach art classes at the gallery Monday through Friday, for a few hours each day."*

**Mom:** *'Wow, you're right—a lot has happened. And . . . what did you tell Mrs. Ridge?"*

**Me:** *"I told her that I wasn't a professional artist and that I've never gone to art school or taught anyone how to paint before, so I wasn't qualified. But she still wanted me to do both the commissions and the classes . . . so I said yes."*

*(Mom stayed quiet, let me keep talking, get everything off my chest and out my mouth)*

**Me:** *"I have no idea what I'm doing, Mom, but I couldn't shake this feeling I got . . . that I'm supposed to do this. It was the same feeling I had when I got Aunt Carol's invitation to stay here for the summer. It's hard to explain—but I just can't help but wonder if this is why I'm here: to do something I've never done before and to help others do the same. Maybe it was crazy for me to sign up without knowing what I'm getting myself into, I know—"*

**Mom:** *"Brave. It was crazy brave, Josie. I'm proud of you for saying yes. Even though I'm sure it wasn't an easy answer to give, I know you can do this. You've never not been able to do something you've set your mind to."*

**Me:** *"I'm scared of what others will think of me, Mom. I'm either in a wheelchair, or I'm on crutches. What if they judge me because of that? I know I'm supposed to do this—I do. But I keep wondering how I'm actually going to do it . . ."*

*(I paused, needing to fill my lungs with oxygen before the sound of sobs —of hearable grief—filled my ears instead)*

**Mom:** *"I don't know if anyone knows how they're going to do something, Jo. Most of the time, they don't—they just . . . do it. They do it scared, not knowing what will happen or what others will think.*

*It's okay to be scared, Josie Girl. It's human. But don't let your fears stop you from doing this, okay? Prove them wrong, just as you've always done your whole life. You're a fighter—fight."*

*(I sniffled, cupping the phone receiver in both hands)*

**Me:** *"I miss you, Mom. It's so different being away from you and Dad. I know it's only been a few days, but it feels like it's been a lifetime. I miss your hugs that make everything better."*

**Mom:** *"Not as much as we miss you, Jo. The house isn't the same without you—and it won't be until you come home. But your dad and I . . . we're both prouder of you than you could ever know. This time apart is just a season—but we've still got a whole lifetime of being together behind us and ahead of us.*

**Mom:** *"Now. Go do it, Josie. Go fight. Okay?"*

I needed to go back to the art gallery and do what Mom said. *Go do it. Go fight.* There was a giant of fear waiting for me in that room . . . waiting for me to come, to have a standoff like David and Goliath did. There were so many reasons I didn't want to load up my sling with stones and hurl it into the giant in front of me—reasons of me not being qualified, not being the best suited for this position, having health conditions that limited what I could do.

But I couldn't give up before I'd even started, even tried.

The orangish-grey sunset clouds chased after me as I walked down the last street that took me to the art gallery. With the exception of one left turn, it was a straight shot to the gallery from the house.

What would have taken others five minutes to walk took me ten because of the pace my crutches allowed me to walk at.

There it was—just ahead. A road paved with gravel greeted my feet as I turned left, started down a path that was quiet and still. Just me and pebble-sized rocks and green grass on either side and the gallery ahead.

I stopped short of the front door. My fingers dove into my dress pocket, found the key Mrs. Ridge had given me yesterday when she stopped by and told me she'd started advertising my art classes around town and left a sign-up sheet for people to fill out and bring to her if they were interested, and gave me the key to the gallery and told me I could go there at any point and time.

Cold metal pressed against my fingers as I put the key in the lock, turned it, stepped inside. I just . . . stood there with my back against the door, and I blinked in the box-shaped room. I saw it—this place —different this time. Maybe because I wasn't just here today and gone tomorrow, but because I'd be here for a lot of today's and tomorrow's. I wasn't just in a room where art happened, and I could look at it and admire what artists made, but in a room where I'd be showing others how to create art, too.

I snapped mental photographs of specific areas of the room. Where I'd be teaching. Where my students would be working. Where the easels and cans of paint and the stacks of white canvases would be kept.

Everything in me wanted to ask, *what do you think you're doing?*

There were a hundred ways I could answer that question. But that was why I was right here, standing in an empty room, fighting my giant of fear with a sling and stone. To change those answers, to transform them from wonderings to knowings.

*This—this is what I'm doing.*

# CHAPTER 12

**JULY 03, 1951**
(Present Day)

My stomach was a nervous mess of butterflies that fluttered and tumbled round like a cyclone in my belly.

I sat beside Mrs. Ridge again on the grey sofa, just as I had several days ago. Except today was different. Instead of two cups of coffee on the table in front of us, there was a single sheet of paper, stained with pen ink on it. I knew what was on it without having to read it. Names. Names of people with faces I couldn't place who'd decided to take a chance on me, to sign up and show up for my art classes that were starting next Monday.

"Here's the sign-up sheet. I compiled all the names onto one list. It also has their ages and experience they've had with art." Mrs. Ridge handed it to me, and I think we both noticed at the same time how my fingers were a little shaky, kind of like the aftermath of an earthquake. But she didn't say anything about it, and neither did I. The only noise was that of the paper, the sound of crinkling and crumpling of its folded edges.

*(First/Last Name) (Age) (Experience)*

*Rose Lewis – 23 – yes*

*Alice Johnson – 17 – yes*

*Timothy Allen – 32 – no*

*Helen Morris – 26 – no*

*Roger Peterson – 30 – yes*

*Betty Walker – 19 – no*

*Henry Young – 45 - no*

*Elizabeth Scott – 56 – yes*

*Patricia Harper – 15 - yes*

*William Ridge – 22 – yes*

I silently counted as I read each name—*ten*. My breath was as shaky as my fingers were.

"Did you really think no one would sign up, Josie?" She wasn't mocking me, wasn't making light of my obvious surprise that people *had* signed up. She just wanted to know, honestly, if that's what I'd really thought would happen.

I'd asked myself that question a hundred times, silently wondering, would anyone take a chance on the girl they didn't know, the one who either sat in a wheelchair or used crutches to hold herself up? The one who didn't have experience teaching art to anyone except herself? The one who was just as much of a stranger to them as they were to her? The one who that, maybe some saw as defying the rules, both spoken and unspoken, for women in the 1950s?

Maybe it was unconventional for me—just a twenty-year-old woman, barely an adult now—to be teaching art classes at a public place outside of my home without proper training. Maybe it made *me* unconventional. But if me doing what I knew I was supposed to, regardless of whether that was inside the constrictive boundaries placed around women or skirting the edges of them, then . . . so be it.

"I don't know. I hoped some would . . . but I didn't know. Do they know about me?"

Mrs. Ridge's eyes were question marks waiting for me to explain.

"Do they know about me having no teaching experience or any kind of formal art training and that I have a physical handicap?" Maybe some people wouldn't care about those things. But for every person that didn't, there was someone who did. That was one of the harshest realities of living in a broken world with broken people who judged another's brokenness without even taking the time to understand it. "I don't want the people who signed up to come and wish they had known those things beforehand. I want them to have the choice to accept me for who I am or not to. I want it to be *their* choice whether they stay or leave the class."

Mrs. Ridge put her hand on my shoulder, gently. I felt her fingers squeeze the skin under my rose-budded cotton dress. It felt as if her hand had always belonged there on my shoulder. "I understand that, Josie. But I also want you to know . . . I wouldn't have asked you to do this if I didn't believe in you. And I know I'm not the only one out there who will believe in you. Even if some leave the class, the ones who stay are the ones worth investing in because they believe in you."

Belief is at the root of everything. If we don't believe in someone, how could we ever believe in what they have to offer us? Their skills, their talents, their friendship, their advice, their words of constructive criticism and guidance? Maybe that's why faith is so important. Faith is the *root* of belief. If you believe in someone, you have faith in what they can offer you. But some people don't chance it—because faith often requires believing in what you can't see right then. It's blind trust. It's walking in the dark and trusting the person guiding you not to let you stumble or fall and bring you safely to the light.

Belief is vulnerable—but it's powerful, too. Because once someone believes in you, it changes everything.

"Josie, would you like to have dinner with me tonight?" Her invitation made me smile in spite of everything weighing down my heart and mind.

"I would love that." Mrs. Ridge reminded me of Mom in so many ways—her kindness, her genuine care and concern, her smile that couldn't help but make me smile back in return.

"At six o'clock? Oh—and you'll be able to meet one of your new students." Mrs. Ridge grabbed the list. I watched her eyes dart around the page until they landed on the last name entered on the sheet of paper.

She pointed to the last name: "My son."

*William Ridge.*

# CHAPTER 13

The last thing I remembered was Dad mumbling one word before I fell into oblivion: *hospital.*

Was that where I was now?

My eyes opened, and my pupils dilated thick black. I felt like Alice in Wonderland, tumbling down the rabbit hole into the dark unknown. Not knowing how long I'd fall or how hard I'd land, or what waited for me at the end of falling. I kept seeing glimpses of the bottom of the tunnel. But what I saw there? It didn't make sense to me. Everything was in reverse—dark places were bright, and bright ones were dark. How could there be more light where there should have been total darkness?

I didn't know—but I wanted to reach the light. I stretched out my arms while I free-fell in the dark, willing my fingertips to touch the light. But when I did . . . something happened.

I wasn't in a tunnel following in Alice's footsteps; I was in a bed. There were people I didn't know hovering above me. There were voices I didn't recognize coming from around me.

"She's waking up," someone whispered.

I didn't even know I'd been asleep. All I knew was that I was in a room that wasn't my own. I was wearing clothes that weren't mine. I was surrounded by people in white uniforms that I didn't recognize. I was somewhere I wasn't supposed to be.

The hospital. In a hospital bed. Wearing a hospital gown. With doctors and nurses. With an IV going through the vein in my left arm and patches on my chest that connected to a heart rate monitor machine.

A nurse came close and asked did I know my name? *Josie Carter*

How many fingers was she holding up? *Four*

Did I know why I was here? *No*

The nurse with the name tag that read *Dotty Bursley*, who had been trained to intentionally speak softly to patients and keep her words slow and body language calm, started to explain to me what had happened. I noticed her hands were relaxed at her side but ready to reach out and grab hold of my shoulders if I started to freak out and try to move more than I should. I knew the drill. The routine. How to react and respond to hard news.

I'd been in the hospital more times as a kid than some had been in their whole lifetime.

"Two days ago, you were at the park with your father when you went unconscious. You've been in critical condition since then. You were running an extremely high fever because of an infection in your leg that was caused by a sliver embedded in the skin just above your right knee. We drained the infection, and that allowed your fever to reduce enough to where you could wake up."

Dotty paused, gave me a moment to process all that she had just told me. But I was too weak, too numb to do anything but lay there and listen. My brain felt anesthesia-induced, like it was stuck in a place of the right nerves not triggering the appropriate emotional responses I should have been having in that moment. Anything— sadness, fear, anger, shock.

When it was clear that I wasn't going to say or react in any way, Dotty went on. "Do you remember cutting your leg on anything? Whacking it against something that could've made a cut?"

It took me a few seconds to realize that Dotty had asked me a question and was waiting for my answer. My head felt tired even at the thought of forming words. "Don't . . . remember," I said, weakly. "Can't feel my legs. Wouldn't know if I cut it."

Dotty sensed my exhaustion, and I watched her glance at the heart rate monitor, check its reading: *115 bpm*.

"I have one more question for you, and then you can see your parents for a short time, alright? Just nod your head for *yes* and shake it for *no*." Dotty made sure I understood her instructions before going on. "According to your medical file, you were diagnosed with polio at the age of five. The file shows your polio resulted in permanent paralysis in your legs and feet—meaning that you can't feel anything or walk on your own without using crutches or a wheelchair. Is that correct?"

I nodded my head. I'd gone over four years of knowing what it meant to have half of my body be physically numb. I knew I wasn't the only person out there to receive a polio diagnosis and have permanent paralysis. I knew I wasn't the only one who had gone to countless hospital appointments, seen the top doctors, tried the recommended treatments to help my body, and have them all end with a two-word apology—*I'm sorry*—because there was nothing anyone could do to help.

Pain is universal. But suffering . . . it's individual. Everyone knows what it feels like to hurt and be hurt. But the pain one experiences in that moment can only be felt by that person, no matter how similar their medical history may be.

Hearts break in similar ways but never identical ones.

"Each night before you go to bed, I need you to check your legs for cuts, scratches, or anything that doesn't look normal. I know you can't feel your legs and feet, so you wouldn't be able to feel if anything hurt you. But it's important you check every night. With polio, you have to be extremely careful about not getting infections in your body. It's *very* important you check your legs each night before you go to bed. Understand?" Dotty's eyes were kind but serious—and I knew that I must have been dangerously close to something even worse happening because of that infection in my leg. If Dad hadn't been there . . . if he hadn't taken me to the hospital . . .

How had I not noticed?

Dresses that fell just below my knees were both a blessing and a curse: they kept me covered, but they also concealed what I never thought to check for—splinters or any kind of cut that shouldn't be there on my numb skin.

*How did it get there? . . . Was it the desk in my bedroom?*

I remembered whacking myself against it a few days ago when I got thrown off balance on my crutches. Had my imbalance caused this mess?

I nodded again, pulling myself out of my thoughts and focusing on the nurse in front of me.

"Okay," Dotty said. She came close to me, brushed away a stray piece of damp and sweaty hair that stuck to my cheek. "For now, you need to rest. Your parents will be in to see you soon, alright?"

My eyes closed before Dotty shut the door behind her.

# CHAPTER 14

**JULY 03, 1951**
**(Present Day)**

It was still light out when I walked two houses down to Mrs. Ridge's. The sky was more orangish than blue, and the clouds more greyish than white. The whole afternoon I'd wondered what Mrs. Ridge's son was like. A sign-up sheet of paper can only tell you so much about a person, and it had offered four things about him:

He was Mrs. Ridge's son.

His name was William.

He was twenty-two.

He had experience with art.

After ringing the doorbell, Mrs. Ridge answered it and smiled at me. "Come in, Josie. I'm running a little behind on dinner—I have a chicken in the oven, and it needs to cook for a few more minutes." She led me to the dining room and pulled out a chair for me. "I'll be back in a few minutes. Will should be here in just a moment."

Before I had time to think, a boy with copper-colored hair and a lanky figure bounded down the set of second-story stairs that opened to the dining/living room. His eyes were what caught my attention the most—blue like the sky with dark green flecks like evergreen trees. The blue in them made me think that he had a happy and bright side to him. The green in them made me think he had gone through something hard and painful.

Without a word, he crossed the distance between us in several long strides and sat at the birchwood table across from me.

I didn't know what I expected Will to be like—charming, outspoken, maybe even flirty. I didn't have much experience with boys, but from what Sophie had told me about the boys at her school over the years, I think I made presumptions that William—or Will, as his mom addressed him—would fit into one of those three categories. But he was none of those things. He was quiet, serious even, but his eyes hinted that beneath his rough exterior was the heart of a playful boy. Maybe that's why in my head, when he came bounding down the stairs, I thought of him as the copper-haired boy. Because even though he was tall, I saw the boy in him—the boy that was playful and kind but also carrying a lot of hurt. Its presence was as noticeable as the dark circles under his tired eyes.

"I heard that you've had experience with art?" Maybe it was a stupidly obvious question to ask because we both knew he did. But I didn't know what else to say.

"Yes," he said—and I could feel his eyes silently laughing at me for asking that question. Not mocking me for it, but laughing because we both knew he painted, yet I'd asked anyway. "And you teach art?" Maybe it was the way his eyes crinkled when he smiled softly that made the blue in them stand out brighter, a shade that looked happy.

"Yes." I couldn't help but smile in return, and I exhaled a breath that felt . . . comfortable. Like what would've taken minutes for others to talk about in order to break the ice took him and me one question each.

He leaned back into his chair, and he looked at me with curious eyes. "So, tell me a few things about yourself."

"Well, I'm Josie, but I go by Jo, too. I paint. I'm staying at my aunt's house over the summer and teaching art classes. You?"

"I'm William, but I go by Will. No one ever calls me by my full name except for my mom when she's mad at me." We both laughed. "I'm studying business at university in Canada. I'm home for the summer and, apparently, attending art classes."

That word—*apparently*—drew me to the light like a moth. "Apparently?"

He shrugged his shoulders and bluntly said, "It was my mom's idea. She told me you'd agreed to teach art classes, and since I was home for the summer and not busy studying, why didn't I take them? I haven't painted in a while, but I still know how—and my mom kept telling me I should take classes. So, I am."

"To please her." I knew that's what Will wanted to say but didn't out of politeness.

His eyes were focused on the swinging door straight ahead of where he sat. Only a few feet separated us from the kitchen door his mom had disappeared inside of. "She wants me to be an artist like my dad was."

I noticed it again: how when Will's dad was mentioned by either Mrs. Ridge or Will, it was using past tense adjectives—*was* an artist. I wondered where he was . . . whether he walked away from his family as Sophie's dad had done, or whether he was even alive. But either way, he wasn't here where he should be. And whether that was because of a choice he made or something out of his control, I wondered if his absence was what I saw in Will's eyes—pain and longing for his dad—and what I'd seen in Will's mom's eyes—pride when she spoke of her husband but loneliness, too.

"And . . . you don't want that?"

"Painting may have been my dream when I was younger, but it's not anymore." He could've stopped there, not explained anything else. But he filled in the missing blanks I hadn't asked him to answer. "When my dad died, that dream died with him . . . but it's still my mom's dream for me. I'm better at learning business than I am at learning art, though, and I'm okay with that. And it's easier on my hands being able to negotiate business deals with someone rather than holding a paintbrush all day."

Will set his hands on the table, and when I saw them, I knew it was a vulnerably brave thing for him to do. His fingers were like gnarled old tree trunks, curled with arthritis. I'd seen many old people with arthritis, including my grandpa before he died, but . . . Will's? His hands looked like they belonged to an eighty-year-old grandfather, not a twenty-two-year-old boy who shouldn't even know what that aggressive a form of arthritis was like to live with.

I looked from his hands to his face, and where others may have shown him pity, I gave him admiration. Because it takes an incredibly brave person to reveal the parts about them that aren't perfect, that aren't always beautiful but sometimes seen as ugly to those who don't understand the beauty that runs deeper than the scar lines. Will was brave—one of the bravest people I'd ever met.

I knew there was a story there . . . about Will's hands. But I also knew that was a chapter Will, if he wanted to, would share with me someday. Some chapters are like that—they're not to be opened unless the person who is living them wants to share the pages with the reader. Right now, Will had allowed me to read more lines than I ever dared to imagine he would, and I was grateful for his openness . . . it made me feel less alone in my own struggles.

"For what it's worth... I think your dream is a good one." Will smiled at that—a smile that made him look twelve instead of twenty-two.

"What about you?" he asked me. I noticed Will tilted his head just a fraction to the right when he asked a question—and he kept it like that, hanging with curiosity, while he asked and listened to my answer.

"I don't know yet. I guess I'll find out along the way." I honestly didn't think I'd ever be the one to find my dream. My dream would find me, sneak up on me in the moment I least expected it to, and it'd just be there . . . and I'd know it was for me. I already knew I wanted to do something in the world of art, but oftentimes, dreams become hobbies in the face of harsh reality. Reality didn't always allow for the dreams in my head to turn into dreams I lived out outside the walls of my imagination. All I knew then was that I was here for the summer because I felt . . . called.

My Sunday school teacher had once told me and a group of wide-eyed and captivated third graders that if we ever heard a whisper—something so quiet, we had to be even quieter than the whisper and listen so carefully to hear it—not to ignore it.

*"That's where God whispers,"* Teacher Billy had said. *"He doesn't always shout; sometimes, He whispers to us and shares the most special secrets with us. Secrets about the plan He has for us and the way He wants us to go. All God wants you to do is to listen and follow when you hear that whisper."*

I'd heard that whisper to come. I'd answered it. And it led me here.

Nothing happens without a purpose—even if the purpose is so small that it can't be seen with the naked eye or whispered so softly that it can't be heard with the human ear. Everything has purpose. Every day has purpose. Everyone has purpose. In a small world of chance, there's always a bigger world of purpose.

"Sounds like an adventure." There was this gleam in his eye that didn't make me feel bad for not knowing my purpose in life. He made me feel okay about it—and that this adventure I was on of discovering wasn't a bad thing, but maybe a good one.

And that maybe I'd found a friend at the start of this adventure: the copper-haired boy at the dining room table.

# CHAPTER 15

JULY 09, 1951
(Present Day)
*Telephone conversation*

**Sophie:** *"Josie—it's Sophie. I only have a few minutes before I need to be somewhere, but I wanted to call you and wish you luck on your first day of teaching."*

**Me:** *"I'm so glad you called, Sophie. Is it bad that part of me wants to find a way to get out of teaching? I feel so unready for this."*

**Sophie:** *"It's not bad, Jo. It's . . . human. I know our personalities are different. I'm more outgoing than you are, but it's never easy for me to put myself out there in a situation that's new to me or something I'm scared to try and do. That's why I called. I'm here—to remind you that it's okay to be scared. Don't let fear stop you from doing what you're called to do. You're stronger than what's scaring you—remember?"*

*(Sophie's voice went from soft and certain to bubbly with laughter)*

**Sophie:** *"Jo, if you could put up with me the past fifteen-sixteen summers we've spent with each other, you can do anything."*

*(I laughed, too, my voice carrying across thousands of miles to reach her in that London hotel room)*

**Me:** *"Thank you, Sophie. You always know when I need someone to set my head straight and keep me on track."*

**Sophie:** *"That's what friends and family do. We help each other when times are hard or scary or anything, really."*

*(A brief pause)*

**Sophie:** *"I need to run now. Mom's waved at me to get off the phone for the past minute straight. Call me tomorrow and let me know how today goes, alright? I love you."*

**Me:** *"I love you too. Talk tomorrow, Soso."*

*Soso*—I'd learned from one of my junior high school private tutors (who was also a linguistics expert) that *so-so*, with a hyphen between the two *so's*, meant 'okay' in Japanese. Somehow, I'd missed the part of Miss Janet's explanation for what it contextually meant—as in not terrible, but not good—and I'd started calling Sophie that one day. Because to me . . . Sophie made everything okay.

It stuck over the summer we spent together where I was twelve and Sophie was thirteen. After I learned what *so-so* actually meant and I told Sophie, we both laughed over it. Even though it was grammatically incorrect the way I used it, we both knew what I meant by it—not that Sophie wasn't terrible, but not good either; but that she made things okay.

I hadn't called Sophie that—*Soso*—in a long time. It felt foreign on my tongue now in spite of being familiar for so long. But that's who she was to me—she was my *Soso*.

Maybe it was silly for us to let the nickname stick, but we were both young, and it made us laugh, and it just . . . stuck. And what might have made others cringe to hear or deem 'corny' still made us smile because it was more than just a nickname to us—it was a nickname that came with a boatload of memories we made together.

I wondered where Sophie had to be that morning—afternoon for her, with the time change—as I tucked my crutches beneath my arms and headed to the art gallery for my first day of teaching.

# CHAPTER 16

**DECEMBER 24, 1940**
(10 Years Old)

"Josie Girl—what are you doing out of bed? It's almost midnight."

I knew I should have stayed in bed—but I couldn't sleep. My cotton sheets were a tangled mess from all the tossing and turning I'd done. But no matter how hard I tried or how long I kept my eyes closed, I couldn't fall asleep. My body was too restless. Even though three months had passed since I was last in the hospital with a fever that scared the doctors and nurses and took years off my parents' lives, my body still had lingering effects ... nightmares.

I got scared that there was something wrong again—that the infection the nurse warned me of was coming back. Maybe I'd gotten hurt again before Dad lifted me into bed three hours ago. Maybe I'd whacked my leg against something and cut it, or more slivers and infections ...

My eyes had been wandering lost in the dark for hours, and I wanted—needed—light. Light that would show me I didn't need to be afraid of the fears I faced in the lonely hours of the dark night. So I'd slipped out from beneath the covers, climbed into the wheelchair that was right next to my bed, and wheeled myself out into the family room. A Christmas tree with soft, flickering lights had greeted me. I needed the light tonight. Needed to stay close to it and be reminded that I was okay.

I was still there an hour later. Not able to sleep and not wanting to leave.

"I can't sleep."

Mom sat cross-legged on the floor next to my wheelchair. Having Mom beside me made me feel less afraid. It always did.

"Are you feeling okay?" she asked.

The yellow lights on the tree were just bright enough for Mom to see me nodding my head. I could see the worry lines on Mom's face. This wasn't the first night I hadn't been able to sleep. My parents told me they thought it might be insomnia—and that it would pass, and I'd be okay and just to sleep whenever I could. I wondered if it was something more. I think Mom and Dad did, too, but they never said anything.

My voice was a tired whisper. "Nightmares again. Just can't sleep." I wondered why Mom was awake, too. "Why are you up?"

"I've stayed up until midnight every Christmas Eve for a long time now—since I was twelve, I think." Mom let out the softest laugh—a laugh that went back in time, traveled through years of memories to reach the one she was remembering right now.

"Why?" I met Mom's face in the dark, and she met mine, and I knew there was a story behind the reason she stayed up until midnight each year until Christmas came at the stroke of twelve.

My eyes silently asked her—*will you tell me the story?*

Hers answered—*yes.*

"When I was growing up, my dad—your grandpa Joe—was a fisherman. He'd sail off in a boat for weeks, sometimes months, at a time and fish deep in the ocean. He'd come home and sell his catch and set off again days later. I remember one time when I was eleven, I stayed awake until two in the morning so I could ask him one more question before he left. Your grandpa Joe always left very early in the morning, so we said our goodbyes the night before. But I needed to talk to him, so I waited until I heard his footsteps come down the hallway, and then I jumped out of bed.

"I remember he looked so startled when he turned around and saw me standing there. It was almost Christmas, and I wanted him to promise me that he would be home for it, that we could celebrate and open presents together as a family. He knelt down in front of me and promised me that he would. I asked him, '*But where do I find you if you're not home on Christmas?*' He smiled at me and said, '*Just look for the light—that's where you'll always find me.*'"

Mom's hand fingered through the dark until it found mine, held my fingers gently in hers. "I didn't understand what he meant then, but I kept looking for the light and trusting that he would show up on Christmas. And he did—a few minutes after midnight on Christmas Eve. But you know what, Josie Girl?"

"What?"

A few seconds ticked by before Mom said anything else, and I sat there, not wanting to shatter this moment by asking Mom to tell me sooner than she was ready to.

"What, Mom?" I said as patiently as a girl my age could.

"I didn't find out until the next Christmas when I was twelve, but your grandpa Joe almost didn't make it home that time. There was a storm that night while at sea—a really bad one—and he got blown completely off course. He didn't know which way was home or how far away it was. But he told me that he looked up—looked past the rain and the clouds, to the furthest thing his eye could see: the *stars.* They showed him the way home. Their light was what saved him and what allowed your grandpa to keep his promise to me." She squeezed my hand. "Did you know that's why we named you Josie—and call you Jo—after your grandpa? Because you're light—the brightest light your dad and I have in our life."

"But I can't see it, Mom. If I really am a bright light, then why is everything still so dark?" Mom understood what I was saying. If I was light, then why did I have to fight so much darkness—the thoughts that tried to tell me there was no hope left for me getting better, getting stronger, getting healthier?

Mom wrapped her arms around me, held me and all my questions close to her chest.

"I saw it, Josie. When you were in the hospital, I begged one of the nurses to let me see you one more time before your dad and I had to go home for the night, even though it was past visiting hours. She finally agreed, and when I slipped into the room to see you, it was so dark in there. I didn't want to turn on the lights and wake you, but my eyes hadn't adjusted to how dark the room was, and I was afraid I'd miss my step and trip and fall onto your bed. But the heart rate machine you were hooked up to—the screen was flickering with light. And it was just enough for me to see you, to kiss you goodnight. It was the light I needed to see—because it was the light that showed me that my little girl was still alive. That she had a heartbeat. That she would be okay. The light on the screen was reflecting the light that's in you."

Mom's eyes were shimmering with tears, and I knew mine were, too. I didn't really know what to say, so I did what I'd learned was sometimes best: I didn't say anything. I just sat there beside Mom, wrapped in her loving embrace.

"Remember, Josie Girl," Mom whispered close to my ear. "It's always darkest before morning. But every day, it's always the light that breaks the dark. And at night, when it's dark, the light's still out there—the moon, the stars, these Christmas tree lights. It's always there."

The clock hanging on the wall, just right above the Christmas tree, chimed midnight—Christmas was here.

Mom started humming one of my favorite Christmas carols: *Silent Night.* And maybe tonight . . . it really was a silent night. Just me. Mom. And light. A memory we painted together with the new set of painting materials my parents got me for my Christmas present.

A memory worth remembering.

# CHAPTER 17

**JULY 09, 1951**
**(Present Day)**

They were here, and so was I.

The ten students who'd signed up sat on the fold-up chairs that were set in the middle of the room, facing me and the desk I sat behind at the head of the room. I watched them—how they talked to the person sitting beside them and laughed and smiled. Even Will, too. He talked with a man who was Timothy Allen—three years Will's senior. I realized that was one of the advantages of living in a small town of 3,600 people: everyone was like a neighbor to you. And the odds of running into someone you knew—whether here in the gallery or somewhere in town—were very high.

Their conversations allowed me a moment to gather up my courage. I knew what I needed to do next: get their attention and wheel myself around the desk in plain view. Right now, my wheelchair was made invisible by the desk, making it seem like I was sitting in a chair. I was, in a sense. But it was a chair on wheels that traveled with me almost everywhere I went.

I took a breath and . . . did it. Wheeled myself out of my hiding spot. Let ten students—strangers—see me as I was and for who I was. And as the noise died away and silence filled the room, everyone looked at me, waiting for me to say something. I felt so vulnerable.

I glanced at Will in the corner seat and wondered if that's how he felt last week at dinner—when he put his hands on the table in a vulnerable position. And how I felt, too, when after dinner was over and I was about to head home, Will's mom grabbed my crutches and helped me to my feet, and Will saw me in a vulnerable state, too.

But . . . it felt almost as if when Will looked at me before showing me his hands, he was able to draw something from me—strength, maybe?—that made him feel safe enough to be honest with me. I'd watched him at the dinner table and how he struggled to hold his fork and knife sometimes in his hands because his fingers couldn't grip them how they should. I'd heard his cutlery clank against the china plates more than once. He'd watched me hobble on crutches, struggling to support the weight of my half-numb and paralyzed body.

We were both vulnerable and yet . . . it felt safe to be.

Will gave me the slightest of nods, and I felt the courage to open my mouth and say something.

"Good morning—and thank you for coming." I held my hands together on my lap so no one would notice how they were trembling. "Before we spend the next two hours together, I thought I should tell you a little bit about myself since I know I'm a stranger to most of you. Here are a few things about me: My name is Josie Carter, and I'm twenty years old. I was born and raised in Pennsylvania. This is my first time in New York, and I'll be staying here over the summer. As most of you probably noticed—I'm in a wheelchair. I've been in one since I was six years old. I was diagnosed with polio at a young age, and it resulted in permanent paralysis in my legs and feet. I love art, and I've painted since I was a kid. I've never had anyone teach me how to paint, and I've never taught anyone how to, either."

I paused long enough to draw a breath and continue. "I know most people don't start off their introductions by sharing their disabilities and how they're unqualified. But someone I know still believed I was capable of teaching art even after I told them what I'm telling you—that I'm limited in both what I can do and what I can offer you. I don't want any of you to feel obligated to stay if this isn't what you signed up for. But if you're willing to try and learn, I'm just as willing to try and teach you what I've learned. I may not know the answer to every question you have—but I'll answer the ones I can."

I looked around the room and saw the same ten faces still meeting mine. But I think I saw them differently this time because at first, I saw ten people who could all stand on their own two feet. But now? I saw ten people who all sat in a chair and were broken in some way, like me. I lived with disabilities and the trauma I'd experienced because of them. Others in the room lived with the trauma of a broken heart. Others lived with the trauma of broken families and abusive relationships. Others lived with the trauma of anxiety and fear. Just because some traumas were visible and others weren't didn't mean that it didn't break us just as bad. And our brokenness, even though visible on the outside for some and invisible on the inside for others, could bring us together. Because even though suffering is individual, it's corporal. It unites.

And as I started teaching the basics of art to the beginners in the class and allowed those with experience to go ahead and start painting, I saw a group of people who were willing to learn and let the girl in the wheelchair teach them what she knew.

"Why did you do that?"

Will kept pace beside me as we left the art gallery at noon. We lived two houses from each other and would be neighbors over the summer, so when he asked if he could walk me home, I was grateful for his company. Will had proved to be a friend to me in the short time I'd known him.

I looked over at him. "Do what?"

"Why did you tell everyone that you were unqualified and have health disabilities?" I could tell that Will wasn't asking because he was judging me for that decision, but because he wanted to understand the *why* behind it.

"I guess . . . I just don't want to be afraid of who I am or feel like there are things I need to hide about myself. My inexperience. My wheelchair. I want people to see me for who I am and what I am—and it's up to them from there whether they believe in me or not." I'd spent too many years feeling like a stranger in my own skin because I wasn't comfortable being me: the girl in the wheelchair that painted.

"But what would you have done—if they hadn't believed in you and walked away?" Whether Will realized it or not, as soon as that question came out of his mouth, he started massaging his fingers. Like he wasn't only rubbing out the ache and pain holding a paintbrush had caused his hands, but rubbing out memories where someone hadn't believed in him and something he wanted to do . . . or believed he could do something that he didn't *want* to do.

"Honestly? I probably would have done what I've always done . . . let myself cry, and then moved on from it."

There isn't a certain number of times for someone to be hurt by another's words or actions to where it doesn't hurt anymore. Hurt doesn't work like that. It doesn't go away after a certain number of times it has dealt a heavy and hard blow. Hurt is painful—and pain is real. And you can't heal what hasn't been acknowledged hurts. Unless you let yourself feel the pain that was inflicted on you, you'll never experience the healing that follows it.

"My dad once told me that when someone hurts me, I need to stay true to who I am, not letting the things others do to me harden my heart." Dad's words had helped me to take the verbal stones people had hurled at me and not retaliate but build something with them—a home. A place where good could be brought out of bad things. "I can't say for certain that's what I would have done if people left the class, but it's what I would have tried to do."

Will nodded slow at my words—almost as if he was acknowledging that he was right there with me and did the same, too.

"Who taught you to paint?" I asked him. When I thought about the painting he'd started today and would work on for the next few days—a mountain with its head sticking high into the clouds and its feet planted at the bottom of an endless ocean—I could see why his mom wanted him to become an artist. Will had talent. But just because someone has talent at something doesn't meant that *has* to be their dream.

"My dad did." Will's face was happy and heavy at the same time. Talking about someone you loved and lost made you proud and sad to speak of their memory. "Every fall, he would travel across the country to different art galleries and museums to sell the paintings he did that year. Sometimes he took me with him, and there was one time we were flying somewhere—it was such a long time ago, I don't remember where—and our flight was delayed for a few hours. I got so bored as an eight-year-old kid just sitting in the airport and waiting for time to go by. My dad grabbed a notebook and asked if I wanted to learn how to sketch a fire-breathing dragon."

He stopped just long enough to smile. "Sketching, painting—that became something I did with my dad. Most of my childhood memories of him are the two of us doing that together. For my dad, it was his passion in life. For me, it was a hobby—and a way I could always connect with him."

"What about you?" I was grateful that Will asked me questions and didn't rely on me to carry on the entire conversation. His questions and the way he asked them put me at ease and made me feel . . . comfortable. Like I was talking with a childhood friend.

The road to home was just ahead—and a two-story Victorian-style house waited at the end of it. Our conversation and our time together were coming to an end. "I taught myself. I did it one day, and—I don't know—it just made sense to me. The colors. The brushes. But it wasn't always easy. I learned the most by making the most mistakes and teaching myself how to correct them."

Will stopped in front of the white-picket-fence leading to his house. "See you tomorrow." His question came out also as a question, wondering if we could walk and talk together again.

"See you then."

We put a bookmark on our conversation and not an end to it. I think in that moment after we said goodbye, we both knew that we'd have many more conversations ahead of us. That the copper-haired boy and the wispy-haired girl were only on the beginning pages of the chapters that would write themselves over the summer.

I didn't mind one bit—and I didn't think Will did, either.

# CHAPTER 18

I could still perfectly see the salt-and-pepper bearded man's face when he showed up at my doorstep thirty minutes ago. How his eyes widened a little when he realized that the customer who'd phoned for a taxi from *Grange Avenue* was a handicapped young woman who would need his help getting into and out of a taxi.

I wanted to see the town and sketch what I saw from the backseat of the yellow taxicab along the way. One of the art commissions Will's mom gave me was for Honeyville Baptist Church—the church she'd attended growing up, where she got married, where Will went to Sunday school through his childhood years.

The taxi driver told me his name was Bennett Brown, but he went by B.B. He invited me to call him the same. When I told him my name and why I was here for the summer, he grinned and told me that the fifteen-year-old girl in my class—the one whose name was Patricia but went by Pat—was his niece. B.B. told me that Pat had just started taking art lessons a year ago when she got into high school, and she loved it—and that she was so glad she could continue taking classes while school was out for the summer.

She loved to paint.

B.B. loved how happy it made her.

I loved her passion for it.

B.B. pointed a finger out the left window of his driver's seat. "Up here on the left is where the church is. It's closed—only open on Sundays and Wednesdays—but I'll pull over so you can get out and take a look around."

B.B. stopped in front of a building with white clapboards and stained-glass windows. I wondered if the church in front of me was like what Sophie was seeing on the London streets: old English architectural structures that, with one glance, made you know that there was a lot of history that had taken place inside its walls.

I could understand why this was a place you'd want to go to each Sunday and get married in and have your kids grow up in and why Will's mom wanted me to capture this place in pencil sketches and paint colors. It was a reminder that even in a world that was marred with the stains of war and violence, there was still beauty in it. Places like this that had stood the test of time for over one hundred years were proof of that lasting beauty.

B.B. helped me out of the car and handed me my crutches. He led me to the front door of the church. It was locked, but I could see through the stained-glass windows near the door. "If you want my two cents on this, you should definitely paint the church building itself. But there's something inside that you should paint, too—on the back wall behind the pulpit."

He stepped back and let me take his spot in front of the window. I immediately saw what B.B. was referring to. It was too big and captivating to miss.

"Is that a painting?"

B.B. nodded from behind me. "It is. I'm not a churchgoer, but Pat told me about that painting. The church has been doing some renovations in the sanctuary room over the past two years, and that painting was one of the things added to the room." He laughed a straight-from-your-gut kind of laugh. "I remember later that week when I saw Pat and my sister's family, she couldn't stop talking about the painting. I haven't seen it for myself until now, but the way Pat kept going on and on about it, I felt like I could picture exactly how it really looked in my head."

I laughed at that, too. I had been that kid who could talk forever about art—paintings I wanted to paint, others I'd seen and couldn't get out of my mind, shading and colors and designs that got my mind rolling and my hands working.

When I looked at the painting, there was something familiar about it. Not that I'd seen the painting somewhere before, and I was beginning to remember where I recognized it from, but the painting itself—the people in it, the boat they were in, the stormy sea they were on. I knew the story it was wordlessly telling.

Jesus. His disciples. A boat on a stormy sea. Fear and faith, colliding.

A silent reminder whispered across the tempest and sea: *It's okay to be scared. It's okay to struggle with fear and doubt and wrestle with faith. It's okay to be human. It's okay to be broken and wonder why Jesus is sleeping and why He hasn't ended the storm already.*

Life isn't like an algorithm that's predictable, and the outcome is the same. It's hard. Unexpected. Complicated. Scary. And maybe the storms in life aren't there to throw us off course, but to help us stay on course. To help us stay alert, awake, eyes open wide to the things that matter in life and the moments ticking by. To wrestle with fear and doubt and come out with a stronger faith in the end.

I stepped back from the glass window but pressed into the imprint it left on my mind and heart. "Thank you for showing me this, B.B. It's perfect—and exactly what I want to paint."

His lips parted into a wordless smile that said, *you're welcome.*

Something golden blonde, like sun rays, caught my attention in the background behind B.B. I focused on it—rather, who it was that walked past the church and whose face I'd seen a glimpse of. A face framed with honey-blonde hair and soft freckles on her cheeks.

I remembered that face.

The seventeen-year-old girl in my class, the one who had experience with painting and was timid and shy and barely breathed a word during the two hours she was in the room with me.

"Alice!" Her name came out of my mouth fast, loud.

Alice stopped and turned, looked behind, and saw me. She stood glued to where she was, frozen like a deer caught in car headlights.

B.B. told me he'd wait for me in the taxi as I walked to Alice. "Hey, Alice," I said. "What are you doing in this part of town?"

Alice pulled strands of her hair behind her ear—a nervous habit, I assumed. She seemed caught off guard by our meeting here unexpectedly and needed a minute to get her head back on her shoulders. "I'm a nanny to three kids who live down the street from here. I was just on my way there. I should go . . ."

"Okay," I said, and offered her an understanding smile. "I'll see you tomorrow."

Alice nodded and walked off in the opposite direction. I couldn't help but stare at the girl whose figure began to blur as she faded from view and wonder—*what is she afraid of?* I saw it so clearly in her eyes now and in her body language yesterday.

Fear chased after Alice like her shadow did.

# CHAPTER 19

**MARCH 17, 1941**
**(10 Years Old)**

"Doesn't it feel good to be outside?"

Mom's voice pulled me out of my thoughts and startled me. I blinked in the ocean waves again from the shoreline. Mom sat on a beach towel, sand imprinted on her legs and feet, and looked up at me where I sat beside her in my wheelchair.

"Yeah, it does." Our Pennsylvania bones were rattled from the cold temperatures last winter. Mom suggested we should go somewhere on a family vacation for a week. Dad agreed and scheduled time off from work. And Sophie came along, too.

Early spring was supposed to be a time where things come back, awake from their winter slumber, thaw from their frozen sheets. But this spring, things weren't thawing—they were hardening. Between Sophie's parents. Mom and Dad hadn't told me everything—they spoke a lot the past month in hushed whispers and worried tones about whatever was happening between Sophie's parents—but I knew things weren't good. Sophie's dad, Jack, always had this side to him that . . . scared me. Whenever our families were together for a reunion or the holidays, Uncle Jack was kind and generous with his money, but he easily got angry—and I knew he said a lot of things he shouldn't and done others no one spoke of. Maybe that's why Mom and Dad never let me stay at Sophie's house over the summer and why it was always Sophie coming to ours instead.

When Dad came to tell me last week that Sophie was going to be staying with us for the next few weeks, I knew things were bad. Because if Sophie couldn't stay in her own home with her parents— a place that should always be safe—something had broken in their family. A month and a half later, I found out what it was: their marriage. They divorced. And Sophie went home with her mom after the child custody battle while her dad packed his bags and left without saying goodbye.

A few days after Sophie got here, my parents realized that we needed to get away for a bit. Sophie needed to be distracted. I needed to be in a warmer environment—I'd gotten sick so many times over the winter because it was too cold for my body to stay warm. Mom and Dad needed a break from work stress and the strain of dealing with Mom's older sister's marriage unraveling at the seams.

So, there we were—at a beach house rental in St. Petersburg, Florida. Me, thawing out my frozen bones. Sophie, thawing out her frozen heart. Mom and Dad, thawing out their frozen minds. The four of us were trying to welcome spring even though we knew it was temporary. Once we got back home, it would still be winter.

Sophie's laugh was contagious—and I realized that was the first time I'd heard her laugh since she got here. Sophie had smiled, laughed more on the inside than she did on the outside, but she never sounded happy, looked happy, since she showed up on our doorstep with two suitcases in hand.

I followed the sound of Sophie's laughter and spotted her and Dad in knee-deep salty water, splashing and spraying each other until the other was soaked. I smiled at that—how Dad made Sophie happy, and Sophie made him happy. I sometimes wondered if Dad hadn't smiled as much because of me . . . my health. Because when you love someone, and they're hurting from something, you hurt with them, too. And you don't stop hurting with them until the pain is gone. But my pain wouldn't go away. Could I ever play with Dad like Sophie did? I wanted to, but I didn't have all the things Sophie did—a healthy body that wasn't broken on the inside and the outside. A healthy body that could walk and run and splash in the ocean waters.

"You okay, Josie Girl?" Mom startled me again. I couldn't seem to focus . . . I kept losing myself in my thoughts, staring out at those Florida waves.

"I'm tired—having a hard time focusing on anything right now."

Mom's eyes focused on me and narrowed with concern. "Do you want to go inside and rest for a little bit?"

"No," I said. "I'd rather stay out here. I want to be outside for a little bit longer." I'd spent more of my life indoors than outdoors, and I wanted to be here—in the sunshine, on the sand, near the water.

"Okay," Mom said, her voice pinched with worry. "We'll all be out here for another twenty minutes or so, and then we need to get showered and ready for lunch."

Twenty minutes—I wanted to make them count. When Dad and Sophie stopped splashing and came ashore, I called out to him.

Dad came over a minute later, bent over my wheelchair, dripping wet water onto my dry bathing suit. "Yeah, Josie?"

"Dad—I want to get closer to the water. Will you help me?" I felt so fragile and scared in that moment. An invisible wall separated me from where I was and the shoreline. I couldn't get to where I wanted to be—just ten feet ahead—on my own. I needed Dad's help.

"Come here." Dad opened his arms to me and scooped me up into them, cradling me several feet above the sand. His footprints sunk into the soggy sand as the shy ocean water tickled his toes and slipped back into the deep. I wanted to feel that—to remember what it was like to feel water and sand running over my feet and in-between my toes.

"Careful you don't drop her!" Sophie's mischievous laughter rolled in like the waves.

Dad pretended to lose his grip on me, and I felt my stomach lurch a little. "Dad!" I instinctively wrapped my arms tighter around his neck, even though I knew he never had and never would let me drop.

"What?" he said, feigning innocence even though the smile on his lips said he was guilty as charged.

A salty breeze sprayed onto my face, and the salt stung my chapped lips. The water was up to Dad's shins now. "Dad." My voice dropped low, quiet. "I want to stand. Will you help me?"

Dad's face grew serious, and the smile that graced his lips was now a flat line. "Hold on to me," he said.

*I'd never let go.*

Dad gripped me under my armpits, suspending me just an inch above the sandy surface. The same water that went to Dad's shins went to my knees. "A wave's coming." His voice was like an invitation for the water to draw close.

I took a breath and held it like I was about to plunge underwater. I didn't know why I did that—maybe part of me still dared to believe that I'd be able to feel the water on my skin and not just know it was washing over me because I saw it with my eyes.

It happened so fast—the wave crashing onto my toes and legs—and that moment was over too soon. I heard the waves and saw them coming, but I felt nothing. Not the coldness of the water or the saltiness of it that stings your bare skin.

Something sharp and familiar stabbed my chest: disappointment.

I didn't know what I was hoping for out there . . . maybe I was just hoping. Without hope, there's no reason for living. Even if the odds were completely stacked against me, giving me a mile-long list of reasons why I shouldn't dare to hope again, something in me still did. Hope gave me purpose, even when reality brought me disappointment. Hope that there was something more out there for me. More than hospitals and wheelchairs and polio.

The breeze picked up, swept over the sand, and picked up the coolness of the waves. I shuddered a little in Dad's arms. I felt him tense.

"Are you cold?"

I nodded against him.

Dad held me closer and tighter to him. "When we get back to the house, you can take a shower and warm up and rest for a while before we go out to lunch, okay?"

The warm water from the shower and the polyester blanket over my body did nothing to warm me as I rested in bed. My teeth chattered like soldiers marching in unison. Even though the door to my bedroom was open, I wished I wasn't alone right then. Dad was in the shower. Mom was in the bathroom, detangling the wet knots in Sophie's hair. I wanted to call out for Mom, but I couldn't get my upper lip to separate from the bottom one.

My vision started going dark, and to my eyes, it looked like someone had drawn the curtains and turned off the lights. But I was staring at a window streaming in sunlight.

*Mom . . . Mom.*

It was happening again: I was starting to pass out. Blood rushed to my head, and in a room that was a kaleidoscope of color, I was colorless. Grey. Pale. Fading.

*Mom . . .*

I fought against the darkness that wanted to envelope my lids with a black seal. I didn't want this to happen again . . . *no, no, no.*

I heard a voice coming from down the hall—Mom. She said something, but I couldn't make sense of her words. They were a cacophony of garbled noise to my ears: *knots . . . brush . . . bedroom.*

I knew if I could hold on for even thirty seconds longer, Mom would be here. She'd see me. She'd know something was wrong. She'd help. But my eyes clamped shut, and I couldn't open them. My body surrendered to the thick oblivion beckoning me to unwelcomed slumber.

The last thing I heard was Mom's footsteps creaking against the wooden floorboards as she stepped into the bedroom.

# CHAPTER 20

Three days into teaching art classes, and all ten students still showed up. They were learning, growing, becoming. My mind couldn't wrap itself around that fact.

I didn't know what I was doing until I just . . . did it. But somehow, it was working. I silently prayed it would work today, too, because I was doing something different than I had the past three days. Instead of having my students work on replicating artwork done by other artists or practicing basic brush strokes, I told them an hour ago that I wanted them to create something themselves. It could be anything—it didn't matter as long it was something original, something that couldn't be accredited to anyone but them. They'd looked at me and seemed as caught off guard as I felt in that moment. Because I hadn't planned on that today, but yet it felt as if somewhere between my head and heart, I'd known I would do this today all along.

I glanced at the clock: their hour was up. It wasn't enough time for some of them to have completed whatever they were painting on their canvases, even for the beginners in the class, but it was enough for a beginning—and enough of a glimpse to know what the end result might be.

I asked each of them to bring their easels to the center of the room and form a circle shape with their chairs. Each of them did without questioning what I was doing or why I asked them to. And there we were—the ten of them and the one of me—in a circle where everyone's work was seen and noticed by the other.

"I wanted us to form this circle because it unites us," I said. "And I wanted us to be able to look to the person on our left and right and see that every single person's artwork here looks different from the other—and that's okay. That's what makes art beautiful: it's unique."

I took a breath, tried to put the words swimming in my head into words. "Pablo Picasso painted something that powerfully changed the world of art after his close friend committed suicide, and Picasso suffered from depression because of that loss. Georgia O'Keefe painted a flower that many saw as ugly because, during the day, it didn't have much beauty—it was prickly and unattractive. But at night, it was stunningly beautiful. People missed the beauty it offered because they weren't patient enough to see it. Jean Francois-Millet painted about peasants and French citizens who gleaned in fields from sunup to sundown just to earn enough to survive.

"Why am I telling you those things? Because the most masterful paintings we've ever seen were painted by artists who had known some form of suffering. They painted with their hearts and not just with their hands. And they created beautiful things out of hard ones. That's the goal in art: to paint with your hands but let your heart—your life experiences, your losses, your victories—be the inspiration behind your work. All the things that make your heart beat, break, bleed, and heal—that's what we paint. That's what makes art unique and beautiful because it's painting a story no one else can tell but you."

Everyone in the circle looked at me with eyes that hadn't dared to blink, but someone's gaze landed hard on me. It caught my attention, and I looked straight across from me.

Alice.

She didn't look at me with the same fearful eyes I saw a few days ago on the church street corner. This time, they were almost . . . alive. Like something I'd said had resonated with her and brought out a side to her she hardly, *if* ever, showed.

But the moment was severed when Alice realized I was looking at her, too.

After a moment of silence that stretched to its breaking point, my voice found words again. "We'll end here today on that note. I'll see you all tomorrow."

Alice didn't look at me again, even when we crossed paths on her way out the door. But I couldn't stop picturing her face in my mind —a still-shot of the honey-blonde girl who'd looked alive and unafraid.

If somehow my words instilled that life and bravery into her—I'd speak for the rest of my life.

# CHAPTER 21

(Present Day)

The smell of *chicken à la king* and fresh biscuits made my stomach growl.

I'd been sitting in my wheelchair on the side of Will's house, watching people grab heaping plates of food and talking amongst themselves. No one seemed fazed by the ninety-degree weather— except for me. I sat where I could find shade, refuge from the blistering sun, at a potluck gathering with people that were perfect strangers to me. Part of me wondered what I was doing here, why I'd accepted Mrs. Ridge's Saturday afternoon potluck invitation when I dropped off the painting of the church I'd completed yesterday. But she'd asked, and I'd said yes, and well, here I was—sitting in the shadows with a plate of food on my lap.

"What are you doing?" The voice snuck up behind me like an intruder, quiet and unexpected.

*Will.* I'd wondered why I hadn't seen him yet, where he'd been.

"Hiding?" I caught the playful tone in his voice as he came around my wheelchair and stood in front of me, a plate of food in his hands, too.

"No," I said, trying to hide a smile that quickly grew on my face. Will brought out a playful side to me that not many people did—a side that remembered what it was like to laugh and smile genuinely. "I'm sitting."

"Mind if I hide with you?" He sank to the grass beside me after I nodded my head, still fighting that smile on my lips while he grinned wide. We were the two kids in the shadows playing hide-and-seek from the group of people scattered across the grassy front yard that didn't even know we were hiding to begin with.

"Why aren't you out there with everyone else?" I'd sat in this spot for the past twenty minutes, and I hadn't seen Will once.

He shrugged, slow. "Most of those people are friends of Mom's from her women's group. I don't really know them, and they don't really know me."

He was hiding from people, and I was hiding from harsh sunlight and memories.

"And?"

He smiled, knowing I'd caught on to him. "*And* Mom told me you were here, but she hadn't really seen you since after you said hi to her when you showed up. So I was looking for you."

Will had looked, and he'd found me. And I was grateful he had.

"I saw the painting you did of the church. Mom couldn't stop talking about it." Will paused for the briefest of seconds. "It's really good."

It's one thing to look at something you've created and wonder and hope that it's good enough. And it's another thing for someone to look you in the eye and tell you that it's more than that. I think everyone needs that someone in their life to affirm and remind them that they're good enough. Will's *it's really good* was that for me— that affirmation that I'd given it my all and done well.

"Thanks." I didn't fight holding back a smile this time.

We ate in silence, Will finishing his food and me lagging several minutes behind.

"Are you done with that?" Will gestured to the plate resting on my lap and the fork I'd abandoned a minute ago, too full to finish what remained on my plate.

I nodded.

Will reached out his hand to take my plate and stack it on top of his empty one. But somewhere between me handing him the plate and Will receiving it, something happened. Neither of us was holding my plate, and we had creamy sauce coating our hands. The leftover pieces of chicken and mushrooms I hadn't finished hung limp on my dress.

I think if I hadn't looked at Will's face, I would have laughed at that moment—the two of us sticky and wet with alfredo sauce. But I had—and I saw that he was nowhere near laughing or smiling or anything. He looked hollow. Here was the broken boy I thought I'd seen in the dark green flecks of his eyes when I'd first met him. The boy whose brokenness was visible in the shadows.

"Will." I said his name, but he didn't look up at me. His eyes were on his hands and his curled fingers, and then I realized . . . he'd dropped the plate. Not me. And that this wasn't the first time he hadn't been able to hold something in his hands that others did without even thinking twice—or once, even—about. Something simple and easy had become hard and complicated.

I understood that.

I felt that.

I lived that.

"Will." His eyes were limpid like a cloudless summer sky. "It's okay." My fingers instinctively reached out to his and barely touched them, hovering an inch above his gnarled skin and veins coated in creamy sauce. If Will broke, I wanted to be there to catch those falling pieces.

"It's okay," I said again—because something inside me told me that Will needed to hear it a second time. And this time, he looked up at me, trying to sort out if my shadow-veiled words were true. *Was it okay?*

He must have sensed the honesty in my words because his eyes didn't stare down at his hands again. They stayed focused on me, on the only words of comfort I could give to him in that moment.

When you're shattered with disappointment or devastation, words fall short. They can only penetrate the surface of what you're feeling. But pain goes deep. Sometimes, deeper than words can go. But reminding the person who is hurting of those two words—it's okay—can sometimes keep them from spiraling even deeper. Not that what had happened to them was okay or the pain it had caused them was okay. But the mistakes and accidents they had because of what had happened to them and how it had limited their ability to do simple things?

It wasn't their fault—it was okay.

Will dropping his paintbrush at class because he'd lose his grip on it was *okay*. Will not being able to hold up a plate right then was *okay*. Me not being able to get in and out of a taxi car by myself or needing help with the simplest of tasks was *okay*.

It's *okay* not to do everything okay and to need help.

"There's a drinking fountain in the back where we can wash our hands." A flicker of light returned to Will's sad eyes as he spoke those words. He was trying—trying to pick himself back up and not stay stuck there on the ground.

Sauce dripped from Will's fingers, staining the green grass a creamy white hue, as we disappeared around the house. Will let me wash my hands, and the cool water felt good on my hot skin. He washed his hands next and, besides the stain on my dress, we'd fixed this. Maybe we couldn't erase what happened like I couldn't erase the stain on my dress. But we'd redeemed it. Some moments are like that: they can't be erased and made new, but they can be fixed and made better.

"Are you thirsty?" Will lowered his head and started drinking the water that spewed out from somewhere beneath the earth.

I felt my blood turn hypothermia-cold, and it took everything in me not to scream for Will to stop, to not drink that water. My hand was a tight fist, and my fingernails punctured into my fleshy palms.

Will took my silence as a *no*. But he didn't know, couldn't understand that a drinking fountain was a nightmare to me. A nightmare I could still touch with my fingertips and get goosebumps and break out into a cold sweat from. And that every time I saw someone drink from one, it terrified me.

A drinking fountain. A park drinking fountain that I had drunk from as a thirsty five-year-old girl was what brought me from standing on my feet to sitting in a wheelchair.

Where I got polio.

# CHAPTER 22

**MARCH 18, 1941**
**(10 Years Old)**

*I know I'm dreaming. My movements are slow, sluggish. My mind is induced with anesthesia-like unawareness. Numbness.*

*I know I'm dreaming because I'm seeing myself from the eyes of someone that's not me—like an out-of-body experience, watching something from the outside and feeling invisible to everything around me. And I'm watching my five-year-old self run and skip and trample grass blades and crunchy November leaves under her feet. I listen to her let out laughter faster than she can suck in air.*

*I know I'm dreaming because I know what's going to happen five seconds from now. Her shoe is going to catch on a tree root, and she's going to fall and have blood and dirt on her knees.*

*I wonder if I can change this, stop what I know is coming from happening. I know it's a dream—but can I change this? Can I rewrite this part of her story—my story—even though I know when I awake, it will be untouched, irreversible?*

*"Careful!" I call out to the five-year-old me, daring to try.*

*But my voice can't be heard. It's like I'm stuck in a bubble, and sounds can filter in, but mine can't penetrate through the paper-thin barrier. So, I watch her tumble and fall hard onto the ground.*

*I instinctively look to the left, where the wooden park benches are, because I know Mom and Dad are there. They come running to her side when they hear her crying and watch her grabbing onto her scraped and dirty knees.*

*Dad's there in an instant, and he lifts her up off the ground, props her up on his lap. Mom's there now, too, asking if she's okay, if she got hurt anywhere else besides her knees.*

*Dad holds her in his arms and stands up. I reach out and try to grab his arm because I know what he doesn't. This moment is like an over-watched TV episode: I know exactly what will happen. I can predict with perfect accuracy what the characters will say, do, and act in every next scene. But my hand is like thin air, and it vanishes through Dad's shirt sleeve, even though I'm pulling and tugging on it and begging him to stop.*

*I'm helpless and watching Mom and Dad both take handfuls of water from the drinking fountain and wash the blood and dirt off her knees. And when she feels the cool water on her skin, and she's stopped crying, she realizes something: she's thirsty. She wants water.*

*No! I scream it as loud as I can, knowing they can't hear me. But I can't hold it inside.*

*Dad's picking her up and lifting her high enough to where her mouth can catch water and swallow it down in thirsty gulps. She's drinking it in like a thirsty fire hydrant, taking water instead of giving it.*

*And then she goes home.*

*I'm in her bedroom now, watching her wake and feel so, so sick . . . and she starts throwing up all the liquid and food in her stomach onto her blankets and pajamas. I'm slow-crawling to the edge of her bed because I need to grab onto the younger me and prepare her for what's coming, so she's not hit with a tsunami wave of shock and devastation like I was. I need to tell her what her parents are reading in the newspaper that night that, if they'd seen this morning, would have changed everything. They're rereading yesterday's headline in the living room, clenched fists wrinkling each corner of the page.*

"CITYWIDE SEWAGE LEAK - LAST NIGHT ON NOVEMBER 20, 1946, SEWER LINES THROUGHOUT THE CITY OF QUEEN VILLAGE, PHILADELPHIA, BURST AT APPROXIMATELY 12 MIDNIGHT. UNDERGROUND SPRINGS AND PUBLIC DRINKING FOUNTAINS HAVE BEEN CONTAMINATED. PUBLIC HEALTH OFFICIALS ARE WORKING HARD TO REPAIR THE DAMAGE. UNTIL THEN, A CITYWIDE MANDATE FOR QUEEN VILLAGE HAS BEEN INSTALLED THAT PUBLIC DRINKING FOUNTAINS MUST BE AVOIDED FOR HEALTH SAFETY UNTIL OTHERWISE STATED."

*I know what's going to happen next: Mom and Dad are going to put the pieces together, realizing that their daughter drank from a public drinking fountain yesterday at the park, and rush her to the hospital when they find her in her room, soaking her blankets in vomit.*

*She's feeling sick because of the water, they realize. Sick because of the feces-and-urine-contaminated water they unknowingly let her freely drink.*

*But I can't warn the little girl on the bed. I'm still crawling towards her by the time Dad picks her up, and the three of them get in the car.*

*No! No! No!*

*I'm in the hospital now, and the younger me is in bed, and the doctors are talking to Mom and Dad. Telling them that she has all the symptoms of paralytic poliomyelitis—her leg muscles are weakening, and she has difficulty breathing and swallowing, and she's running a fever and still vomiting. She doesn't understand what paralytic poliomyelitis is at that age or what the doctors have to do to confirm that diagnosis: a cerebrospinal fluid sample.*

*The main doctor—I can't remember his name now—is trying to prepare Mom and Dad for what was a 'maybe' then and a 'definite' after the test results come back. That she won't get better. That her leg muscles are deteriorating. That there's nothing that can be done to reverse the damage. That soon, she won't be able to walk on her own. Her muscles are losing their strength, and she's slowly losing her ability to feel her legs.*

*I look at the younger me on the bed. She's feeling too sick and too weak to move or keep her eyes open. She doesn't know what the words paralytic poliomyelitis and permanent paralysis and handicaps mean, so she's not scared. All she knows is that she's a sick little girl who wants to get better so she can run and play again.*

*But she won't be running again. She won't be walking again on her own. No, she'll be sitting in a wheelchair or standing with crutches. She won't remember what it's like to have feeling in her legs and for them to be strong enough to hold herself up because those realities will turn into the fading and distant memories of a kindergartener.*

*I'm crying again because I don't want this little girl to have to endure this. I wish I could take this heavy, heavy cross from her and carry it for her. But I can't. Because it's me wishing I can take something from the younger me and give it to the older me—the one watching this moment in my life through a dream. Either way, whether in real life or in this dream, it's still me—and I still have to carry this cross.*

*"Josie?" Someone says my name, and it startles me, makes me jump. The voice is so clear, so close by, but I can't figure out where it's coming from.*

*They say my name again, and I shut my eyes, trying to listen to where the sound is coming from. How to find it. Where to reach it. And when I open my eyes, I'm . . . awake. I'm in a hospital bed, but I'm not five anymore. I'm ten. I'm not invisible, trapped inside a bubble; people can hear and touch and see me.*

*I tilt my head to the left because I know someone's sitting beside me. It's Sophie. I don't know where I am or why I'm here. But if Sophie's here, then I must be okay.*

*But when I meet her face, I see her eyes are red and rimmed with tears. She was crying, is crying. It scares me . . . Sophie never cries. Not even after her dad left, and she became a single child with a single parent. She's always been so strong. But she's crying. And I don't understand why.*

*"Jo . . . " Sophie can't finish her sentence.*

*"Sophie, what's wrong?" I find my voice for the first time since waking up. My throat is dry, my voice is hoarse, and my tongue cleaves to the roof of my mouth.*

*Sophie still doesn't say anything, but she's crying and looking towards the end of the bed, down where my legs and feet are.*

*I look, too.*

*And I scream.*

# CHAPTER 23

"Is there any more blue paint?" Alice's words were a library-quiet whisper, not wanting to disrupt everyone else in the room who was hard at work on their own paintings.

"Yes, let me get it for you." I wheeled myself over to the back of the room, where cans of paint were stacked against the wall. "Here you go."

Alice whispered a soft *thank you* and retreated to her workstation.

I'd been watching her a lot today—probably more today than any other day. Because today, I saw something in Alice that inspired me —passion. I watched her slip into a world of colors, and she made it seem so vibrant and saturated with life and purpose. No one else in the room had that light in their eyes when painting. But Alice did, and her eyes were like beacons: bright and unmissable.

Alice's easel was positioned away from my view, and I couldn't help but wonder what was on the other side of that canvas because whatever she was creating and bringing to life on there was bringing her to life, too. I watched her face fall for the briefest of seconds, and

I found myself wheeling over to where she was. "Do you need any help?"

Alice looked hesitant at first, and I wondered if she would decline even if she did need help. But she surprised me by saying, "Yes. I'm almost done with this painting, but I'm not sure if it's any good. Could you" —she paused— "give me your honest opinion on it?"

I nodded, and Alice sidestepped. She invited me into her creating space, and I knew that was a vulnerable thing for her to do. Because giving someone access to your work and asking them to critique it honestly—that's terrifying. There's always the chance they'll love it and the chance they won't. Always the chance they'll be loving with their words or harsh with their judgment. It's downright terrifying to show someone such a personal part of who you are and what you love. And Alice trusting me in this moment with her work, knowing I could easily build her up or tear her down with my words, wasn't something I took lightly.

Trust taken lightly isn't trust at all. Trust is heavy. You feel the burden of it. And it must be handled carefully—because trust can easily be fractured and broken.

I didn't want to lose the trust Alice had in me right then with careless and thoughtless words. I would honor her trust. And as my eyes found her painting, they stared into the deepest blue ocean waves with bubbly white foam. They were at war with each other— the waves. Beating, crashing, and smashing each other with powerful forces of water. An angry ocean. It was all-together haunting and mesmerizing.

"Alice, this is incredible." It wasn't at all what I expected to see. I thought I'd find effort; instead, I found that coupled with natural talent. Talent that, with time and practice, could be turned into an opportunity to be considered professional. I knew art and the talent it required to make it far. Alice had that, could reach that.

Alice looked genuinely surprised, as if she was expecting me to have a long list of things that needed to be changed in order to improve her work. But the changes I saw that could be made were few and minimal.

She didn't say a word but watched me. Tested the weight of my words to see if they were stable, if they were truthful.

"How did you learn to paint like this?" I kept my voice to a whisper.

"I—I don't know, really." Alice shrugged a little. "I started painting when I was younger. It's just been a hobby of mine for a long time now."

"Keep doing it, Alice. You're talented—really. And tomorrow, I can show you some techniques I learned that I think would help you if you'd like."

I saw a ghost of a smile on Alice's face—and it widened even more after she and everyone else left for the day. When I saw her smile like that, a smile came to my own lips. Because it hit me in that moment how I could help Alice grow and develop her talent.

That thought turned into an idea, and that idea developed into a plan as I walked home with Will.

I needed to walk with Will's mom—and that's what had me showing up unexpectedly on their doorstep, stepping into the living room, and sitting beside her on the grey couch. That's what had me asking her if I could talk to her about the commissions she'd given me.

She nodded at me, slow and curious.

I didn't know where to begin, so I jumped right in. "I wanted to ask if you would let me give the rest of the art commissions to one of my students instead of me doing them."

"May I ask why?"

"My student is very talented. And I know, given the opportunity, she can go far with her artwork. I want to give her that chance to develop her skill and to grow as an artist." Giving Alice this chance —being able to help her, have her trust in me grow, see that smile on her face—made it worth the trade-off. I'd rather lose this chance and give it to her than hold onto it for myself.

I saw so much of Alice in me. Talent and doubt. Capability and low confidence. Bravery and timidity. Maybe that's why I felt so strongly about giving Alice this chance: because she deserved to have someone believe in her enough to give her an opportunity she didn't think she was good enough for.

"I trust your judgment, Josie. If this is something you feel so strongly about, then yes, you can give the commissions to your student." I didn't know how I'd earned her trust and confidence in such a short time, but for whatever reason she believed in me, I was grateful.

"Do you think I could talk with Alice's parents and get their permission before I ask Alice if she wants to take on the commissions?"

Something changed on Will's mom's face. I didn't miss it. It was like watching a flower go from blooming one minute to withering the next.

"Alice's parents died when she was younger in an automobile accident. She lives with her uncle. To be honest, Josie, I was surprised to see her name on the list of students in your class." She paused, trying to collect her thoughts and put them into words. "Alice's uncle has been . . . very protective over her since he was appointed her legal guardian when she was twelve. Especially recently, as Alice has gotten older and wanted to try new things, he's been even more protective. I think he's afraid that something might happen to her, and he'll lose her just as he lost his younger brother and sister-in-law. So, he tries to keep her safe. But that's looked like isolating her from things that could potentially hurt her and not allowing her to pursue dreams that take her outside of the home."

The light met the bulb in my head, and it made sense—why Alice was so timid. Why she lacked confidence in herself and doubted her talent. Why she seemed worried more often than happy. Why she was on her guard and put up walls that kept other people from coming too close.

I understood that—her uncle's desire to protect her from being hurt. My parents had done the same with me. They were scared to let me out of their sight because they didn't want me to get hurt. They wanted and needed to be there because they couldn't let anything else happen to me. But sometimes, holding on does more damage than letting go ever could. Love doesn't isolate. Love isn't fearful. Love isn't controlling. Love is . . . *love*. It believes. It perseveres. It protects. And protecting may mean holding on, but other times, it means letting go.

Mom and Dad had to let go of me in order for me to be here, doing what I was doing—spending a summer painting memories and chasing dreams I didn't know were in me. Dreams of creating and teaching and helping others. I would have missed that if they hadn't let me go. Yes, it was hard for them and for me as well. But hard things are necessary things, too.

Hearing the pieces of Alice's story that Will's mom told me . . . it made me want to help her all the more. Because I understood what it was like to be in her shoes. Maybe not fully, but I understood enough to know I wanted to help Alice grow and chase after her dreams. Even if art wasn't her dream, I still wanted her to have the chance to try it.

"I still want Alice to have the commissions." Determination instilled my words with a newfound confidence that I really was making the right decision by giving Alice this opportunity. "I'll talk with her uncle."

Will's mom looked at me and gave me the same look Mom had given me so many times that I no longer needed words to recognize what it meant: she was proud of me. For doing this—not backing out even when it would have been so easy to. "I'll get you Alice's address and bring it by tomorrow."

My smile was small but wide. "Thank you."

Life often requires that you fight *for* yourself. No one can fight your battles or take on the weight of your problems for you. It's something you have to do for yourself. But you never have to fight *by* yourself.

Alice didn't have to fight alone.

If I couldn't be her sword, I'd be her shield.

# CHAPTER 24

I held the sheet of paper with Alice's address scribbled on it the entire drive in the backseat of B.B's taxicab. It took fifteen minutes from my house to Alice's, but it felt like time was running a marathon on its clock hands, and those fifteen minutes were condensed into five.

Alice's house was near the church I painted—on the same street I saw her walking down while on her way to her babysitting job a week ago from today. B.B. pulled over on the side of the road, the car tires hugging the curb of the sidewalk. He got out of the taxi and helped me do the same.

"I'll wait here for you," he said. "I'll have the windows rolled down, so shout if you need anything—I'll hear you."

"Thanks, B.B."

I took slow, tentative steps toward the front door. The sun was setting and casting exaggerated shadows on the old, modest-sized home. The floorboards on the front porch creaked like old bones. There wasn't a doorbell, so I knocked and hoped that the *rap-rap-rapping* of my knuckles on wood would be heard. I listened. A metal lock turned on the other side of the door. It opened, and Alice's terrified, wide eyes peaked out at me like blue orbs.

"Hey, Alice." She didn't say a word. She just looked at me as if I had something horribly wrong by having knocked on her front door, by standing here and saying hello to her. "Can I come in?" Seconds ticked by before Alice wordlessly moved to the side and opened the door just wide enough for me to step through.

"Is your uncle home? I wanted to talk with him for a few minutes if he's not busy." Alice froze like a statue at that question: silent and unmoving.

But she didn't have to answer.

Her uncle came out of what I assumed was his bedroom and spotted me down the hall. "Can I help you?" He was polite, but confusion creased the skin on his aging forehead.

"I was wondering if I could talk with you for a few minutes? I have a business proposition for Alice that I wanted to discuss with you."

His lips formed a tight line as he glanced past me to Alice for the briefest of seconds. He lumbered past me, his shoes scuffling against the hardwood floor as he entered the living room—and I could only guess if I was supposed to follow him. Alice lingered under the doorframe separating the hallway from the living room. Her hands were at her side, nervously fingering her dress material between her thumb and index finger.

He didn't sit down on the beat-up couch in the room, and he didn't offer for me to, either. A coffee table separated us and he looked down to meet my face. His eyeballs were an explosion of bloodshot, tiny red veins and his face was a scraggly mess of greying facial hair. He looked—and smelled—like he had been drinking alcohol. His visible beer-belly made me think he drank a lot . . . more than he should.

He looked at me, and I realized he was waiting for me to say something. "I'm Josie Carter, and I just moved here for the summer a few weeks ago. I'm not sure if you already know, but I'm teaching art classes at a friend's gallery. I've been working with Alice, and she's very talented at painting. With your permission, I wanted to offer Alice a chance to do paid art commissions for my friend, Mrs. Ridge."

He glanced past me at Alice, and the way his eyes widened, those red veins looking like torch flames, it dawned on me: he didn't know Alice was coming to my art classes. She hadn't told him. And here I was, a total stranger standing in his living room, telling him something that he shouldn't have heard from me.

"Thank you for stopping by, Miss Carter." His breath was stale and permeated with the smell of alcohol. "But Alice won't be accepting that offer. Also, she'll be withdrawing from your class. I thank you for your time, but if you'll excuse me, it's getting late, and I have a busy day tomorrow."

"But—" My voice caught in my throat.

*No.*

This wasn't supposed to happen. I was desperate to say something, to right this wrong I unknowingly made. Words clawed at my throat in desperation, but they couldn't find a foothold out of my mouth. When I looked at Alice, I knew that anything I said would only make things worse, cause more damage that was irreparable. Her facial expressions were an open book of adjectives: fearful, hurt, devastated.

*I'm sorry.* The words didn't make it past my mind as I walked past Alice and closed the front door behind me. B.B. met me at the car, and he didn't say a word or ask how things went. I was out of words but full of tears.

I hadn't made a single thing better for Alice.

I'd only made things worse.

# CHAPTER 25

**MARCH 18, 1941**
**(10 Years Old)**

I physically awoke from my dream on that hospital bed. But I emotionally died there on that wrinkled bedsheet, too. The image in my mind was too horrible, too graphic to be a nightmare.

"Jo." Sophie hadn't stopped crying, hadn't stopped saying my name over and over again like a broken record player stuck on repeat. That's what loss does to you: it cuts through your skin like a serrated knife. And sometimes, all you can do is cry and endlessly repeat yourself.

I'd stopped screaming, but my mouth was still a wide *O*-shape, reeling from the shock and horror. My legs . . . I'd lost them.

There wasn't anything there from the knees down—just a stump of what would have been my lower legs and feet.

They were gone. Amputated. Taken away from me. And now, not only had I lost the ability to walk on my own, but I'd even lost the ability to *stand* on my own two feet. I was dangerously close to vomiting as I faded in and out of consciousness, my pupils dilating the light from the room and the darkness behind my sockets every few seconds.

Arms wrapped around me, but they weren't Sophie's. They were too long, too strong, to belong to my twelve-year-old cousin's thin frame.

"Josie Girl." Those two words broke something in me.

*Mom.* She and a swarm of medical staff gathered around my bedside after my screams sifted under the closed door like a putrid aroma and down the hallways.

"I'm so, so sorry . . ." Those three words devastated me. They were a confirmation that I really had lost my legs. That this wasn't some horrible trick or hellish nightmare that I could escape from.

Mom's tears soaked the shoulder of my thin hospital gown. Mine were wet on her clothes, too.

No explanation, no reason for *why* I had to lose my legs and feet would make this moment hurt any less. I think Mom knew that because she didn't say a word. Didn't explain the why. Didn't try to reason with a ten-year-old girl's mind when her heart was broken.

I didn't need to know that I could have possibly died if I hadn't gotten this amputation. That if my parents had pleaded with the doctor to just repair me and not fix the problem, I'd spend more of my life in a hospital bed than anywhere else. That, when I recovered, I might be able to get prosthetic limbs so that maybe, with physical therapy lessons coupled with time and patience, I could stand on legs that didn't belong to me.

I didn't need to know that.

I needed to be held.

*God . . . where are you?* I begged to know. Because when life shatters you beyond repair, where is God in those moments?

Mom was here. Sophie was here. Dad was here. Doctors and nurses were here. But where was God? Where was He?

Something in me whispered He was right here beside me. Holding on to me tighter than Mom. Letting me cry on His shoulder and Him on mine. But part of me couldn't accept that, couldn't believe that when my grief went beyond belief.

I looked past Mom at what I lost—at the tree-trunk-stump-limbs that I would now live with for the rest of my life. How could losing limbs I hadn't been able to feel for years hurt this bad now? How could I have feeling, pain-stabbing-and-heart-wrenching-feeling when I was paralyzed, my limbs medically labeled as 'numb; feelingless'?

Grief doesn't make sense, and that's why *now* it hurt. That's why *now* I felt emotionally what I lost physically.

How was I supposed to get through this? My body had been waging a war against itself for the past six years, and I was losing. Miserably, horribly, losing. I hated my body as much as it hated me. How was I supposed to heal when the hurt wouldn't end and the complications and life-threatening infections set in before I could even catch my breath? How was I supposed to eventually move past something that always moved with me? Even at a young age, I knew I wouldn't heal from this. Maybe someday, I would heal *through* it. But right now, I was hurting *in* it.

Just like when I was five and in a hospital bed, I knew things would never be the same. Just like when I was ten and in a hospital bed once again, I knew that moment would change my life. And I knew that right now, in a hospital bed again for the hundredth time, that today my life would forever be different.

I lost something—something that could never be replaced, and I'd never get back.

And that loss cut deep.

# CHAPTER 26

I hardly slept that night.

Insomnia did that to me—kept me up during the long and lonely hours of the night when I should have been fast asleep. Kept me beating my fist into my pillow and tossing and turning till the bedsheets were a wrinkled mess beneath me.

From yesterday's sunset to today's sunrise, I couldn't get Alice off my mind. Her uncle. What happened and what would never take place now. I hadn't just lost an opportunity to help Alice— I'd *lost* Alice. And I was a tumbleweed of emotions blowing in all directions, wondering if I'd made a mistake. If I'd said the wrong thing and missed saying the right one. If I'd messed up and would ever get a chance to undo the damage I'd done.

The what-ifs exhausted my mind just as badly as a sleepless night did my body. But morning was here, and I didn't have a choice but to pick myself back up and head to the gallery.

The sky was somber and grey and dripping wet with rain as I stepped out the front door. But amidst the grey, my eyes filtered something different . . . color. At the end of the walkway, beside the mailbox on the sidewalk. Red—a red umbrella.

The red umbrella came closer and found me and my pair of crutches on the front porch. Will. He peered out from beneath the umbrella drenched with summer showers and smiled at me.

"Will, what are you doing here?" He motioned for me to come under the umbrella, and he guided the canopy of leather over the two of us. How long had he been standing out here in the rain, under the shelter of his red umbrella, waiting for me?

His reply was honest. "I heard about what happened yesterday with Alice. Her uncle called my mom last night and told her that Alice wouldn't be coming to your classes anymore or taking on the art commissions, either." His spoken words silently spelled out the ones he didn't need to say to be heard: that I needed a friend.

We were like two penguins wobbling close together under the umbrella to keep dry as we stepped out onto the street.

"I'm sorry that happened, Jo."

Tears gathered fast and unexpected like storm clouds in my eyes, but I blinked them away. Will was still a stranger to me in so many ways. Yet, in spite of that, I felt safe being broken in front of him. I didn't know why, exactly. Maybe because he understood brokenness, too.

"Did I do the wrong thing by talking to Alice's uncle? Did I make a mistake?" I needed to ask that question to someone besides myself. Because when I asked myself, I got nowhere. I was stuck in a merry-go-round of *I-don't-knows*. I needed someone else to tell me the honest truth.

Will's eyes were serious and lost in thought. "I think it depends on the reason you talked to her uncle. Why did you?"

"Because I wanted to help."

"Then I don't think you did the wrong thing." He gave me a small smile.

"Life doesn't work like that, Will," I said, shaking my head. "Just because I was trying to help doesn't mean I did the right thing."

*Life doesn't work like that.* Effort doesn't always result in the desired outcome. Sometimes helping doesn't change things for the better. That's the risk in helping: it will either help or hurt the person receiving it from you.

"Just because you tried to help and it didn't work out the way you wanted it to doesn't mean you did the wrong thing either, Jo."

"I'm not giving up on Alice." The words popped out unbidden, a promise of sorts, surprising even myself. I wasn't going to give up on Alice now. Just because it wasn't easy to help didn't mean it was impossible. And maybe Will was right—maybe just because it didn't end the way I wanted it to didn't mean it was actually the *end*. Sometimes ends aren't endings at all. Maybe at first glance, they are. But if I looked closer, pressed in deeper, I'd find something unexpected at the end: a new beginning. A new chance to help Alice.

"I wouldn't expect anything less from you." He gave me a lopsided grin that could have parted the clouds up above and made the sky smile blue. "Oh, and Jo?" We were steps away from the art gallery now. "I know you can't carry an umbrella. So let me hold it over you on the rainy days, okay?"

He could have just let me take a taxi or walk in the rain without an umbrella. But Will chose to be a friend instead.

I smiled for the first time that morning.

"Okay."

# CHAPTER 27

B.B. was slowly but surely becoming a friend to me. We were making memories together in that cab as he took me where I needed to go around town—the bank, the grocery store, then home. I wasn't just a customer to him, and he wasn't just a taxicab driver to me. He was a friend.

I had a brown paper bag full of groceries on the car seat beside me. The noon sun was bright and staring at me through the window with its searing rays. The streetlight ahead was flashing red, and B.B. halted the cab to a stop. Cars drove by, and some people strolled down either side of the street on the sidewalk. I was beginning to recognize the neighborhoods in the city after several times of B.B. driving me here and there. The church was up ahead on the left side of the road.

The light turned green, and the taxi started moving again. My face got close to the window, not caring about the blinding sunlight or its heat radiating off the glass panes. I wanted to see the church as we passed by it. I hadn't gone past the church doors that were wide open on Sunday mornings since I'd been here. I wondered if Will and his mom still attended services there.

Just up ahead, barely past the church, I saw the girl with honey-blonde hair, and it was like déjà vu. Alice.

"Could you pull over for a minute?" I asked. I needed to get out of the cab and talk to Alice. It was almost as if God was giving me a second chance right now to see her. A chance I didn't expect but one I wasn't going to let pass by.

B.B. pulled over and helped me out.

"Alice!"

She turned around and saw me. Surprise made her eyes buggy.

"Can we talk?" My words were oxygen-deprived from rushing to catch up with her on crutches, and I breathed hard and heavy. "Please?"

"Okay . . ."

"I'm sorry about what happened the other day. I didn't know you hadn't told your uncle you were coming to my classes—"

"It doesn't matter." The one-shoulder shrug she gave me was cold and angry. "This isn't the first time something like this has happened, and I doubt it will be the last."

That was the longest sentence Alice had ever spoken to me. A sentence full of sharp words with even sharper edges. Raw honesty.

"Alice, what's going on with your uncle?" On any other day and in any other moment than this, I would never have asked her that. Her walls would have been too high for me to scale and too thick to penetrate. But they were down right now, completely unguarded.

Alice raked her fingers through her hair. "He's like this with everything I want to do—he shuts it down. Doesn't let me do it. I didn't tell him about coming to your art classes because I knew if he found out, he'd make me quit—and he did. The only reason my uncle let me take this babysitting job I have over the summer is because we need the money." Her voice was wound tight like guitar strings with emotion. "I know my uncle loves me, and he's trying to protect me. He doesn't want to lose me . . . but he's holding on too tight. He feels responsible for his brother's death, and I've tried to tell him a hundred times what happened wasn't his fault. But he doesn't believe me—and I don't know what to do."

Her honesty stirred a desperation within me. "I want to help, Alice."

Alice's bottom lip quivered, trembled as she fought back a rush of emotion. She looked so vulnerable. But beneath the vulnerability, I saw something raw and real and beautiful: courage.

Being brave doesn't mean you're not vulnerable or afraid. It doesn't mean having it all together. Being brave sometimes means letting someone hold you together when you're falling apart. Asking for help doesn't make you weak. It shows that you're mature enough to recognize that you can't do this life on your own. I knew I couldn't. Will knew he couldn't. And now, Alice knew she couldn't, either.

Her voice threatened to crack like a lake of frozen ice under the hot sun. "Then teach me."

Beads of sweat zigzagged like a snake down my neck from the hot sun as I stood there, processing what Alice was asking. Helping her meant teaching her. But that meant risk. Going behind her uncle's back, teaching her even though he told me not to. But if I didn't help Alice? That meant leaving her when she needed a friend the most.

My jaw muscles clenched down hard, and they butted up against my cheek. "I'll teach you, Alice."

Her eyes were shimmering lights as we came together, worked together, and made a plan to stick together. Alice went to her babysitting job, and I returned home. But it wasn't goodbye this time as we parted our separate ways. It was 'see you soon.'

Maybe the potholes in life that catch us off guard aren't there to throw us off course but to help us stay on course. To be alert, awake, eyes open wide to the opportunities around us. The other night at Alice's house—that was the pothole. But today, outside the church —that was what allowed me to steer on course, to really know how to help Alice.

The honey-blonde girl's walls were down.

And she'd let me in.

# CHAPTER 28

**NOVEMBER 04, 1941**
**(11 Years Old)**

I was eleven today.

The red marker on the kitchen calendar circling today's date—November 4<sup>th</sup>—was a confirmation of it. This birthday was so different from last year's. Harder. Not as happy. Not as magical.

I woke up that morning and, instead of cramming spoonfuls of my favorite cereal—Rice Krispies—into my mouth faster than I could swallow them, I picked at my cereal, watched the chunks soak into the milk. Last year I couldn't wait to eat breakfast because Mom only let me have sugary cereals on special occasions, and I couldn't rip into my birthday presents until I'd eaten. Today . . . I didn't care about bowls of cereals and bow-tie presents. Because I knew once I finished that bowl of cereal and opened the gifts that waited for me on the living room coffee table, there was somewhere I had to be.

Mom had teared up last night when she came in the room and told me that my physical therapist appointment was scheduled for tomorrow—now today—and that she tried to cancel it, but they couldn't fit me in anywhere else this week. No parent wants their child to have to spend their birthday trying to relearn how to walk. To function. To live again.

I'd been going to physical therapy for months, and I was no closer to walking with my prosthetic legs than I was before. I had already been informed that I would never be able to walk again on my own, even with my prosthetic limbs. But if I kept trying, kept going to physical therapy and doing the exercises I was given, I should be able to stand and walk using crutches. Those crutches, according to my therapist, would hold me up and bear the weight my body couldn't anymore.

Some day. One day. Always far out. Never now.

I didn't want to spend today in a sterile office walking back-and-forth across a room. Didn't want to hold on to the metal railing to keep my body up as I rebuilt the muscles I had left in my upper legs, tried to train them to balance and hold themselves up on my attached lower limbs.

Bitterness spilled all over me and stained my heart, and it wasn't the kind of stain that would come out after being washed and cleaned. It was the stubborn kind of stain that refused to come off no matter how hard it was scrubbed at.

I just . . . wanted to be a kid again. To live a normal life. To not be in the top percent for the rarest diseases and have to live the rest of my life making it through each day knowing that the next would never be easier than the other. My health struggles would never go away. They were chronic. There. Part of me. And that made it hurt to face each new day.

I think the most common approach to hurt is this: we tell ourselves that somehow tomorrow will be better. That today's emotions will dissolve with the passing of time. That the future will be brighter and promising. That's what I started out telling myself. But what happens when it doesn't turn out that way, and we're left to sort through a pile of disappointment and false hope? How do we move on? How was *I* supposed to?

I didn't know. I sank against the breakfast table, eating soggy cereal and trying not to cry on my first day as an eleven-year-old. But I'd still chosen to wake up that morning, to keep going. Maybe that's how I was supposed to make it through—just keep trying. Whether that day was a success or failure, I couldn't allow myself to give up.

I set my spoon down on the table beside my bowl and gave up on eating my cereal just as Mom came into the kitchen, told me it was time to go.

Time to try again.

Every Tuesday morning for the past few months, I sat in a sterile office with peeling wallpaper and worked with my physical therapist, Dr. Hobbs. Yellow sunlight filtered through the white window blinds. I squinted at the light, blinked it in with every other step I took.

"Try it again." I'd already spent half an hour slow-walking back-and-forth as far as the metal railing would take me. My arms shook, and my body ached.

"I keep trying it again," I said, snapping like a broken pencil. "How much longer do you expect me to keep trying for?"

"Josie." Dr. Hobbs pinched the bridge of his nose, let his eyelids rest heavy for a moment. He was trying to find the patience to deal kindly with me. "You have a chance some people don't have in your condition. You have a chance to walk with your prosthetics. But it's not going to be an overnight process—you have to keep trying."

Salty tears burned my eyes. "You don't get it, do you? My other doctor and surgeon already told me that I'd never be able to walk again, even with my stupid prosthetics. My body's not strong enough to do that."

His eyes narrowed into slits as he stared at me. "Prove them wrong."

Those three words didn't challenge me; they angered me.

"You don't understand what it's like to be *me*. You don't know what it's like to try and try and try and . . . nothing. Nothing happens. Nothing changes. Nothing gets better." The words spewed out my mouth like a rapid-fire machine gun. "Why do you keep telling me I can walk someday when we both know I can't? It's easy to tell people what to do when you don't understand how hard it is to keep trying—"

"That's where you're wrong." He held out his hand towards me, and it silenced me long enough for him to continue. "It's not easy to tell you or anyone what to do because I *know* it's hard to keep trying. I *know* it's discouraging and painful. Put yourself in my shoes for a minute. Don't you think it's hard for me to have patients coming to me every day, needing helping that I don't know if I can give them?"

His voice was rough and raw, but I deserved it. I had never stopped even for a second to consider if this was hard for Dr. Hobbs. Pain is self-isolating, and it wants you to focus only on yourself and not give a thought to how your pain affects those around you. Even if you're the one in pain, those who know you and love you are hurting, too.

"I may not know what it's like to be in your shoes, Josie. But I've gotten a taste of what it's like—and that's why I'm here, and you're here every Tuesday." He reached out, set his hand on my shoulder. It was as heavy and burdened as I felt in that moment. "I wish I could promise every person who comes in this room that they'll make a full recovery—I wish that more than anything. I can't promise anyone miracles, Josie, but I can promise you I will never give up on trying to do everything I can to help. But you need to help yourself, too."

He blurred a little in front of me, like a water-streaked camera lens. His words had cracked my broken heart open wide, and it was exposed, and that terrified me—because something that's exposed feels, while something that's hardened is numb.

"Will you try?"

# CHAPTER 29

JULY 21, 1951
(Present Day)

We had a plan.

Alice and I hadn't parted ways until we made sure of that. But our plan had loopholes in it that needed to be filled—and that's what had me at Will's house, about to ring the doorbell.

"Jo?"

Will's voice came from behind me outside, and my heart skipped a beat in my chest.

"Will, you scared me. What are you doing out here?"

"I was helping my mom with some gardening in the backyard." There were dirt imprints on his knees and his hands. He sported a grin. "I think the better question, though, is what are you doing out here?"

"I was looking for you, actually. I wanted to talk to you about something." He raised his eyebrows, curiosity lining the features of his face.

"Does this have something to do with Alice?" The way he hovered inches above me, looking down at me with those searching eyes, made me feel so small.

I nodded, and he said he wanted to wash the dirt off his hands, and then he'd be back.

"Come inside, and I'll meet you at the kitchen table," he said, just before disappearing through the door and down the hall to the bathroom.

I wondered for a moment why Will wanted to talk in the kitchen rather than the living room, but when he met me in the kitchen, opened the refrigerator door, and pulled out a tall glass jar of lemonade and a plateful of cookies, I understood.

"So," Will said, his back to me as he pulled open cabinet doors and reached for two glasses. "What's going on with Alice?"

"I ran into Alice yesterday while in town, and we talked for a little while." I traveled twenty-four hours back into my memory, remembered all the things Alice had told me and what I'd said to her. "We actually *talked,* Will. We've hardly had a conversation, much less an honest and open one. Alice told me a lot of things . . . about her . . . her uncle. I told her I wanted to help, and she told me how I could."

Will handed me a glass of lemonade, and I accepted it from him and took a nervous sip. He sat across from me, waited for me to explain.

"Alice asked me to keep teaching her."

I filtered surprise and even a tiny bit of shock on Will's face. "She asked you to do that? But her uncle already took her out of the class —"

"I know," I said too quickly, too strongly. I took a breath and tried it again, slower, softer. "I know. Alice didn't ask me to let her join the class again. She asked me to teach her privately while she's at her babysitting job."

"Does her uncle know about this?"

"No."

Will's sigh was heavy and long. "But you're going to teach her anyway?"

"Yes," was my quiet whisper. "Will, Alice's uncle views anything she wants to try as her jumping in front of a moving train. But it's not. It's Alice wanting to board that train and see where it'll take her in life. For her uncle, Alice wanting to paint and pursue her dreams means that it could take her somewhere dangerous. He's afraid to let her do anything. But Alice wants to paint . . . I think she needs to, Will."

"I don't like doing it this way," I admitted. "I don't like going behind people's backs. I wish there was another way—but there isn't. Alice needs me to help her. To stand with her. To teach her. If I don't, who will?"

"I understand, Jo. I do. Just . . . be careful, right?" His eyes pleaded with me not to just *say* I would be careful but to actually *be* careful.

"I will." I took a breath and was about to tell him the reason why I was here, sitting at a kitchen table sipping lemonade and eating cookies with him, confessing to him my plans with Alice. But I hesitated.

"I feel like there's something else you need to tell me," Will said, not missing a thing.

"I need your help, Will. Alice wants me to teach her at one o'clock for an hour while she's at her babysitting job. She already talked to the children's mother—Mrs. Chambers—and asked if it was okay for me to be there. Mrs. Chambers said it was, but that Alice must make sure that her children are being taken care of and not neglected because Alice is distracted. Can you go with me . . . and help keep an eye on the kids while I teach Alice?"

"You want my help?" It was like Will was confirming that I'd actually just asked that of him because he was so caught off guard.

"Yes," I said. "I'm sorry to ask you, Will. I . . . I really need your help. You're the only person I could ask."

Will's face softened at those words, erased a few of the lines surprise had written along his forehead. "I'll help you, Jo, but I'm not really good with kids."

"If you can get along with me, you can get along with anyone." I smiled, and he did, too.

"Count me in then. I'll help how I can."

"Thank you." Words couldn't really express my gratitude in that moment, but I hoped they were enough. That Will understood how much his helping out meant to me. "Meet me outside the church on Monday at 12:45."

"I'll be there."

# CHAPTER 30

**JULY 22, 1951**
**(Present Day)**
*Telephone conversation*

**Sophie:** *"Hello?"*

**Me:** *"Hey, Sophie—it's Jo. Did I do my math right? Is it one p.m. there in London?"*

**Sophie:** *"It's 1:05 p.m., but yes, you did your math right."*

*(Sophie laughed, knowing her technicality made me roll my eyes)*

**Sophie:** *"Time zone changes are so confusing. What is it—a little after eight in the morning there?"*

**Me:** *"Yep. My day's just starting over here."*

*(A brief pause of silence ensued on both our ends)*

**Me:** *"How have you been, Sophie? We haven't talked in a little* *while."*

**Sophie:** *"I'm sorry I haven't called sooner; things have been really busy. I feel like Mom has something planned every day, except for Sunday. The other day, we drove past Buckingham Palace—it was so beautiful. And yesterday, we went to see Big Ben—it was huge! I overheard someone say that the clock tower is three-hundred-and-sixteen feet tall. Can you imagine how high that is? Mom and I were there when the clock chimed, and it was so, so loud. I've never heard anything that loud before. I wouldn't be surprised if all of London could hear it."*

**Me:** *"Wow—that sounds really great, Sophie. I'm glad you're having a good time there. If anyone deserves that trip to London, it's you. And don't apologize for not calling sooner. I figured you'd been busy, but I still wanted to make sure that you're doing alright."*

**Sophie:** *"That's sweet, Jo. Thanks for thinking of me. I've been thinking about you a lot too. How have you been doing? Are classes going alright?"*

**Me:** *"I've been doing okay. Honestly? Things have been hard, especially the past few days. But I think they're starting to turn around for the better."*

**Sophie:** *"What's been going on?"*

**Me:** *"I was having a problem with one of my students—not her necessarily, but her uncle. Do you know Alice Johnson?"*

**Sophie:** *"Yes, I do. She and I were in the same choir group for about a year when I was in middle school. I didn't get to know her very well—*

*our paths never crossed, really—but I've seen her and her uncle around town a few times."*

**Me:** *"Well, to make a long story short, Alice wants to learn art."*

**Sophie:** *"Let me guess—her uncle said no?"*

**Me:** *"He did . . . but I think Alice and I have worked a way around that."*

**Sophie:** *"Are you sure that's a good idea, Jo? Don't get me wrong—I trust your judgment, but please make sure to be careful."*

**Me:** *"You sound just like Will. He told me the same thing yesterday before he agreed to help me."*

**Sophie:** *"Will's helping you?"*

**Me:** *"Yes—I'll tell you more about it when we call next time. But he's been a good friend to me. I need to go in just a second . . . Will's mom invited me to join them for church this morning, and I'm still in my pajamas."*

**Sophie:** *"Jo? Before you go . . ."*

**Me:** *"Yeah?"*

**Sophie:** *"I just wanted you to know that I'm so glad you're there—at my house—for the summer. I knew it was the right thing for you to do, and I'm proud of you."*

**Me:** *"Aw. Thanks, Sophie. Call me in the next few days, alright? I* *want to hear more about what you're up to there in London."*

**Sophie:** *"It's a plan. Love you, Jo."*

**Me:** *"Love you too. Talk soon."*

# CHAPTER 31

**OCTOBER 22, 1942**
**(11 Years Old)**

It's funny how the most unexpected things in life can illuminate your purpose. For some, they find their life calling within the doors of the church, through the words a pastor says. For others, they find it through words of affirmation of a talent or gift. For me, it was a two-day-old newspaper clipping.

Maybe it was mere chance I came across it on the living room coffee table where Dad sat each night reading the headlines. Maybe it was providence that the words on the front page, on the left column, caught my eye. Maybe it was God whispering for me to pick up those sheets of ink-stained pages and read them. Whatever it was, I stopped and read those one-hundred-fifty neatly printed words.

The clipping talked about a woman named Peggy Guggenheim whose gallery had just opened two days ago on 30 West 57th Street in Manhattan, New York. Her gallery was known as 'Art of This Century,' and she was helping raise money for war bonds through the art she sold.

She was a single woman making a difference. Changing lives. Helping her country. Not by fighting on the front lines or being in a position of power in the government—but through art.

I reached for the phone on the coffee table and dialed Sophie's number, desperately hoping she would answer it. She did—and I rattled off what I'd just read in the newspaper faster than she could make sense of what I was saying. I practically begged Sophie to go to the gallery's opening. She was in New York—it couldn't have been more than a few hours' drive to get there. She could see what I couldn't and describe everything to me.

I didn't remember how our phone call ended—all I could remember was Sophie telling me she'd talk to her mom about it and would call me back. I wished more than anything that *I* could be there. I wanted to meet Peggy Guggenheim. Talk with her. Shake the hand of someone who was making a difference in a war-torn world through her love of art.

And it hit me like a tsunami wave slamming into me: I wanted that.

I wanted art—painting—to be something I could use to make a difference. Maybe not on a grand scale like Peggy Guggenheim. But I wanted to change lives through what had changed mine—however few or many lives that meant. Isn't that how it starts for everyone at some point? A hobby becomes a talent; a talent becomes a passion; a passion becomes a calling.

I needed art. Spending hours in my room painting my heart out on a canvas wasn't optional. Mixing my emotions—the good ones and the hard ones—in colors of paint wasn't optional, either. I needed to create beauty out of my struggles because that helped me get through them. I couldn't *not* paint. It wasn't just something I did for a period of time and then moved on to the next thing I wanted to attempt. No, I needed to paint every day. That desire had become a desperation this past year. Maybe I was still reeling from the trauma of surgery and amputations and physical therapy and pain.

Maybe my calling had been birthed out of my pain?

That thought made me stop and think hard. I didn't think I ever would have picked up a paintbrush if I hadn't lost my ability to walk. I wouldn't have stuck with it if I hadn't already lost so much. Maybe it was a hundred reasons that brought me to this point, confessing my dream under a whispered breath as a young girl just shy of her teen years in a quiet living room to a newspaper clipping.

In that moment, I realized just how desperately I wanted and needed to paint for as long as I could. And for the first time in a long time, I felt something. It wasn't pain—it was hope. Hope that didn't disappoint or hurt me. Hope that gave me a future dream and a present way to work towards it—practicing, never giving up, always trying my best.

*Hope.*

# CHAPTER 32

I'd barely eaten a ham sandwich after finishing at the art gallery before I darted out the door to go teach Alice. Will and I had gotten to the church seconds apart from the other.

Alice told me the house I was to find was close to the church—and Will confirmed that by pointing to the end of the street, gesturing with his hand that we would take a left, and our destination was the third house down on the right side of the road.

"You're pretty distracted, aren't you?" Will's comment pulled me out of my mental daze. "You've hardly said a word, and you haven't answered any of the three questions I've asked you in the past five minutes. And" —he gently reached out and touched my arm— "you're about to turn right when you're supposed to go left down this street."

"Oh." A shaky sigh made its way out of my mouth. My stomach knotted. "Sorry, I'm just nervous."

"You're nervous? What about me?" His eyes crinkled as he smiled. "Who knows what those kids are like. While you're painting, I may be running for my life for the next hour."

I smiled at his humor. It made some of the anxiety bubbling in the pit of my stomach dissipate. Sometimes all it takes is laughter for anxieties to seem less scary. Didn't the Bible say something about laughing in the face of fear? Maybe that's what it looked like— laughing even when you're scared. Not because things aren't hard or scary, but because there's someone to laugh with in the midst of them.

"I hold you personally responsible for any and all injuries I might receive in the next sixty minutes." There was the playful boy in Will —the one I knew was there when I saw the blue in his eyes—and it made us both laugh.

Our playful banter lasted until we reached the two-story brick-and-mortar home. The mailbox at the start of the walkway leading to the front door spelled its occupant's name in chunky-sized letters: *Millie Chambers.*

"Just remember why you're doing this, Jo, and you'll be fine." His whispered words close beside me instilled in me the courage to ring the doorbell with shaky fingers.

Alice answered the door and led Will and me into the drawing room. She was quiet, withdrawn, again. I wondered if she was second-guessing her choice, wondering if she should have asked me to be here and teach her, if she was as nervous as I was doing this.

"Mrs. Chambers just left a few minutes ago—she's a waitress at one of the local diners—but she asked me to say hello to both of you." Alice's voice was quiet, like the confidence and conviction she'd spoken with a few days ago to me had buried beneath the surface once again. "We can work in here, Josie. And Will—the nursery is just in the next room. The kids are in there right now playing. You can go ahead and go in—they know you're coming."

Will opened the door and ducked beneath the doorframe that was painted white. High-pitched voices called out Will's name. I couldn't guess their ages, but they sounded happy to see Will and that their play partner had arrived.

The noise that filtered through under the door—happy sounds and belly laughter—filled the silence that strangled the air between Alice and me in the drawing room.

"Should we get started?" Alice's nod was confident, like she was confirming both that she was willing to start and determined to do this.

It's terrifying and fulfilling at the same time to stand on the precipice of a decision and know that if you go forward, you can't go back. I felt both those emotions then, too. Because I knew that once I started teaching Alice, there was no way I could undo that. It was cemented in time, in my memory, in Alice's life, and mine. It was terrifying to wonder and to second-guess myself in the moment that I was making the right decision. But when Alice laid a plastic tarp across the wood floors, pulled out an easel and canvas, paint colors and brushes, and set to work, and I saw the artist in her eyes come alive—it was fulfilling.

Alice had asked me to watch her paint and point out any mistakes she was making, any ideas I had for improving her work, or any helpful tips or pieces of advice I could give her. So, that's what I was doing—watching and wondering how Alice had such a gift for art.

"Have you ever tried glazing?" I asked as she stopped to mix paint colors on her palette.

"No—what is that?"

"Glazing is basically when you take a transparent color and paint it over a section of your painting that's already dry. Visually, it lets you add elements to your painting to enhance it, like shadow effects.

Also, if you used a transparent yellow paint color and added it on top of a dry pink color, it will change the color to orange. That basically allows you to create a different color on top of the original one, so if you don't like the colors you chose, you're not stuck with them." I felt like a talking dictionary of art terms and definitions. But if I could take what took me years to learn and discover and share it with Alice during our time together, I would. "Glazing gives you a lot of creative freedom to experiment with shading and coloring."

The wonder in Alice's eyes could have lit up a night sky. "Where did you learn how to do that?"

"By watching others and reading for myself. When I was younger, I decided that I wanted to be an artist—and I worked hard to make that dream a reality. I read every article I could get my hands on that featured artists and their painting techniques. I got every Norman Rockwell's *The Saturday Evening Post* magazine cover I could find and tried replicating his work. But I had to learn for myself, too. I experimented with different ideas in my head. Pushed myself farther than I thought my talent could take me." I hadn't meant to keep rambling on like that, sharing pieces of my story that weren't exactly necessary to answer Alice's question. But her eyes were anchored on mine, not darting around distracted or disinterested, and I knew I had a captive audience in her.

So I went on sharing the rambling thoughts in my head and the memories in my heart. "My mom once told me that I had to know *why* I wanted to paint. Because the reason behind that *why* was what would keep me going through the setbacks and the breakthroughs. I knew I'd found my purpose in life—because I hadn't been able to let go of it. No matter how hard it sometimes was to hold on to my dream, it was even harder to stomach the thought of letting it go." Painting was something I'd spent years working towards and chasing after; hundreds of days fighting for while simultaneously fighting for my health. On the days where I couldn't do much, I still did something. And in the face of nothing, something—*anything*—is a lot.

I recognized the flicker in Alice that would turn to a flame if she kept fanning it. Even though she had to birth that fire herself, I could still do something—I could hand her the match to light it with when she was ready.

Alice nibbled on her lip, a quietness sinking over her as she internalized the pieces of my story. She turned back to her art, picked up painting where she'd last left off.

We needed to be here, the honey-blonde girl and me, doing this. Sitting side by side, breathing in the smell of paint. Bringing colors and beauty from paint tubes. Making something out of the empty canvas before us. Reaching for the sky when the world told us to stay grounded.

This was life: doing something great, something memorable, with something little.

At the end of the hour, Will emerged into the drawing room with three kids—James, age eight; Wayne, age five; and Judy, age three—hanging like monkeys on his arms. The smile on Will's face was a visible confirmation that today was supposed to happen. And tomorrow, it was supposed to happen. And for every summer day I was here, it was supposed to happen.

# CHAPTER 33

After finishing at the gallery, I stopped by to see Will's mom and drop off another commissioned piece of artwork I'd finished that morning. She had commissioned me for six pieces, and, excluding the one I was about to hand over to her, I had four left to complete before the summer's end.

We were sitting on the grey couch again, and it was starting to feel like home. Will's mom took the painting. Lonely people walking down street sidewalks and across walkways filled the canvas. "I love it, Josie," she said. "There's nothing I'd like you to change about this piece—it's perfect. How are things going at the gallery?"

"Going well," I said. "My students have learned a lot already, and I think they're enjoying the class."

Her smile was warm, inviting, gooey like melted chocolate that matched the color of her brown eyes. "And how's Will doing in your class?"

"He's . . . doing good. Will's a good painter." I meant that—he was good. Will had a talent for it. But I knew it was hard for him. I'd seen his eyes narrow and his brows furrow when his hands ached from holding a paintbrush. Rheumatoid arthritis didn't just hurt on the inside. I saw the pain his unnaturally curled and bent fingers were in each time he painted.

I knew Will was doing this not for himself but for his mom. To please her. To make her proud. To be like his dad. But his heart wasn't in it. It was in business—finances, business deals, negotiations, deadlines, meetings. All the terminology I didn't understand fascinated Will because *that* was his passion in life. Maybe for a time, it was to be an artist like his dad. But times change, dreams change, people change, and that's not always a bad thing.

Pride colored her eyes with a bright sparkle at my words. Everything in me wanted to tell her that being an artist—taking these summer classes, painting five days a week—it wasn't his dream. He didn't want it for himself. But I couldn't be the one to tell her that, to shred her dreams for her son beyond recognition. Will would have to tell her that someday, not me.

"I'm so glad to hear that. I told Will taking this class would be good for him."

I offered a kind smile, laced with compassion, as my response.

"Also," she went on, "I have something I wanted to ask you. This weekend, Will and I are going up to my sister's house in Albany. Every summer, my family and extended relatives get together for a reunion, but in the past few years, it's morphed into more of a family-friend gathering. I know it's last minute, but would you like to come with us?"

"Are you sure?" I had nothing planned for this weekend, but I didn't want to barge into their reunion when I didn't belong there.

"I'm sure, Josie. I'd love it if you came. Will would, too. He's not close with many of his relatives, and I know it would mean a lot for him to have a friend there."

Her kindness touched my lonely, cookie-crumbling heart. I hadn't said a word about it to anyone, not even when Mom and Dad called me last night, and we talked for an hour on the phone, but I was lonely. It was hard . . . being away from home. From my parents. From Sophie. From the familiar places and faces and things I knew.

But Will and his mom—they were making this small town in New York feel like a second home to me.

"I'd love to go."

Two days and a three-hour car ride later, I was in Albany.

# CHAPTER 34

**JULY 28, 1943**
**(12 Years Old)**

Ten months—that's how long it had been since I decided I wanted to be an artist.

But I'd left that dream in the attic while Sophie had been here for the past three weeks. My hands needed a break, and my lungs needed something else than dusty attic air. My mind needed to be cleared, allowed a moment to rest.

Also . . . I hadn't told Sophie yet—about my decision. I hadn't told my parents yet exactly, either. They'd pieced it together, no doubt, seeing me spend hours after tutoring lessons holed up in my room, in my own world with paint colors and brushes. Mom and Dad hadn't asked me outright, but I knew they could sense the change in me. That I'd found something that made me come alive on the inside and outside that I wanted to do forever.

I didn't know why I hadn't told the three of them yet. Some dreams are special, and they lose their specialness when they're shared with others at the wrong time. I knew there would be a right time, but now wasn't it. And until that changed, I was perfectly content with chasing after my dreams alone.

Sophie snuck up behind me. "Wanna do some stargazing?"

We both knew my answer was yes. The first night after Sophie arrived, we wrote down a list of all the things we wanted to do together in the three August weeks she would be here. Late-night talks while sipping hot chocolate even though it was seventy-five degrees outside. Listening to our favorite Bing Crosby records. Laughing over nothing and everything until our stomachs hurt.

We were down to our last night and the last thing on our list— stargazing. It was Sophie's idea. I didn't understand why she wanted to spend our last night together that way, but she smiled—really smiled—when she said to me, "Stargazing—let's do that."

So, there we were—sitting outside on the grassy lawn next to the driveway when we probably should have been asleep in bed.

"Things are going to change a lot after tonight, Jo." Sophie took two breaths—one, two—before she said anything again. "I'm not sure if I'm ready for that."

With the breaking of tomorrow's dawn, Sophie would be getting on a train and going back home. But when she got home, she'd be there for a week before she repacked her bags and headed off to Maryland, the place she would be calling home for the majority of the next four years. A few nights into her stay, Sophie had told me that her mom was sending her to West Nottingham Academy, a boarding school for boys and girls. There were two reasons for that decision.

One: It had been two years since Sophie's parents' divorce was finalized and her dad left their family. Sophie hadn't seen him since —but she hadn't been able to adjust to him not being around, even after all those months of him not being there. When you live every day of every year with both your parents, the absence of one of them —it's not something you get over. Not then, not when you grow up, not ever. Maybe in time, you adjust to it. But you never get over it.

Two: Sophie's mom had to get a job to support the two of them. So from the time Sophie got home from school and went to bed—she was alone. When Sophie got up in the morning for school, her mom was still fast asleep from her late-night work shift at a local diner. Their schedules were as opposite as night and day, and it was hard, especially for Sophie. Being alone is . . . lonely.

So, at the beginning of this summer, Sophie's mom decided to enroll her at a boarding school, where she would start and finish high school. In the middle of summer, Sophie agreed to go. And at the end of summer and the beginning of fall, Sophie would be there, in Maryland.

"I know." Change, even good change, isn't easy. It's hard. It's unnerving. It's scary. But I could see that beneath the depths of worries Sophie had and the unreadiness she felt, she knew it, too: she needed to go.

"I'm not good with change." She let out this nervous breath of laughter, attempting to laugh instead of cry.

We both looked up at the sky, and an empire of lights blinked down at us. They looked so small up there when in reality, they were bigger than both of us down here. Maybe that's what our troubles look like when they're put into perspective—smaller than we think they are.

"I'm not either." I'd never been good with change. Maybe because most of the changes that happened in my life had been bad more times than they'd been good. And it hit me then that that's how I felt about the change that had taken place in me these past ten months. My dream to paint. It was the best change that had happened in my life to date, but it both excited me and terrified me at the same time.

"Come on," I said, abandoning my spot next to her and hobbling back to the house as fast as my crutches would take me.

Sophie quickly caught up with me. "Where are we going?"

"I want to show you something." I wanted to show her the changes that had taken place in my life so she could see that it's okay —it's okay to be excited and terrified with change.

And that led us to the attic.

# CHAPTER 35

JULY 28, 1951
(Present Day)

The one-hundred-sixty-five miles it took to get to Albany was time stretched to its breaking point—infinitely slow and long.

Will's mom drove, and Will sat beside her on the black leather passenger seat. I'd stared out the backseat window of the car and gotten lost in the maze of green trees and highway roads and white clouds dotting the blue sky like landscape. But the view out the window had suddenly gone dark, and it wasn't until Will's mom gently spoke my name that I realized my eyes were closed. That I'd slipped into deep slumber halfway into the hours-long drive.

"Josie, we're here." Her voice sounded distant, dream-like to my ears. She and Will slipped out of their sides of the door.

I rubbed the sleep out of my eyes, tried to stir myself with the heel of my hand. The back door next to where I sat opened, and I blinked in bright sunlight and a silhouetted form.

"Here." Will lowered himself and reached out his arms for me, braced his hands under my elbows. I placed my hands on his arms, allowing them to anchor me as I dragged the lower half of my body out of the car. My prosthetic legs refused to cooperate like a stubborn child. Will held onto me until I settled into my wheelchair.

This trip I'd decided to leave my crutches behind and only use my wheelchair since I'd be inside most of the weekend. The world felt so big, and I felt so small in it. The inches I lost when I went around in a wheelchair rather than standing on my crutches felt infinite.

The three-story-tall house stretched far into the sky and wide across the grassy earth. Its outer shell was covered in white paint, encapsulating glass windows. It looked like it belonged on a country estate, not in the middle of a New York town with almost one-hundred-thirty-five-thousand people. Even though the house didn't have a voice of its own, it breathed these silent words to every onlooker: wealthy.

Will's mom had told me that her sister—older by two years, five months, nine days—was one of the wealthiest families in Albany and that her home had dozens of rooms, so making space for one more person—me—would never be a problem. I didn't think I believed her then how rich her sister really was. But I did now—and I could only imagine what the inside of the house looked like.

I didn't have to imagine for long because soon, the front doors opened, and I slipped into a world of glass chandeliers, ornate rugs, and tapestries on the walls.

A dozen eyes were on me, and dozens of words whispered about me —questioning why a girl in a wheelchair showed up on the doorstep of a family-friend reunion.

Will stood beside me while his mom left to greet her sister, his aunt Emmy. I was grateful that Will was there with me because I knew, unlike everyone else staring at me with curiosity or judgment shaping their eyes, I had a friend who stood by me and was glad I was here.

Will pointed out some people in the room, told me in a whispered voice of what relation they were to him. The man with the grey whiskers of facial hair—that was Uncle John. The younger man who smiled too much—that was his older cousin, Henry. The girl that attracted the sons of family friends to her like bees swarming to a hive—that was his younger cousin, Kathy. And the lady in the pearl-colored dress with a forever-frown imprinted on her aging face—that was Aunt Emmy.

"There you two are." Will's mom found us tucked away in the corner of the room, avoiding disapproving relatives and less-than-friendly family friends. To the both of us, she said, "We'll be having lunch in about an hour, so we should put our bags in our rooms." To Will, she said, "Your aunt wants you to take your usual room." And to me, she said, "Josie, I'll show you the room you'll be staying in— it's next to mine."

Will crossed the living room, retraced his steps down the hall leading to the front door, and went to get our bags. Will's mom took me past the living room, straight down one hall and left down another. When we reached our rooms, and the door I opened revealed a queen-sized bed dressed in forest green covers and draped with snow-white sheets on the left side of the room and a dresser and sitting chair on the right, I had to ask her again. "Are you sure it's okay for me to be here?"

I'd noticed how Will's aunt had said hello to him and gave him a smile when they crossed paths near the front door, but she hadn't acknowledged me at all.

"I'm sure, Josie." Her smile was both knowing and understanding. "My sister has never really gotten along with anyone, not even me. And the rest of my relatives . . . they have their own little cliques, and they don't always welcome people who are different from them. Like Will. Like me, in some ways. Like you."

"But I'm glad you're here," she went on. "So is Will."

It meant a lot—to be accepted by the two people in this mansion of a home that meant the world to me.

Sometimes the people who are like family to us aren't those we have blood ties with, but those that are our hearts are knit together with. Will and his mom—they were family.

# CHAPTER 36

The only sound that filled my tiny corner was my pencil sketches on notebook paper.

This house—it was like an endless maze of rooms and more rooms and even more. After dinner, Will's aunt said we'd spend the rest of the evening in the ballroom. I'd noticed Will trying not to laugh when he saw my eyes go buggy-wide at that announcement. I'd never been inside a ballroom before, and I didn't know they still existed inside people's houses. But they did, and here I was, sitting in the corner of the room, watching some drink champagne glasses and others dancing to the songs the orchestra played.

"You're hiding again?" A shadow, elongated and familiar, stood beside me. This was the second time now that the copper-haired boy had found me sitting in the shadows.

"No," I said, fighting a smile just as I did the first time we had this conversation.

"Well, I am." Will leaned against the wall. "My mom wanted me to dance with her, and then my cousin, Kathy." I remembered her—the talkative and popular cousin. "Kathy was talking so much that she didn't realize she was stepping all over my feet for three minutes straight."

We both exchanged a smile, and Will grabbed a chair and sat down next to me. He spotted the notebook and pencil on my lap. "What are you working on?" Curiosity had him leaning closer towards me.

"I'm sketching a scene I'll paint once when I get back to my aunt's house."

Will caught the lines and shadows on the page. "Of this?" he asked, referring to the ballroom and the people in it.

"Yes," I said, my pencil moving slowly, purposefully across the bottom of the page, sketching the marble flooring.

"Do you always paint stuff like this?" *Stuff* meant people, places, memories of mine.

"Yeah, I do. I've painted a lot of memories I've made over my life."

"Even when they're bad?"

Bad memories—I'd painted countless of those over the years. Me in hospital beds. Me in a wheelchair. The angry freckled boy at the park. Courtroom memories of Sophie's parents' divorce.

I nodded—*yes*.

I wasn't holding on to the bad memories, but I wasn't letting go of them, either. Because letting go means forgetting—and I didn't want to forget the things that had hurt me because they were the same ones that made me stronger. Braver. Instilled a stubbornness in me that kept me going, fighting, pushing through.

"I wonder if my dad did that, too." I didn't know if Will meant to say the words aloud or just think them in his head, but either way . . . he'd thought them, said them, and I heard them.

"Do you have any of his paintings still?" I wasn't sure what one did when they'd lost someone close to them. Did they pack their belongings in boxes and hide them away down in the basement or up in the attic? Did they donate them or sell them off because those items held memories that were a constant reminder that the person they loved was gone?

"My mom has them somewhere in the house, but I don't want to go searching for them, and I don't want to ask Mom where she put them. That's the last thing I want to do right now." He sighed, deep and heavy, above the orchestra music. "If I talk about his paintings, she'll be more convinced than ever that I'm going to be an artist like him."

"Your mom talked about you when I saw her a few days ago. She said she knew she was right when she suggested you take my class over the summer . . . because you're good at painting." I never planned to tell Will about my conversation with his mom, but right now . . . I had this feeling, like a stone sinking in my stomach, that he needed to hear about it.

"I can't tell her yet. Since I got home from school . . . since you came . . . since I started taking your classes, my mom's been happy. I haven't seen her this happy in a long time. I can't tell her now. It would break her heart." His head hung so low. Lower than the sun dared to go as it set behind mountains and hid beneath the ocean shoreline.

"The longer you wait, the more it will hurt her in the end, Will." Things that need to be said—whispered confessions of honesty—will hurt to say and to hear. But it will hurt more, so much more, when they're delayed until the very last possible second. Truth can't be spared until we have no choice left but to confess it.

"How can you say that?"

I double-blinked. Will—he sounded like the angry freckled boy at the park who hurt me with his words over a dirty baseball. That was the first time anyone had been mean to me about my health disabilities.

I closed my eyes out of instinct because I knew something in Will had snapped—and he was about to snap at me with his angry words. I knew as he took a breath that whatever words were seconds away from leaving his mouth would hurt me.

And they did.

"You're in a wheelchair—your whole life has been hard. And it always will be that way. Things aren't going to suddenly change for you and get better, so how do you know what it's like when someone has a chance you don't—a chance to be happy again in life—and you have to be the one to ruin it for them?" His words were choppy like angry ocean waves, and his face was torn with something— regret. Regret over every word he knew he shouldn't be saying to me but didn't stop from slipping past his clenched teeth. "How can you sit there in your wheelchair and tell me that waiting to tell my mom will hurt her more in the end when you don't know what it's like to be anything but hurt every day of your life?"

Will stormed out of the room, angry like an untamed thunderstorm. And he left me behind with a swarm of bees stinging my eyes with tears and a heart that his words had cut a jagged line into. My heart fractured, howled with pain. It didn't matter that I already knew what was coming . . . it still hurt. Maybe even more. Because I wasn't reeling from the initial shock of his unexpected words. I wasn't caught off guard and left feeling numb.

I was left to sit there with his words—with the pain they caused and the damage they did to me. With gaping wounds from a friend that deflated my spirit like a balloon deprived of helium.

Fully feeling, fully hurting, fully crying.

# CHAPTER 37

JULY 28, 1943
(12 Years Old)

The attic was my hideaway.

I was there for hours each day, painting until I ran out of sunlight. Mom and Dad had moved my workspace out of my bedroom a few months ago after I'd dripped paint on the flooring and stained parts of it blue and white. The three of us spent a weekend back in March clearing out a space for me to work up in the attic. We moved all the boxes and random things we'd stashed in the attic and forgotten about on one side of the room, stacked against the wall, and the other half of the attic was mine. The large, open window exposed me to sunlight and fresh air, which was exactly what Mom said I needed.

Mom and Dad said they didn't care if I accidentally dripped paint here. It was a space for me to create and make messes—a place where I could slip away and paint.

Five stairs and a door separated the attic from the rest of the house.

"Come on." I looked back at Sophie behind me, wide-eyed with curiosity.

I'd spent months practicing getting up these stairs on my own with crutches. Wondering if I could do it without needing Dad to carry me up them. And I could—because my muscles were slowly, slowly, rebuilding themselves from my physical therapy appointments.

I climbed the set of stairs, smiled between deep breaths. Sophie waited at the bottom, unmoved. She stared up at me.

"I told you I had a surprise. Now come on!" I said—and that was all it took for Sophie to come bounding up the stairs faster than I ever could.

The old doorknob squeaked in my hand. I pushed it open, and my fingers searched the right side of the doorway for the light switch. I made a rule with my parents that I wouldn't use this light to paint by because there had been a handful of times where they found me up here late in the night, fast asleep in my wheelchair with a paintbrush in hand. But I wasn't up here tonight with Sophie to paint.

I kept gliding my hand across the wall, looking for that switch. And then I found it. Flipped it on. And there was light, revealing what was shadowed in the dark.

It was a humble and messy space, my spot in the attic.

"What is all this, Jo?" Her arms were spread wide like bird's wings, gesturing to a collection of items stacked against the attic wall.

"This," I answered, "is an accumulation of months of work."

"Come over here," I said, motioning her to stand beside me. "These are stacks of paintings I've done. And that plastic bin is full of hundreds of paint tubes and dozens of paintbrushes. And that over there" —I gestured to the wooden easel propped up beside the plastic bins— "is the latest painting I've been working on. I didn't have a chance to finish it before you came, but it's almost complete —just needs a few more finishing touches."

Sophie wandered ahead of me on the graffiti-colored floorboards, and I stood back and watched her. She turned back to face me. "Jo, why didn't you show me this before tonight?"

Sophie could see how much this attic of mine meant to me. The evidence of all the hours I'd spent in it was scattered left and right on the floor.

"It's kind of been my secret up until now." Sophie's eyes silently begged for me to go on, to not stop there when I'd barely begun scratching the surface of my honest confession. "A lot has changed for me this year. I haven't really told anyone, but I want to be an artist, Soso. It's my dream."

Sophie's eyes shimmered beneath the yellow ceiling light. "I'm so . . . happy, Jo. I think that's been your dream for a long time now—I knew it was—but now you're seeing it for yourself. You're meant to be an artist."

Maybe Sophie was right—maybe it had been my dream for longer than I knew. But it was buried beneath pain and disappointment and years of struggles. Painting had been a kind of a savior to me when it was all I had as a six-year-old girl. Had she seen the artist in me, even then? But now I knew for myself that painting was all I wanted to do.

It seemed almost like a Biblical paradox to me . . . what I thought was too horrible to even be the tiniest bit redeemed—my polio diagnosis— had undergone a flicker of redemption. Something had come out of it—my love for art. Maybe at first, painting was a coping mechanism for me. It helped me survive the hardest days of my life and instilled a sense of purpose in me. But now? Painting was everything to me. And that was the flicker of redemption—the treasure—I'd found in the wastebasket of the broken pieces of my life story.

"Why haven't you told anyone?" Sophie's gaze was soft, and her words were gently voiced.

"Because I'm excited . . . and I'm scared, too," I admitted. "This—me having this dream—is a good change, and that's why I'm excited. But I'm scared, too—change is scary."

She read between the lines: *Change is hard and exciting and terrifying and scary. It's okay to feel all those things at the same time. I'm right here with you, and I understand.*

We stood side-by-side at the window, staring out the glass pane, quiet. The starry sky glistened outside. I kinda laughed under my breath, knowing what was about to come out of my mouth was far-fetched, more impossible than possible.

"Do you think I could paint something as beautiful as that someday?"

"I think you could paint a hundred things as beautiful," Sophie said.

The dreamer in my heart swelled with pride against my chest.

"Don't let go of your dream, Jo, unless you're sure that it's the wrong one. But if it's the right one? Hold on to it and chase after it as fast and as hard as you can. You do that for me . . . and I'll do that for you."

That night was sealed with a handshake and a promise us two—the almost-high school girl and the dreaming artist—would never forget.

# CHAPTER 38

The ballroom and Will's angry words were eighteen hours behind me now. But I was still stuck in my head, trapped in yesterday's memory, in my assigned guestroom. I'd stayed behind that closed bedroom door on Sunday morning for as long as I could, not showing up at the breakfast table. The only reason why I'd shown up for lunch was because goodbyes followed the meal.

And there I was, thanking Will's aunt for lunch and for letting me stay the weekend, trying to mask my bitterness and hurt with anything that resembled gratitude. She gave me a polite smile, nothing more than that. And after she said goodbye to Will and his mom, the three of us left Albany behind and began the long drive home.

Will didn't say a word to me as he helped me get in the car. I didn't say anything to him, either. The silence between us was louder than any noise could ever be.

I closed my eyes thirty minutes into the drive, kept them that way the rest of the way home. Will's mom started talking to him about the weekend, about my art classes, about his plans after he graduated college. His answers were short and non-descriptive. He wasn't acting like himself, and neither was I.

When we'd gotten home and parted ways last night, Will left wordlessly without a goodbye, and so did I. I cried myself to sleep until I woke up the next morning—today—with my face looking like a train wreck and fifteen minutes until my two-hour class began.

I didn't want to brave a smile on my face and pretend as if the weekend had never happened and that things between Will and I were okay. I knew there was only one way I was going to get through today, but I'd spent hours this morning in a tug-of-war battle, most of me resisting but part of me willing.

I needed to let go of the hurt Will had caused me. I needed to stop replaying it in my mind. He'd hurt me once in real life, but he'd hurt me a hundred times over again in my head. Somehow, I needed to forgive the copper-haired boy . . . without waiting for an apology.

But I didn't want to. I was hurt and angry and upset—and I had a right to feel all those emotions. I didn't want to let go because his words were still so fresh in my mind. But maybe that's when we're all supposed to let go—while the pain is still fresh, before it takes root in our hearts, makes us bitter and hard on the inside.

Will had taken a wrecking ball through our friendship, and with an apology or without one, how were we supposed to start over? The pieces left of our friendship were a shattered mess. How were we supposed to glue them back together? Maybe we weren't. Maybe, with or without an apology, we were to let go of the old pieces and start over with new ones. Start again. Because if Will hadn't been the one who hurt me yesterday, it could just have easily been me hurting him tomorrow. One of us would have hurt the other—we were both so very human. And that's why I was wrestling so hard, so much, this morning . . . because I needed to forgive Will.

Forgiving someone allows you to start over again. Differently than before. And it may be a harder kind of different in the beginning, but in the end, it's a better one.

When ten o'clock came, and Will opened the door and slipped inside, I forgave him . . . because his friendship meant more to me than a handful of angry words ever could.

"Excuse me—Miss Carter? Could I ask you something?"

The girl three years my senior with a name that matched the color of her dress got my attention—Rose Lewis.

"Of course." This was the first time Rose had asked that outside of wanting me to answer a specific question she had about her artwork. She had my attention.

"Three of my friends from out of town are visiting for the next few weeks, and I told them about your art class. They asked if it would be okay if they dropped by tomorrow and met you. Would that be alright?"

"I'd love that." I was surprised and touched that Rose had mentioned my art class to her friends. She had always been responsive and hardworking in the class, but she was soft-spoken most of the time.

"Great." Her smile was wide and grateful, like a ray of sun breaking through a sky of grey clouds. She grabbed her handbag and left, ending our conversation like that.

I left a few minutes later, but when I reached the door, I stopped. I almost dreaded turning the knob and stepping outside, not knowing if Will would be there, as he had been since the beginning, to walk home with me. He was so withdrawn today . . . so quiet, still so not himself. He barely looked at me, and when he did, his eyes didn't light up, and his mouth didn't go wide with a smile. He just looked and blinked in my existence as a passing stranger would have.

I opened the door, stepping out under the hot sun and air sticky with humidity. But the space Will had stood in every day waiting for me, the same spot where his shoes dug into the dirt, was empty.

He wasn't here.

When I went forty-five minutes later to the church where Will and I met at before going to see Alice, he wasn't there. And when I rang the doorbell, and Alice answered it, and I stepped inside, she told me Will had gotten here early and was already with the kids. He had shut himself behind that white door before I had a chance to see him. And an hour after that, when I finished with Alice and was waiting for Will to reemerge, Alice told me that Will had said for me to go ahead without him, that he had some errands to run around town.

But I knew those were excuses dressed up as straightforward explanations. He didn't have errands to run, but that was the only thing he could say without outright saying that he didn't want to see me.

His rejection and his excuses hurt. Part of me wanted to grab onto him and shake some sense into his shoulders. He was the one who had hurt *me* with his words and not the other way around, but I wasn't running away from him. I wanted to know why he avoided me like the plague.

The closed doors he hid behind told me that today . . . it wasn't a day for answers.

# CHAPTER 39

I was sitting in a diner booth with a cream tablecloth across from a woman I'd only known for two hours and twelve minutes—Catherine Davies.

Rose had me meet her along with two other friends minutes before my class started. At the end of class, Catherine was the only one out of Rose's three friends to pull me aside, ask if she could take me out for lunch and talk with me more. I'd told her that I only had a short time—about thirty minutes—but Catherine had smiled and said that was all the time she needed. So here we were, two perfect strangers in so many ways having corned beef sandwiches and milkshakes together.

"I know you don't have much time before you need to get going, so I'll get right to the point." The lilt of her French accent was soft and clear. "I'm sure you can guess by the accent, but I'm from France—Paris, France. I've spent the last several years traveling to small towns around America during the summer season when citywide festivals and fairs are happening. I'm staying with Rose for the next month, and she told me about the fair that's taking place here a few weeks from now.

"Miss Carter, after watching your art class today and how you interact with your students and help them, I want to ask: if I sponsor you and make all the arrangements, would you be willing to host an interactive art exhibit at the fair? I've made some connections, and if you're open to doing this, I can make it happen."

I almost felt embarrassed sitting there, listening to her talk about the summer fair happening in a few weeks that I didn't even know existed until now. No one had mentioned it to me, and I hadn't even thought to ask about it. But it made sense—a small town and summertime often resulted in a fair.

My initial embarrassment was overshadowed by my genuine surprise. Sitting here at an ordinary diner booth on an ordinary Tuesday afternoon, being offered the unexpected from a French girl six years my senior traveling across America and working with town fairs.

The clock was ticking, and I was running out of time before I needed to leave and before I made my decision. Because if the fair was really happening in a few weeks, that meant I would have to give Catherine my *yes* or *no* today. My *yes* would mean that both she and I would have to start preparations now, this week. My *no* meant she needed time to find someone else in town to host the art exhibit.

I didn't know what the right answer was—and I didn't want to give Catherine a *yes* when it should have been a *no*, or a *no* when it should be a *yes*. So, I did the one thing that came to mind. I asked Catherine if she could give me her telephone number and I would call her tonight with my answer. She agreed—and we both slipped out our respective ends of the booth and went our separate ways. But our conversation—her offer—followed me even after Catherine left, and for every step that it took me to get to Alice, and for every step after that it took me to get home.

188

"Yes."

That was the one-word answer I would call Catherine later with, and the decision I told Will's mom I made.

I didn't want to do this—the art exhibit—but that's why I decided I *would* do it. The feeling of dread in my stomach wasn't because I knew that this opportunity wasn't mine for the taking. I knew it was—but I was scared to reach out and grab hold of it. I was hesitant to do it because I *knew* I should, and that hesitation, that initial resistance, is what made me decide—*yes*.

The way Will's mom looked at me—looked right through me—made me think she could understand how hard that *yes* was for me. How hard I had to fight for it. "You know I'll do whatever I can to help, Josie. You just let me know what I can do, and I'll get it done."

I thanked her—because I knew that was an offer I'd take her up on in the weeks to come.

"Josie, before you go . . . can I show you something?"

"Of course." I followed her down the hall, past the kitchen where Will and I once sat and had cookies and lemonade, to a room that was too small to be a bedroom—a closet.

She opened the door and reached for a box on the second shelf. The box was big, heavy, and I wondered if she could manage to drag it off the shelf and set it down on the floor without needing Will's help. My eyes scanned down the hall to see if Will was nearby, but a thud on the ground told me the task was already completed.

She pushed back the old and dusty cardboard flaps, opened the box. She sank down to her knees to reach in and pull out whatever she wanted me to see in there.

I saw three things.

#1—A pearl-colored wedding dress, folded and wrapped carefully, at the bottom of the box.

#2—Photos dressed in glass with dusty frames, resting on top of the wedding dress. A couple stared deeply into each other's eyes, sinking in the ocean of love they so visibly had for the other. The other photo was with the same couple looking a little older, a little more worn with the passing of time but a smile never leaving their face, and a young boy standing beside them.

*Will.*

He couldn't have been more than five-six years old then. But he looked so happy, so full of life, standing there beside his parents. In a photo void of color, I could still make out the bluish hue of his eyes.

#3—A painting full of color. Out of those life memories kept in that box, that was the one Will's mom pulled out, held out in her two hands for me to look at. It was of a hospital—I could tell that much by the size of the building and its all-white exterior. But behind the hospital, beyond those walls of white, was color: a rainbow.

A sign in the sky—a promise.

I looked from the painting to Will's mom, searched her eyes for answers. Who painted this, and what was the story behind this work of art?

"My husband, Hank, painted this over twenty years ago. I won't get into the details, but my husband and I were going through a very hard time in our lives . . . and we desperately needed something to change. We needed something—anything—good to happen." She paused, and we both took a breath, inhaling memories and dusty air. "A year went by, and then it happened. The good we needed—it happened. I'll never forget the day I found out I was pregnant with Will. My husband and I both broke down in tears in the kitchen when I told him. Later that same day, I was washing dishes in the kitchen, and I looked out the window, and there was a rainbow out there—the most bright and beautiful one I'd ever seen. I showed it to Hank, and he looked at me and told me, 'Storms can last a long time, but they can't last forever. See, honey? It's just like I told you —after the rain always comes the rainbow.'"

"Will was your rainbow."

The rainbow in the sky was a promise in a mother's womb.

"He was . . . and he always will be." The love she had for her son— it went deeper than I ever thought it did. I wondered if Will knew how much she loved him—because her love was greater than any disappointment or hurt he could cause her.

"Josie," she said, slow, thoughtful. "I know enough about art exhibits from my husband's time as an artist to you know that you'll need artwork to display. I would be honored if you would take this one and display it at the fair."

"Are you sure?" I knew this painting—this tangible memory she could hold in her hands—was vulnerable to display. Because it honored the work of someone who was no longer alive and would be referenced in the past tense. He lived, he painted, he loved.

"Yes." Her voice was fragile and yet resolved at the same time. "He deserves to be remembered in this way. It would mean a lot to me . . . and to Will, too. I'm proud of Will for wanting to follow in his dad's footsteps and be an artist—and I think seeing his dad's paintings at the exhibit and taking your art classes this summer will inspire him to keep working towards that dream after he finishes college."

I felt a hollowness in me at those words. And I felt as if I understood for the first time why Will hadn't said anything to his mom, had put off that dreaded conversation for as long as he had. If I were him, I would have done the same, too. It's not easy when your dreams change, and they collide with the dreams those closest to you envision you living out.

"I'll tell Catherine that I already have the first painting I'll need for the exhibit when I call her later tonight."

She smiled at me, and I tried to smile back, but my smile fell short on my lips. The old floorboards creaked somewhere behind, close to the hallway entrance, and I knew to whom the sound belonged.

Will—the boy whose heart had just broken at the words of his mom.

I looked behind me: he was gone.

# CHAPTER 40

APRIL 06, 1944
(13 Years Old)
*Telephone conversation*

**Me:** *"Hey, Sophie. How's school been this week?"*

**Sophie:** *"It's been okay. You know my science teacher, Miss Rolland?"*

**Me:** *"Mmhmm."*

**Sophie:** *"She paired me up with two other students in my class for this semester's final project. We have to design an experiment as a group to present to the class."*

**Me:** *"Who did she team you up with?"*

**Sophie:** *"Maria Allen and Fred Casey. Maria's nice, and we get along, but Fred? Jo, he's so stubborn and always thinks he's smarter and better than everyone else in the school. He's impossible to be friends with, much less work with on projects."*

**Me:** *"I'm sorry, Sophie."*

**Sophie:** *"Me too. These next few weeks are going to be long and torturous."*

*(Sophie sighed deeply; a pensive breath full of frustration)*

**Sophie:** *"Any advice for me?"*

**Me:** *"Well . . . Fred's not the only one who can be stubborn. You can be, too, Sophie. So be stubborn back—and don't let him dictate your group. Make sure you're making group decisions. And if he's not cooperating, then don't cooperate either. Don't move forward until you three are on the same page. If you don't stand up to Fred, then he'll take advantage of you and Maria."*

**Sophie:** *"That makes sense. You know how some people say, 'Kill them with kindness'? Well, I'll kill him with stubbornness because that's the only thing I think will work."*

**Me:** *"When do you three start working on your project?"*

**Sophie:** *"From next Monday. Our deadline is April 28th, so we have a few weeks before our project is due."*

**Me:** *"Okay—keep me updated on how it goes and what's happening with Fred."*

**Sophie:** *"I will. How's painting going, Jo?"*

**Me:** *"It's going good—I've been trying a different style of painting that's become pretty popular. It's called 'abstract expressionism,' which* *is kind of a fancy name for painting something that isn't a portrait or landscape drawing. You basically just put your canvas on the floor and take old paintbrushes—with bristles that are caked over—and you fling paint at the canvas. That's it—and that's why it's called abstract because it's not an object or shape or anything, just random colors mixed together to create something unique. It's easier than painting portraits or landscapes because it's not as detailed or hard to do, but it's not my favorite style."*

**Sophie:** *"That's because you like to be challenged. And because you like to paint things that have a purpose and are part of you—not just flinging some random colors on a canvas."*

**Me:** *"Well, it was a learning experience, anyway. But tomorrow, I'm going back to my acrylics and finishing that painting I told you I started last week—the one of the Bing Crosby record we couldn't stop listening to when you were here last summer."*

**Sophie:** *"That feels like a lifetime ago . . . I can't wait to see you in a few months. Let's listen to that record again when I visit, okay? Especially 'Sunday, Monday, or Always'—I love that one."*

*(Sophie quietly hummed the chorus, snapping her fingers to its rhythm)*

**Me:** *"It's a deal."*

**Sophie:** *"Good. I need to get some homework done before I head to bed later, but, Jo, I wanted to ask—how have your physical therapy appointments been going?"*

**Me:** *"They've . . . been okay."*

**Sophie:** *"Just okay?"*

**Me:** *"Dr. Hobbs told me last week that I've made a lot of progress and can walk a lot better now with my prosthetics. I've rebuilt a lot of muscles that had weakened, too."*

**Sophie:** *"Jo, that's amazing. I'm proud of you. But . . . why don't you sound happy telling me that?"*

**Me:** *"Dr. Hobbs also told me that he doesn't think I'll be able to walk on my own—ever. All my physical therapy appointments have allowed me to do is walk with crutches . . . and that's all they'll let me do."*

**Sophie:** *"Aww, Jo . . . I'm sorry. That's so hard. I wish I could be there with you right now and give you a hug."*

**Me:** *"I wish that, too."*

**Sophie:** *"Don't forget how far you've come or how much you've accomplished. You've come so far in spite of all the setbacks you've faced. I know it's so discouraging to get that news, Jo, but don't let it beat you down. Keep trying, and don't give up. The only thing worse than failing is giving up too soon. I can't promise you that you'll be able to walk again, but you've beaten the odds—all of the impossible odds—stacked against you."*

**Me:** *"You're right. It's hard, Soso. I won't give up, but . . . it's not easy holding on."*

**Sophie:** *"I know. Keep holding on as best as you can—and I'll do everything I can to hold you up, too, okay?"*

**Me:** *"Okay."*

**Sophie:** *"I've got to go now, Jo, but I'll talk with you next week, alright?"*

**Me:** *"Sounds good. Sleep well tonight."*

**Sophie:** *"Love you always."*

**Me:** *"Love you forever."*

# CHAPTER 41

**AUGUST 01, 1951**
**(Present Day)**

Three times today, Will had avoided me. He didn't walk home with me from the gallery. He didn't show up at the church. And when I got to Alice's, he had already shut himself in the nursery with the three kids. His absence hurt more each time he avoided me, not less. I missed him and how things used to be between us, even a week ago. But I wouldn't push him to talk to me; I'd wait until he was ready.

"Alice, before we start your lesson, can I ask you something?" I reached for the bag I'd carried from home, strapped across my left shoulder, now sitting on the floor beside my chair.

Alice nodded, and I pulled out a handful of papers. She eyed them and looked to me, curious. "I was asked to host an interactive art exhibit at the town fair, and one of the first things I need to get done is that I need to have original paintings there to display. I've been working on some ideas, and I wanted to ask which ones you think are best."

I handed them to her. "These are just the basic pencil sketch outlines. I did around ten or so."

After my phone call with Catherine last night, I felt a sense of urgency and inspiration to get some ideas down on paper. Her accent got stronger when I told her my answer—*yes*—and she said how happy she was I'd agreed to work with her. And from there, we spent an hour on the phone, brainstorming ideas, coming up with a plan, deadlines to meet, and schedules to keep.

Alice quietly fingered her way through the stack of pages I handed to her. She separated four pages from the ten. "I really like these," she said.

The first was of the attic, where I learned to paint. The second was of the train I boarded on that rainy day from home to New York. The third was of the beach house I stayed at with my parents and Sophie. The fourth was the night sky full of stars Sophie and I had stared up into.

"I'll start working on these when I get home." Alice smiled—and it was one of the few times it was a truly genuine smile. Something was writing and unfolding itself between the honey-blonde girl and me—a chapter of friendship.

The nursery door opened as I finished with Alice. My heart thumped hard against my chest when Will stepped out of the room. Three kids clung to him like wild monkeys, pulling at his arms and begging him to stay. Alice pulled them off one by one with a promise of afternoon snacks. As they said their goodbyes and disappeared into the kitchen with Alice, I caught Will's gaze.

I knew I should do or say something. But my feet were taped to the floor, where I stood in the middle of the room, and I couldn't move. Words escaped me, and so I stood where I was—silent and unmoving and heart thumping.

"Jo." Four days—that's how long it had been since I last heard his voice. "Can I take you somewhere? My car is parked out front."

I didn't know why he was talking to me or where he wanted to take me. But if I let this chance slip by because I was too stubborn and too wounded to give him a second chance, I would regret it. I didn't want to walk away from our friendship when it would have been easy to; I wanted to stay and fight for it when it was hardest to.

I nodded my head, and we climbed into his car, retraced the route to both our homes, and turned down streets I had yet to travel down until we reached a place that Will said was called Sandy Creek.

Will parked the car and helped me out. There was an old, hollowed-out log close to the creek, and we found a place beside each other on it.

"It's really pretty here," I said, the words dry in my throat.

And it was that—was pretty. There was a kind of peace that blanketed this spot in the world—just trees, running water, grass, and birds in the sky. It was beautiful and rare, and I wondered why Will brought me to this place. It wasn't a spontaneous idea; it was an intentional decision.

"Do you see something up there—in the trees I'm pointing to?" I followed his hand and curled fingers pointing to the left, to a cluster of oak trees with lobed leaves about fifty feet ahead.

I squinted my eyes, tried to find what Will wanted me to search for up in the tree branches. And then I found it: something stood out, something with a defined shape and build and color.

"Is that a treehouse?"

"It is," Will said with this remembering look in his eyes. The story behind the treehouse was somehow tied into the copper-haired boy's story. I could see it on his face—memories.

"Did you build that?"

"Not on my own." His eyes went from the treehouse to me. "One summer afternoon when I was ten, my dad told me that he wanted to do something special together and asked me to pick something— it could be anything, big or small. I decided that I wanted to build a treehouse with him." Will laughed under his breath. "I was so optimistic that first day my dad and I started to build the treehouse here at Sandy Creek. I'd never used a hammer before, and I smashed my thumb more than once. My dad showed me where to nail the boards down and how to actually *make* a treehouse that we could be in without the roof crashing onto our heads or the bottom dropping out from under our feet."

Will's face had traveled back in time. Back to when he was young, and his dad was alive. This was the first time he had ever talked to me about his dad like this—sharing memories.

"It took us a few weeks of hard work, but we got it done. When we took my mom to see it, and she climbed up the stairs and stood in our treehouse, I was so proud. My dad gave me a lot more credit for that project than the three of us knew I deserved. He told my mom I practically built it on my own. We all knew that wasn't true, but he never told me anything but that he was proud of me for the work I did." He paused, his words stumbling to a screechy halt. "I think . . . that was his way of telling me that even if I didn't build well, I *learned* well—and that's just as important. And he was proud of me for that. The summer after we built the treehouse, my dad died from colon cancer."

"I went up in the treehouse yesterday," he said. "I haven't been up there in years. But I needed a quiet place where I could think . . . and there are a few things I wanted to tell you."

"Okay," I said.

"I'm sorry for what I said to you." The timbre of his voice cracked. "I was angry because I knew you were right. And I ignored you because knowing you were right meant that I was wrong—but I wasn't ready to talk to my mom. I know you were only trying to help me, and there's no excuse for what I said. I know I hurt you, Jo —I'm so sorry."

I reached out my hand, set my fingers on top of his. Sometimes having a hand to hold means more than words can. "I already forgave you."

His arthritis-crippled fingers gently wrapped around mine and squeezed. He took a slow, steadying breath, keeping his emotions in check and tears at bay. "I talked with my mom this morning . . . about a lot of things. My dad. My plans for after college. Painting." He paused. "I couldn't keep doing this to my mom and to myself— hoping that my dream for painting would come back so that I wouldn't have to break her heart and disappoint her. But it's not my dream, and I realized last night that I can't keep holding on to the false hope that maybe it would be mine again someday. It won't, and it's not meant to be. I told my mom that today—told her everything."

I wanted to ask how his mom had taken that news, but, at the same time, I didn't want to ask because it wasn't my place to know unless Will wanted me to. So, I waited and listened.

"She told me she was proud of me," Will said, after a moment of silence and time slipped by, "for chasing after a dream that was my own rather than compromising and living out one that wasn't mine anymore. That she was proud of me for doing anything I felt called to do, and she was sorry . . . for unknowingly placing that burden on my shoulders to be exactly like my dad."

I was dangerously close to tears now, too, because I knew how desperately he needed that confirmation that it was okay to have his own dreams in life and affirmation that his mom was proud of him, no matter what he chose to do or be. The older one gets doesn't change that—that wanting and needing to be reminded that those closest to you are proud of you.

"Your dad is proud of you as well, Will, even if he can't tell you that himself." Because not even death can change some things. They're cemented in time, forever—beyond life and death. "And for what it's worth, I'm proud of you, too."

"Thanks, Jo." The words were whispered in sincere gratitude.

A treehouse was built here twelve summers ago, and a friendship was rebuilt here twelve summers later.

# CHAPTER 42

**AUGUST 03, 1951**
**(Present Day)**

Rose caught up with me after class, seconds before I was about to walk out the door and meet with Catherine at the diner, and asked if she could talk to me for just a minute.

"Catherine told me you'll be hosting an art exhibit at the town fair," Rose said. "I know you'll be needing some original paintings to display there, so I worked on one yesterday and this morning. If you like it, I wanted you to have it."

Rose handed me her painting of a white picket fence with green ivy and baby pink roses. They wrapped themselves around the wooden posts and an open mailbox, revealing rusty hinges and dozens of white envelopes stacked in a neat row. It was beautiful, and I not only left minutes later with a painting but with an idea, too.

"The painting Rose did gave me an idea."

Alice, in a way, had become the second most involved person putting together ideas and plans for the art exhibit. Each day I came, Alice wanted to know if I had any updates—if Catherine had said anything, if any more plans were put into place, if I'd made any progress on the paintings I was working on. And she just . . . became as much a part of the project as I was. She was just as excited to hear about any developments that had taken place since we last talked as I was excited to tell her about it.

"I talked with Catherine about this at lunch, and she agreed that it was a good idea."

Alice was all ears and eyes, trained intently on me. "What is it?"

"The town fair is a community event—a team of individuals pairing up and working together to make it a success, and I want the same to be true for the art exhibit. I've been scrambling trying to get all the paintings done on my own, but the one Rose gave me earlier made me realize that I can involve other people in this project. Like her. Like my other students. Like you."

No one got paint stuck to their skin, to their soul, like Alice's fingers were a rainbow of colors, unless art was a passion and not just a hobby. Colors breathed life into her, and she breathed life into them.

"You want my help?" Her eyes were big owl-eyes, slow blinking.

"If you're willing, I could really use your help. This project is too big for me to handle by myself." I was beginning to feel the weight of it digging trenches into my stress-knotted shoulders.

"I'll help, but my uncle can't know about this." Her fingers wrapped tighter around the paintbrush in her hand, knuckles a little whiter.

"You can do this—" I stopped, shook my head like I was erasing the words I said. "*We* can do this."

The determination in her eyes instilled a greater confidence in me. Today, I found a helper—one I needed more than I thought I would.

The copper-haired boy was my companion again on the way home. Things were different between us than they were a week, two weeks ago; but they were better. After our time at the lake, I felt like we understood the other better, could empathize in ways we couldn't before.

"Jo, are you okay?"

His voice startled me out of my thoughts, my mental coma where I was lost in an endless to-do list of things I had to get done. I was starting to feel torn, worn, stretched thin from the reality of everything that would be happening in the next few weeks.

The sigh that slipped between my teeth was shaky and not okay.

"Do you want to talk about what's bothering you?" he asked, giving me room to talk or space to stay quiet. He genuinely cared and wanted to know what was weighing me down so that, if possible, he could lift a little bit of the weight and help me carry it. Will had let me do that for him—help him bear the burden he was weighed under, almost crushed by, with his mom. So now, I let him do the same for me.

"I'm worried and stressed about the fair. I've been so busy; I don't know if I've even told you yet that I was asked to host an art exhibit at the fair. There's so much to do, and if things were different, it would be a lot easier to get done."

"If what things were different?" Will hung on that last sentence.

"Next week, Catherine—she's the one sponsoring me for the art exhibit—wants to take me to the fairgrounds to get started on my booth. Which means she'll have to drive me there and back, or I'll have to go by taxi. If I could drive, I wouldn't have to ask others to go out of their way for me. I'm so frustrated by all the things I can't do." My words felt like vomit in my mouth, and I needed to get it out, all of it out, even though it was messy and ugly to say and to hear.

Being limited and feeling helpless was a bitter pill to swallow. It felt like that pill had lodged itself somewhere in my throat, and I was choking on it. The effects of my health weren't easier now at twenty than they were when I was diagnosed at six or when my legs were amputated at ten. It was hard every day, but on some days, it was harder. Today was that day where I almost didn't care about the good that had come out of my pain, and I just wanted to beg God to rewrite my story. I wanted the hardest parts of the chapters I'd lived already to be erased and rewritten. I wanted an easier life, a normal one, a better one.

You never get used to hurting. It gets old, and it gets hard, but it never becomes easier to go through and live with.

"I'm sorry, Jo. I understand. I know it's hard." Instead of empty platitudes, words that hurt more than they helped, he gave me three things: empathy, understanding, and acknowledgment. An *I'm sorry* for what I had to go through. An *I understand* because he had health struggles, too, and he knew what it felt like to wrestle with them. An *I know it's hard* to acknowledge that the burden I felt was heavy and real, and it wasn't me being weak or wimpy under the weight of it.

"I know you're limited in what you can do, Jo. Everyone is, in their own way. Just because other people don't have your same health struggles doesn't mean they're unlimited, you know? Even now, you're doing things that some people can't—like teaching art classes and helping Alice and hosting an art exhibit at the fair." His gaze didn't leave mine. "Keep doing what you're doing—and I'll help how I can."

He stretched out his hands in front of me. "My hands may not be good for much, but yours are—and your legs may not be good for much, but mine are. We can be for each other what we can't be for ourselves. I can help carry boxes, and you can unload them. We can help each other."

Even two broken halves—his arthritis and my polio—still equaled a whole when put together. Maybe our pieces fit differently than others whose halves weren't broken because theirs didn't have sharp edges or missing pieces, but ours still fit. Maybe our limitations were opportunities to work and grow together rather than alone.

"I'll take you up on that." He didn't make me feel bad for asking and needing help, and I hadn't felt that way with many other people in my life.

"Good. I'll help however I can. Just let me know when and where, and I'll be there."

"Thank you, Will." This was the Will I knew—the one who could reach me where I was, stuck in the dark. He was the light for me.

That's what a true friend does—they always try their best to pull you out of the dark. But if they can't, they sit there in the shadows with you and don't run off when it's exhausting or inconvenient.

"Anytime."

I knew he meant that.

# CHAPTER 43

**MARCH 18, 1945**
**(14 Years Old)**

I shouldn't have broken the rule Mom and Dad implemented—no painting in the attic after sunset—but I did. After Dad hugged me and Mom kissed me goodnight in the living room, they assumed I went back to my room and was fast asleep. Their voices were reduced to whispers as they walked down the hall, past my bedroom to theirs, as to not have the sound of their voices wake me.

But I heard their whispers from behind the closed attic door.

When I heard their bedroom door close with a soft thud of wood hitting the doorframe, I flicked on the attic light and, ever so quietly, cleaned my paintbrushes and then mixed spring colors on a palette.

I needed to be up here tonight. Because today was . . . hard.

March 18th—it was a horrible day to have locked within the vaults of my memory. It was filled with painful and terrible events instead of happy ones. Memories I wish were forgotten rather than the first thing that came to mind when I opened my eyes every March 18th morning.

I lost my legs four years ago today to emergency surgery and amputation. I'd finally gotten the courage to ask Dad why I needed to have my legs amputated. For four years, I didn't want to know because the event was so ... traumatic. Not talking about it and not knowing *why* it happened had helped me to cope with the loss. But today, I wanted to finally know the story behind that fateful March 18^th day.

*"Do you remember the week before we left for the beach house and how you fell on the sidewalk after your physical therapy lessons and scraped both your knees pretty badly?"* Dad had asked me.

I'd nodded. I hadn't even known my knees were oozing blood until Mom grabbed tissues from her purse and pressed it against the wound. That's what happened when you were paralyzed and couldn't feel anything: you didn't feel pain.

*"Your knees were pretty scraped up, but you seemed okay. When we got to the beach house in Florida, especially that day at the beach before you passed out, Mom told me how tired you were and that you were having a hard time focusing and responding to her questions. We just thought you were overly tired from traveling,"* Dad had said. *"But those abrasions on your knees, Jo—they weren't healed ... they were infected with bacteria. That's why you were so tired and chilled and feverish. The ocean water went on your cuts when I picked you up and held you above the water. You passed out because your blood sugar severely dropped because of the infection—it's called* necrotizing fasciitis*—and the saltwater made the infection so much worse. That's why your legs had to be ... "*

Dad hadn't been able to finish that sentence, but I didn't need him to. I knew what that word, that set of trailing *dot-dot-dots*, was: amputated. I felt sick to my stomach, like someone had taken their fist and pummeled hard into my gut. *Paralytic poliomyelitis . . . necrotizing fasciitis ...* how much more?

*How much more, God?*

That question left me aching, restless, unable to sleep. It'd been over a thousand days now of living without my legs, but I swore every year I felt ghost pain resurrect itself within my missing limbs —and they hurt like they did when I was recovering from amputation in a hospital bed. Maybe a girl my age shouldn't have used the word 'swear,' and painted it on the canvas in front of me, but there wasn't another word I could think of. Harsh words fit with harsh truths, paintings like the one I was doing then.

Mom tried to make today special, make it so we would have good memories to hold on to while we were still reeling from the aftermath of devastating March 18<sup>th</sup> news. She took me to the Philadelphia Museum of Art. I liked to go there every so often. Seeing all the paintings on the walls by artists who all struggled in some way gave me hope that I could be an artist in spite of everything that limited me.

But today, they were just paintings on the wall. Colors and shading and lighting didn't jump out at me, catch my attention and make me want to rush home and try to mimic their style. Today, they were just colors. Just paintings. Just that.

I tried to smile because I knew Mom was trying her best to make today a good day. But the smiles fell flat on both our faces when she wasn't looking at me, and I wasn't looking at her.

When Dad came home from work and told me the story I'd asked him to recount to me, he hugged me close, held on to me longer and tighter than he normally did, and told me that he loved me. And when he came in my room to say goodnight to me almost an hour ago now, I saw his red-rimmed eyes just before he turned off the light—Mom's, too.

Maybe that's why I was sitting here after eleven at night, not sleeping and feeling this urge to paint words and feelings on a page. Because grief was keeping me awake, and it was keeping my parents awake. Mom's muffled cries wafted like a sad aroma into the attic.

Grief stabs with the same knife, but it cuts different holes into us. We were all hurting in different but just-as-hard ways.

So, I was stabbing back at grief with a knife of my own—this paper, this brush, these words and colors. Even though today hurt, it was a reminder, too. A reminder that I was still alive. That I was still fighting. That I hadn't given up. That my life still had a purpose because God wouldn't keep me for a moment longer than it did.

These words, like the words of a journal entry, I painted onto the page in front of me:

*Grief: you're real, and I feel you cutting into me tonight and every hard day I live. And I know this isn't the last time you'll stab me hard. I know next March*

*$18^{th}$ won't hurt any less than this one did. But I made it through today, a little stronger than I was yesterday. And I know I will again next year, and for every*

*March $18^{th}$ that I live.*

# CHAPTER 44

A bump on the road and gravel crunching under the thin tires jolted me back to the present.

Destination: Town fairgrounds.

Time: Roughly 2:30 in the afternoon.

Current whereabouts: Sitting in the back seat of a 1941 Pontiac Streamliner car with Rose in the driver's seat and Catherine in the passenger seat.

"Almost there," Rose said, turning left down Grove Street. Empty plots of land dressed either side of the road bare and colorless. Construction for the temporary attractions and booths of the fair began on the brown soil with sparse green grass.

The car came to a halting stop, tires ceasing to crunch gravel, as Rose pulled over on the side of the road, told us she'd be back to pick us up at three-thirty.

"*Merci* Rose," Catherine said, French words slipping out in place of English ones.

"*Au revoir.*" Rose waved goodbye before turning back on to the road, leaving a plume of dust in the air from car tires spinning over the dirt on the road.

"Welcome to the humble beginnings of the town fair, Miss Carter." Catherine's arms swept across the landscape dotted with people and structures and noises and beginnings. "Construction just started on Saturday, so there's not much we can do today," she said, and pointed to the half-built booths. "But I wanted to bring you here today so you can get a feel for the place and an idea of what you'll be working with."

Someone barked orders from not too far away: "Put those tarps on the north section of the field. Bring a couple of hammers over here —and as many nails as you can find. Tape this here, nail this there, hang this over there."

There was a large white pop-up tent to the right, and Catherine started walking towards it. She pulled back the flap and let me go in ahead of her. My eyes squinted as they blinked in dimmer light. The floor space was full of supplies that would be damaged or rendered completely useless if there were unexpected summer rain showers between now and the fair's opening day.

Catherine reached for a clipboard with a list of names and booths and attractions that would be included at the fair. Her eyes scanned the list from left to right, looking for something.

"Here's your entry on the list." Catherine moved the clipboard closer to me, and I read the line her finger pointed to—the fourth one from the bottom.

*Booth #6 – Art Exhibit – Josie Carter*

Seeing my name on that pencil-scribbled list made everything more real. It was written there—a record of my booth number, what I was doing with it, and my name. This wasn't me dreaming as a teenager of becoming an artist someday and making a difference. This was me at twenty years of age, living out that dream and having something to show for it—teaching art, doing this art exhibit. My name on that list was a tangible confirmation that God knew what He was doing by bringing me here, even if I didn't.

"It makes it more real, doesn't it—seeing your name on there?" Catherine said, sensing this was a weighty moment for me.

I nodded.

"When I first started sponsoring art programs in Paris after the war ended, and I would see my name on the list printed alongside the other sponsors, it did two things to me. First, it made me proud of what I was doing, helping bring back beauty and good things to a country that needed it after the war. Second, it scared me because I was doing something I had never done before—and the first time stepping out and doing something you don't even know how to do is always scary."

What she said brought me back to the memories of a starry sky, an attic, and Sophie. How when both of us were on the brink of change, we were two girls who were terrified and excited at the same time. That's how I felt again now—except Sophie wasn't here to remind me that I was strong enough and brave enough and stubborn enough to not let my fears get the best of me. But I realized now that I was brave on my own . . . and I didn't need someone to tell me I was to believe it for myself.

"Tell me, Miss Carter, how old are you?"

My head tilted a fraction, taken back by her question. "Twenty."

"You've seen a lot in your twenty years of age, *n'est-ce pas*?" My high school French class allowed me to understand simple words, simple phrases. *Haven't you?* she asked me.

*You've seen and lived and gone through so much in your short time on earth, haven't you? More than what some people go through in a lifetime you've gone through in two decades.*

*Yes—yes, I have.*

Her eyes searched my face, and I saw something in hers I hadn't before: someone who was as well-acquainted with pain and grief as me.

"Yes."

"And yet . . . here you are, in spite of everything." She said it like I was the magic in a fairytale, making the impossible now possible, the unbelievable now believable. Teaching art classes and hosting an art exhibit as a young woman with polio in a small town where no one had done it before? It felt like the kind of thing that happens only in storybooks—where magic and impossible and unbelievable meet and make something beautiful and miraculous, even. I never expected that for myself.

"That takes courage, *non?* To do what you're doing here." The smile she gave me lit up her pea-green eyes. "I've met a lot of people over the years in my travels across Europe and America, and I can honestly say I haven't met anyone like you. And I'm glad I haven't because you're too special to be common. But I'm sad, too, because the world would be a better place if it had more people like you in it —people who are brave enough to take what life has handed them and change the world in big and small ways because of it."

"Thank you, Miss Davies." It was people like Sophie and Will and Catherine that gave me the courage they saw in me. It was people like them that made the world a better place for someone like me.

Butterflies started tumbling around in my stomach like wet laundry set for the dry cycle. Three weeks from today, this booth and this event and everything that would come out of both would really be happening—August 25th, 1951.

Soon.

"I talked with the foreman earlier today, and he said that the booths will be done by Sunday," Catherine said. "Could we meet before then to discuss your ideas for the art exhibit?"

"Of course. What about the day after tomorrow—three o'clock at the diner?"

"*Parfait.* It's a plan."

# CHAPTER 45

**AUGUST 10, 1951**
**(Present Day)**

"Where do you want me to set the box?" Will asked.

Will beat my three-word question—*"Can you help?"*—with a four-word answer when I told him about Catherine's call. I'd asked if he could help me take a box of paintings over to the booth that I'd filled with paintings of my own and Alice's and two from my art students, Rose and Patricia. He'd looked at me and said, *"You know I will."*

I felt proud when we reached Booth #6, and I told Will that this was the one—the booth under my name—and he smiled at me, understanding what that meant to me. The booths on my right and left—#4 and #5—belonged to a Mr. Jones and his hot dog stand and a Mr. Phillips and his dart-throwing attraction.

"Set it on the counter space over there." The whole of that 10'x10' booth was completely void of anything—decorations, painted walls, something to indicate what the booth was or its purpose there. Just an empty wooden shell on the outside and inside that needed to be filled and painted over and brought to life for two days before it was torn down after the weekend fair.

"Okay," he said, setting the box down and attempting to wipe dusty air off his night-sky black slacks.

"Will, can I ask you something? If this fair is such a big deal for the town, how come no one has been talking about it? I didn't even know it existed until Catherine asked me to do this booth." I had been wondering that—*why?*—since Catherine brought me here last week.

He shoved his hands into his pockets with a thoughtful shrug. "I don't know—it's been a tradition here for a long time. We don't really talk about it or advertise it. It's kind of like Christmas—you know when it is without people telling you about it. People show up on the third weekend of August every year from here and other cities close by—Watertown and Fairmount. I guess it's an event we don't have to publicize because it's always been there, and everyone who lives here knows about it."

His explanation made sense: a small town with not a lot of people doing the same thing every third weekend of August. But for me, coming from a city where there were over two million people, and events like this were advertised in newspaper headlines or fliers passed out on street corners, it seemed backward. But better, too, because instead of having news shoved into your face or shouted into your ear, you got the chance to find out for yourself.

"I'm going to make a list of things I'll need if that's okay, and then I'll be ready to go." *Budget* was one of the things Catherine wanted to meet about, and I needed to show up with a list of items I would need for the booth.

There was a reason Catherine never called me 'Josie' but 'Miss Carter' when I told her she could call me by my first name. *"I respect you a lot, Miss Carter, not just for your artistic talent, but for who you are as a person,"* she'd said. *"I see you as I would any other artist I've teamed up with over the years—as an equal, as a professional, and I call you Miss Carter to give you that level of respect you're entitled to.*" And if Catherine really saw me as an equal, as a professional, then I needed to live up to that. And right now, that meant making a list of everything I could need and presenting that to her—not just showing up and recalling the mental list of items I made while on my way to meet her.

"Take your time, Jo. I'm going to look around for a little bit. I'll meet you at the car." He wandered down a row of booths, and my mind wandered down a row of columns on a piece of paper that went from empty to full of penciled words.

# CHAPTER 46

**JUNE 29, 1946**
**(15 Years Old)**

Summer was here again—and Sophie came with it. For the next month, she would be here before heading home, spending the remainder of the summer with her mom before going back to boarding school a few days shy of September. Sophie was two inches taller since last I saw her, and her wheat-blonde hair was two inches shorter, floating just above her shoulders.

We were both a little older, a little wiser, a little stronger. But still . . . us. The halves of our hearts that we gave each other when we were young still fit together, even though separated by age and space and time. We were just as close, as whole, now as we were then. Maybe even more so now because we understood *time* more—how quickly it comes and goes. How summer takes forever to arrive, and when it does, it flies by and declares itself autumn. We knew that time was a gift like this summer was and that we needed to make the most of it, not let it pass by.

We were doing that—making the most of it—tonight: two cousins in the same room, separated only by the floor space between their beds, exchanging whispers of dreams and hopes and secrets in the dark.

"Jo." Sophie's voice was more than whisper-quiet, and I would have missed it if not for the even greater stillness of the house at night.

"Yeah?" My voice dropped quieter out of instinct, matching hers.

"There's something I wanted to tell you . . . about something that happened to me in March."

"What is it?" My eyes were open in the dark, wide with endless possibilities of what had happened to Sophie.

"Do you remember that time I told you about the spring prom at my school?"

I nodded in the dark, forgetting that Sophie couldn't make out the up-down bobbing of my head. "Yeah . . . you said you weren't feeling well that week, so you decided not to go and to rest instead."

"I lied." Her words were like a cold blast of air in the face on a winter morning: chilling, numbing, skin-chapping. "I didn't go because . . . I was invited to go."

I held my breath. "Who invited you to go?"

Sophie gulped down a pool of saliva. "Fred Casey."

And it was like a lightbulb moment for me. How slowly and subtly, whenever Fred's name—the stubborn and annoying boy Sophie was teamed up with for a class project—was mentioned over their Thursday evening phone calls, Sophie's voice wasn't laced with frustration. She said it like she said any name that belonged to someone she cared for. But it was such a subtle change I hadn't thought twice about it until now, and I realized how far back that change had gone—to the Thursday we called, and Sophie told me that the three of them—her, Fred, and Maria—had gotten an $A+$ on their science project. In the weeks they spent working together that April in 1944 . . . something must have changed because Sophie said his name differently when she told me how much Fred had contributed to the project, that he'd spent more hours than she and Maria combined at the library researching facts and getting information. How could I have been so hung up on their grade that I missed that?

"Why didn't you want to go with—" I stopped. "Fred likes you . . ." My sentence trailed off not so much as a question but a statement.

"Yes." That answer was like holding a grenade in Sophie's hands: it terrified her. "The reason he acted so obnoxious and stubborn last year when we worked on that science project together? I thought it was just because he was an annoying showoff. But he was acting like that because he liked me . . . and he still does. It's kind of a given that you don't invite a girl to a dance unless you like her."

"Do you like him?"

"I don't know, Jo." Sophie ran her fingers through her hair, and she tore her way through the curls and knots from her head to her shoulders, flustered and upset. "Fred's changed a lot since I met him and—I don't know—maybe I've changed, too. We *are* good friends . . . but I'm scared to ever be more than that. Fred just turned seventeen a few weeks ago, and I'm not much younger than him, and it's scary, Jo. We're both old enough to be married in a few years, and I think Fred is realizing that—that we're both growing up and that he doesn't have to put off telling me how he feels about me because he *is* old enough to talk about his feelings now."

Her voice was like soft rain: quiet and sad. "I just knew that if I went, Fred was going to tell me how he felt about me. I'm not ready for that kind of change, Jo."

I was still trying to understand the *no,* trying to figure out why Sophie was so sad and scared when it was clear in her words that she cared for Fred, maybe as much as he did her. So, I gently asked, "Why not?"

"What if he's like my dad?" Her voice cracked with raw emotion. She hadn't talked about her dad since he left three years ago. He had never stopped by, never wished her a happy birthday or a Merry Christmas, never cared enough to call or to be involved in her life in any way. He just . . . moved out, walked away, never looked back. I didn't even know if Sophie was aware of this because she didn't say a word to me about it, but her mom had called my mom last year, and even though I didn't directly hear everything that was said, being in the same room allowed me to put the pieces together: Sophie's dad had remarried a year ago, and the only reason Sophie's mom found out about it was that a family friend was invited and told her.

That deep-rooted fear that all men were like her dad—not faithful or safe—hurt Sophie to confess to me. Three years of silence about her dad didn't mean she had moved past and healed from that trauma; it meant she was still hurting from it, still going through it, still dealing with it. Trauma comes back on hard days and unexpected days, and maybe it doesn't always take the form of grief, but sometimes of fear. Like Sophie's did, now.

I reached out my hand, and Sophie found my fingers in the dark, grabbed tight to my hand, squeezed it hard, left us both white-knuckled.

"If I let myself care for Fred and he turns out to be like my dad . . . Jo, I can't go through that again. I can't let someone into my life and then be alone again after they leave me and break my heart. It's better to be alone than to feel that kind of pain again."

I wished more than anything I could tell Sophie that I understood how she felt and that I knew exactly how hard it was to wrestle with that fear. But I couldn't. I had a dad in my life who hadn't walked away when times got hard. But I didn't have someone who cared about me the way Fred cared for Sophie, and I didn't know what it felt like to want to care for someone in that way but be afraid to. But I did know this: I knew what it was like to wrestle with fear and be afraid to open your heart to something because of past pain and disappointment.

*What if he's like my dad?* That question, that what-if, that horrible not knowing.

"What if he's *not* like your dad?"

No one knows what the future holds but God alone. And that's a terrifying thing . . . because God allows heartbreak. Hurt. Loss. Abandonment. He hates those things just as much as Sophie and I, but in a broken world, bad things happen. And yes, God brings good through it, but that doesn't mean He wishes we had to go through it, and neither do we. God had let Sophie's heart break when her dad walked away. Maybe He would let it break again if Sophie let Fred into her life, and he turned out to be like her dad. But there was still the chance, the hope, that Fred Casey wasn't like Jack Perry.

"I just dunno," Sophie breathed softly in the dark.

"If you care about Fred, that means he's not worth letting go because you're afraid. Even if you're only friends for now and never anything more than that later, isn't it worth it still?" I said. "I know you're scared . . . but take it one day at a time. Don't think about tomorrow or what could happen. Think about today and what's happening now."

"I'll try, Jo," she breathed.

"If Fred really cares about you, he's not going to let one *no* to a spring dance stop him from asking you again or telling you how he feels."

Sophie squeezed my hand once, twice, then let go. "I don't think I'm ready to grow up yet, Jo."

I wasn't ready for her to, either.

# CHAPTER 47

**AUGUST 13, 1951**
**(Present Day)**

Beige paint stained my hands and caked itself onto my arm. I had never been a clean artist—and painting walls instead of pictures didn't make a difference: I was still just as messy. So was Will, standing on the step ladder, painting the top corners of the walls that I couldn't even reach if I had my own legs to stand on.

"You're dripping paint on my arm," I said, wiping wet paint off where old paint had already crusted and dried fast from the heat on my sleeveless skin.

"Sorry," he said, hiding a smile, and I couldn't have believed him less.

I was the artist who was a mess, and he was the wall painter making me messier, but it made the two of us smile. We were tired and hot and smelling like sweat and paint, but we were happy working together.

"Can I have more paint?" he asked, lowering his paint can down to my level where he could exchange it from his grasp to mine.

My back ached from being bent over, outstretched arms painting the wide walls that went further than any canvas I'd painted on before. I bent over even further, reaching for a gallon of paint and unscrewing the lid, filling Will's smaller can to the brim.

"Here," I said, raising it up to him. He thanked me and grabbed for it, and when he took it from me, painted sloshed out and down onto my arm again.

"Hey!" I said, feigning frustration but fighting back laughter.

This time, he looked genuinely surprised. "I'm sorry—that was a total accident."

I was back at it again, scraping and flinging wet paint off my arm.

Will came lumbering down the step ladder, setting his can of paint on the counter. He reached for a stained rag, handing it to me.

I took it from him. "I'll accept this apology."

"But not the other one?" His raised eyebrows were reaching close to his hairline.

"No," I answered—and he knew exactly why.

His eyebrows settled as his lips turned into a smile, and he laughed, climbed back up that step ladder, went back to work.

The two of us, we settled into this playful banter that was comfortable and brought out the smile in the other. He brought out the best in me, and I felt safe showing him the parts of me that I tried to hide from others. Sometimes people get close enough to you just to see who you are, and when times get hard, they leave because they realize that it won't be easy to stick by you through the highs and lows life throws at you. But Will wasn't like that, even though he could see through my soul like it was window glass. He stayed and that . . . made me feel safe.

"I brought you two some water." Will's mom slipped into the booth and set two plastic bottles on the counter. My tongue stuck to the roof of my mouth as I eyed them, suddenly aware of how thirsty I was. Will and I downed those bottles of ice-cold liquid with desperate gulps in seconds.

"How's it coming?" she asked.

"Good," Will said, the corners of his mouth lifting in a proud smile.

"So I see," she said, laughter tugging at her lips as she glanced at my right arm covered in paint. Her gaze moved to the booth walls slowly coming to life, one day at a time. "It looks good. You're both doing good." She wasn't looking at either Will or me—just nodding her head at the work we'd done.

She turned to me. "Josie, I wanted to invite you to dinner tonight. Will can bring you after you two are done here for today?" Her eyes left mine and found Will nodding his yes, that he could take me, and then found mine again. "Also" —she reached for something carefully folded and held behind her back— "a few of the women in my church and myself made a banner for you to hang on your booth."

She unfolded it and held it out for me to see, knowing I couldn't finger it because of the paint sticking like glue to my hands. A painted sign with lettered words that spelled out *ART EXHIBIT* captured my eye with its use of summer colors—sage green, yellow, and white.

"I love it." My smile stretched as wide as the banner. "Thank you."

"I'm so glad." Her joy was genuine and warm like the sun. "Will, is there a place you can keep the banner where it won't get lost?"

"Yeah," he said, "I'll find a spot for it in the tent."

In the exchange of the banner, I saw Will's hands tremble. The paper in his hands flapped like bird wings in a windy sky. His face was streaked with pain, but he didn't breathe a word about it . . . just went to the tent and found a place for the banner.

"Is he okay?" I whispered to his mom as he walked away, quiet enough so he wouldn't hear me asking.

Her front teeth snagged onto her bottom lip, bit down hard. "When Will uses his hands for a long time at once, his arthritis can be extremely painful . . . he just needs to rest his hands for a while. That's the only thing that helps, really."

I nodded, both understanding and hurting. I'd spent most of my life suffering the unfair consequences of my health disabilities. But it was different watching someone else hurt from theirs and not being able to take away or shoulder that pain for them. It hurt that I had been the cause of his pain today, even though I knew Will would have told me it had been worth it.

"Thank you for telling me. We should probably both stop for the day anyway. I'm feeling pretty tired myself." I smiled to reassure her.

She thanked me with her eyes as Will came back, and we called it a day. She went to her car, and he and I went to his. His hands trembled like mini earthquakes on the steering wheel his ten fingers lightly held onto.

"I'm sorry," I whispered from beside him.

Apologizing for someone's pain doesn't make it any less painful and any more okay. A sorry doesn't erase what's been done, but it adds something. Because it sees and acknowledges the hurt and damage that's real.

He stilled, staring at his gnarled hands on the steering wheel. "No worries, Jo. I'm used to it." The copper-haired boy's breaths were as shallow as low tide. He shrugged his shoulders, gave me a weak smile.

There was still so much about Will, about the chapters of his life and the pages of it he'd lived, that I didn't know yet. I knew *about* his arthritis, but I didn't know *why* he had it. I knew he *dealt* with it, but I didn't know what it was like to *live* with it. Sharing your pain is vulnerable; and vulnerability requires trust. And I would never ask him to trust me with anything before he was ready to. But in a world that turned away and tuned out of hard conversations, I wanted to be the one to lean in and listen.

"Some days, I hardly notice it." His eyes traced the road as he drove. "The pain in my fingers sometimes barely hurts, and I forget that it's there. But other times . . . it can be so painful, and there's no way to relieve the pain or to distract myself from it. It's just there."

I understood. Pain can hurt so badly sometimes that nothing helps, nothing distracts, nothing brings even the smallest amount of relief or comfort. It's just there, like Will said . . . unignorably and unforgivably there.

"I was born with rheumatoid arthritis. Simply put, it means my immune system is attacking healthy body cells by mistake, which makes my joints swell and become stiff and painful," he said. "Until I was twelve-thirteen, I didn't have any pain from them. But around then, I started running fevers and was tired all the time. I sometimes had trouble using my hands—making a fist, holding a pencil, bending my fingers—because the pain was so intense."

His breath was shaky, like a dissipating plume of air on a winter morning. "I found out later that some distant cousins on my dad's side of the family had rheumatoid arthritis—it's a genetic disease. My doctor prescribed me corticosteroids to help with the inflammation, and that helps a little. Sometimes hot water or muscle exercises help with the stiffness, too, but that's all. Honestly, on the days where my pain is really intense, nothing helps that much."

I understood his brokenness. And in that moment, I knew he understood mine.

He knew what it was like to hurt and to live each day knowing that the hurt wouldn't go away. Not in six months or six years or six decades. His pain would live as long as he did, and every waking moment was a reminder of that, and the only thing that would change that reality was a miracle from heaven above and God alone.

Menthol-like tears burned my eyes, but I wouldn't cry because he didn't need my sympathy. I wouldn't tell him it would be okay because he didn't need empty platitudes. I wouldn't try to find a silver lining in this moment because he didn't need optimism. He just needed me to listen—to be a silent friend.

Will stiffened again. I wished more than anything that I could drive the rest of the way home, even part of it, so that he could rest his hands. It hurt to watch him so visibly stiff with pain inches from me and be able to do nothing to help.

No amount of rationalizing, trying to find the good in the bad, can change the reality that pain hurts deeper than words can go. Yes, there is good in life, and good things come out of bad ones, but it doesn't make the bad things easier, doesn't make them better.

I left the copper-haired boy in the garage with my gratefulness for both his help and his trust. Both meant everything to me.

# CHAPTER 48

I was starting to get worried when I could count down the number of days left until the fair with two hands. Fears are like that—they pile up last minute when time's running out, and thoughts are like a runaway locomotive, chugging hard and getting nowhere.

Why had it taken me until now to realize that I would be running the art exhibit by myself? Will and his mom both said they would help as they could, but they had family and church engagements in the mornings, so I would be on my own until the afternoon. How was I supposed to do that—show people paintings and tell them about art while helping other people paint pictures?

Catherine had given me a suggestion yesterday, and I eagerly accepted it: charging ten cents for every person who came and wanted to paint a picture of their own. That would accomplish two things: one, the cost of supplies would be covered; two, those who wanted could paint pictures rather than just look at the displayed artwork. I knew it would stir more attention, and maybe more people would come to my booth, and I had smiled at that because I wanted to reach as many people as I could, but I hadn't stopped long enough to think it through. I only had two hands, and I needed more helping hands, and I thought of Alice. Alice—she could do this. Work alongside me. Help me.

My mouth felt as dry as desert sand as I swished the words in my mouth, tried to find the right moment and the right way of saying them before I spit them out. And that moment presented itself right then, while Alice silently mixed paint colors together on her palette where distraction wouldn't mess up her work of art.

"Alice," I said, "can I ask you a question?"

She paused mid-stir for the briefest of seconds, paintbrush hovering just above the half-combined grass-green paint. Questions made her nervous, I'd learned. Sometimes questions resulted in painful answers. Sometimes they caught you so off guard you weren't sure what to say or what to do.

"Sure," she said—and I didn't miss how she looked at me with focused, unblinking eyes.

"Would you . . . want to help me with my art exhibit booth at the fair?"

"You want my help?" The words dropped from her mouth in surprise. Her eyes searched mine, making sure she'd heard me right.

"I do. From eight to noon, I'll be on my own, and I really need the help." She could see the need in my eyes, the need that bordered on desperation. But in her eyes, I saw something else—uncertainty. And it was like a mental smack to my thoughtless head.

"Oh, Alice, I'm sorry—I didn't even think about your uncle." The fair was on the weekend. Of course he would be home on either one or both of those days.

"No, it's okay." She shook her head. "My uncle works at the supermarket every day except for Monday. I'm just worried . . . what if my uncle somehow found out I was at the fair? He'd put the pieces together, and he'd know what I was doing there."

I could have said something, told her how this moment felt like déjà vu and how Will had been afraid of the same thing—his mom finding out his secret and her disappointment in him. I was almost like a secret-keeper to the two of them, and I had been sworn to silence. But Will had brought the truth to light, and he was set free from that burden of hiding in the dark. I wanted the same for Alice, for the honey-blonde girl who was too afraid to come out of hiding, too scared to believe that her uncle would ever give her enough freedom to do something she loved without stopping her and confining her to the four walls of her home.

But it wasn't my place to say something. This was her choice—to take a risk or to not. I knew her mind was spinning with the what-ifs and the outcomes to each one of them, but it wasn't for me to stop the wheels from turning. If she wanted to do this, she would. Beneath the fear beat a heart held together by stubborn courage—I recognized it in her just as I had in Will.

"I'll help." With the exhaling of those words, I let out a breath I forgot I'd been holding in.

"Thank you," I said to Alice—my friend and helper.

# CHAPTER 49

**NOVEMBER 04, 1948**
**(18 Years Old)**

Eighteen—that's how old I was today.

Sophie spent hours on the phone with me in the morning, and she left me with a surprise. "*I'm coming to visit, Jo.*" Her words had traveled across the phone lines like magic. "*I'll be there a week from today—and we can celebrate your birthday together then, alright?*"

I couldn't erase the smile off my face even when my cheeks hurt and begged me to stop smiling. We hadn't celebrated a birthday together in four years now—since Sophie left for boarding school in Maryland. But something had snapped inside of me after I'd set the phone back down on its receiver—hard and sharp like a broken bone.

"Here." Mom pulled out a chair for me, propped my crutches against the wall behind me.

"Thanks," I said, but my gratitude came out dry like stale breadcrumbs.

Mom noticed, and her eyebrows raised for a split second, but she didn't say anything about my November-cold words. She could always tell when something was bothering me, but she never pressed me to share. But she was always, always there when I wanted to.

She slid into her seat across from me and flipped through the old menu with its faded words. Guilt stabbed me hard. Here I was, spending my birthday at my favorite Italian restaurant, *Dante & Luigi's,* and instead of feeling grateful for celebrating with Mom, I was bitter like the sugarless black coffee Dad drank every morning.

"Do you want your usual?" Mom asked, looking up from the menu. I ordered the same dish every time I came—a fettuccine alfredo pasta topped with fresh spinach.

I nodded and reached for the glass of water on the table as the waiter took down our orders and retreated to the kitchen.

"I can't believe you're eighteen now," Mom said, shaking her head in disbelief. "Where did the time go?"

I wondered that, too . . . where the time had gone and why it had propelled others ahead and seemingly left me behind. "It went somewhere, I guess."

"Some good places, but a lot of hard ones." Her words were understanding and caring, not blaming me for being blindsided by the emotions that resurfaced from the unfair things I had gone through in life.

The napkin resting on my lap was trapped inside my closed fist, wrinkled like a wadded-up shirt stuffed in a dresser drawer, and I dug my nails hard into the cotton fabric to keep myself from crying. "I feel like I've been left behind, Mom . . . and I'm tired of trying to catch up."

There it was: my bitterness put into one sentence.

"I've spent the past few years trying so hard to learn how to paint, to become better at it because I love doing it. I *want* to paint. But it feels like I'll never amount to anything . . . that I'll just be the painter in the attic and never be able to do something with that dream. I feel like I'm worthless."

Maybe that's why something snapped inside me when I got off the phone with Sophie: because she had experienced setbacks in her life, but she was past them now. She was living, thriving, and moving ahead in life. School was behind her, and a future with Fred was ahead of her. She graduated with honors and a graduation ceremony, and I graduated with an average grade and a certificate handed to me by my tutor. She had a beau's hand in hers and the possibility of a ring on her finger, and all I had was a paintbrush in my hand. She had a promising future ahead of her, and all I had was a waning dream stuffed in an old attic.

Mom's eyes mirrored mine—full of pain and sadness and enough questions to fill all of heaven with. She reached for my hand on the table, and I met hers halfway across the pale-yellow tablecloth. She gripped my fingers tight.

"Feeling like something doesn't make you that," Mom said, her voice gentle. "You're far from worthless, Jo. Your worth is immeasurable."

I blinked back tears.

"When you're tired, Josie Girl, that's when you rest. Not give up." Her eyes never left mine. "You haven't been left behind—you're so much farther ahead in life than anyone I know. Despite everything you've gone through, look how far you've come. You're stronger and braver than anyone I know—and you've survived what others would never have made it through."

Her words tore open my heartbreak and were like stitches, mending me back together.

"It's okay to fall apart, Jo. It's part of life. Where strength is shown is how you rebound. Keep fighting for what you love."

*Keep fighting for what you love.*

Mom had spent eighteen out of her forty-four years fighting for what she loved. *Me.* Fighting for me through the light of day and the dark of night. She'd asked a broken and calloused first grader to *try*—*try* to paint and not give up on life when things were so desperately far from okay. She had kept me going, kept me alive, kept me fighting and healing through the breaking. She was the reason I had that dream in the attic to be an artist.

She was the reason for so many things . . . because she'd fought for what she loved—me.

Life had thrown me to the bottom of hell, but God didn't let me be there alone. He didn't let me go through anything alone. Because He knew I couldn't make it on my own, and He didn't ask me to, either. Mom and Dad and Sophie—they were my Shadrach, Meshach, and Abednego, standing in the blazing fire of the furnace with me.

"Mom . . ." My voice cracked on that last *m*.

Her lips quivered as she tried to smile. "I've always loved you, Jo. For every second you've lived. And if I had to choose to live this life or an easier one, I would always choose this one. Because you're in it . . . and you make everything worth it."

And I was a dam breaking apart, cracking wide open. How could I ever possibly make hard things worthy ones? What had I ever done to make Mom say that she wanted this life, not another one, because I was in it?

*Love.* Love wider than the universe and deeper than the oceans and higher than the sun and moon and stars in the sky.

I needed to say something beyond Mom's name in a cracked whimper. But words fell short, and gratitude couldn't fit into one sentence or a million.

"I love you, Mom."

"I love you, too," she told me.

And it was like a revelation of love intercepted my disappointment and hit me hard with the truth that I was more loved than I thought. More loved than I hoped. More loved than I fathomed. Loved beyond anything I hadn't done, wished I could do, and hoped I would do someday.

Loved for exactly who I was right then at that restaurant table with a steaming bowl of spaghetti in front of me: *me.*

# CHAPTER 50

It was here. The day I'd spent weeks preparing for and thinking about and now ... all the preparation was behind me.

Rose had lent Catherine her car to drive me here before the fairgrounds opened, said she would catch a ride later with friends and stop by the art booth.

"You'll do good today," Catherine said from beside me. "I have every confidence in you."

Every confidence in me doing something I'd never done—I was grateful for that. I needed that. My years' old dream was coming true today. I was getting a chance, a chance I'd prayed for a thousand times—to make a difference with my love for art—but I was filled with more doubt and second-guessing than ever before. Everything at the art booth was ready for me, but anxiety clawed at my chest.

Ready or not, here it was, and ...

Catherine's parting words followed me from the car to the booth. "*Bonne chance, mademoiselle Carter.*" *Good luck, Miss Carter.*

Will was right—people didn't have to spread the word about this fair because people showed up from here in Adams and from neighboring cities. A sea of hundreds, if not a few thousand, faces and colors and smells and sounds. Little girls begged to go on the carousel ride, and boys flocked around the shooting booth, pocketed nickels from their dad's pant pocket, hoping to win the best prize offered. Hot dogs, cotton candy, glasses of lemonade, and all the traditional foods found at a fair were held in the hands of almost every person there.

And people were here—at my booth. Browsing the display of paintings and paying ten cents to paint anything their minds could create with a canvas of their own. That was humbling . . . and uplifting.

"Excuse me?" The thick New York-accented voice belonged to a young woman—maybe late twenties, early thirties?—in a pale rosebud dress. "I was wondering if you could tell me a little about the artists of these paintings you have displayed and their backgrounds?"

She stilled, and her eyes left mine, noticing things were busy, and Alice was juggling helping three kids paint pictures, and I had a can of paint in my hand.

"Oh—" She cleared her throat. "If this isn't a good time, I can come by later."

I could have said *no* and turned her away. But hope lingered in the woman's eyes, a silent plea for a few minutes of my time if I had it. So I told the woman whose name I didn't know that I would be right back, and I gave Alice the can of paint and told her I would be back to help in just a few minutes. She looked at me and the woman behind me and nodded, understanding that I wouldn't have chosen to do this unless it was important and that I wouldn't leave her for longer than I had to.

The woman with the rosebud dress and I went right up to the booth, where some of the paintings hung on the wall that Will and I painted together. Other paintings were protected in glass frames and set on the counter space. Aligned directly above those frames was the banner Will's mom had made, flapping in the wind.

"These paintings were all done by the locals here, except for the ones I did," I told the woman with the rosebud dress. "Some of the artists are students of mine I'm teaching art classes to over the summer."

"Which ones did you paint?" she asked.

I pointed to three hanging on the wall and two propped on the counter space in front of us.

Her stomach pressed against the wooden counter as she leaned closer, eyes scrunched up to see the easily missed details that come with love of labor. She looked at all five of them, but her gaze settled on one: the one I'd done yesterday and then called B.B. to come pick me up so I could get to my booth and nail it into the wall myself.

"Is that Sandy Creek?"

"Yes, it is." *Yes* . . . A treehouse, a memory. A friendship, a mending. A creek, a renewing.

I had been hit with wild inspiration, and I knew I must have looked like a mad scientist locked in a laboratory. Completely sure of his calculations, his measurements, his thorough detail—sure of everything . . . just as I was. The memory I'd made with the copper-haired boy sitting side by side on that log deserved to be seen, remembered, held in my heart and hands.

"It looks so life-like. You painted it exactly how it looks in person without making it look anything but real. This is incredible." Her eyes were as bright and glimmery as the light bulbs hung on a garland rope across the wall, ready to light up the paintings in fluorescent light when the sun started to set, and the blue sky turn to orange and finally, black.

"And" —her hand with all fingers bent save for one, pointed a little higher, a little more heaven-bound— "who did this painting?"

My voice caught in my throat. "Hank—Hank Ridge."

"It's a beautiful painting," she said, not knowing both the beauty and tragedy behind the rainbow in the sky bringing color to the white-washed hospital walls. The giving of life and the taking of it. The gaining of a son and the losing of a father and husband. "The artist—he lives here in Adams?"

"He did." I couldn't help but wonder . . . was that why Hank's paintings had been put in a box and set on a closet shelf? Because beauty comes with admiration, and admiration comes with questions, and questions result in painful answers. I had never met Hank, but it was difficult for me to tell this woman beside me about him because something inside me ached hard for Will and his mom. Because the painting on the wall and the family photos in that closet box told me two things I didn't need words to know were true: this man—he loved his family, and he loved painting. And those were two things I deeply loved, too.

The woman must have heard the ache in my voice. "Oh . . ." she said softly, knowingly. "It's a beautiful painting. Is that building a hospital?"

"Yes," I said. "That hospital is where his son, Will, was born at. Will's mom gave me the painting to display here today. She wanted to honor her husband's memory and let others see this painting because it was the one piece of artwork he did that he was most proud of."

"Not a lot of artists paint hospitals where their children were born at." That seemed to touch her deeply, and she shook her head, shaking tendrils of wispy hair out of her face. "He must have really loved his son."

And his son had really loved his father, too. Not until one has lost do they realize how much they loved.

"Will and his mom will be here later today helping me with the booth, and tomorrow as well. If you'd like to meet them, you're more than welcome to drop by again. I know they'd love to meet you."

Maybe the three of them meeting would do them a world of good.

"I might just do that." She smiled. "I'll let you get back to what you were doing. Thank you for showing me around. This booth and what you're doing—it's important."

"Oh—" she said. "I'm Emma, by the way."

I reached out my hand to shake hers. "I'm Josie."

"I'm glad I met you today, Josie." She let go of my hand.

"Me too," I said, just before she turned and walked away from the booth into the crowds of people.

This booth . . . it was like my nativity scene—a splintered manger in a humble stable birthing something beautiful in the dirt and grime and blood and howling pain. Paintings hung on splintered walls in a humble booth, bringing life and beauty out of hard things and heartbreak. A sacred space that many people would pass by today and tomorrow, but few would take it to heart, treasure it as Emma had.

But it was worth it. People like Emma *made* it worthy.

# CHAPTER 51

**AUGUST 26, 1951**
**(Present Day)**

"Are you okay?"

I read the concern flickering in Alice's eyes, skirting across her face, as she stopped in front of me. Twelve hours at the booth yesterday and almost four hours today helping people and answering questions and . . . it was catching up to these tired bones, fast. Did I look as exhausted as I felt?

"Just tired," I said.

She gauged me with concern. "Do you want to take a break or—"

"Hi, Josie. Hi, Alice," someone interrupted from behind us—Will's mom. Will quickly caught up to her. "Will and I finished our appointment a little earlier than we expected, so we thought we'd come over now and help."

"Hi, Mrs. Ridge. Thank you . . . I really appreciate that." The smile on my lips felt heavy, tired.

"I'm going to get something to eat real quick," Will said to his mom. "Does anyone want me to bring back anything?"

Two *no's* from his mom and Alice. One nod from me.

"I'll take a hot dog or a sandwich or something if you can find either."

His gaze lingered on my face a few seconds longer than was necessary, and I knew he could see how tired I was. "Do you want to come with me, Jo?"

"I don't know—"

"Go ahead, Josie," his mom said to me. "I'll be here to help Alice."

I wouldn't leave unless Alice felt comfortable being temporarily entrusted with this booth. I looked at her and saw . . . confidence.

"Get something to eat and rest for a bit. I'll be here for another forty-five minutes or so anyway. Take your time," she said, smiling confidently.

A little girl in pigtails tugged on Alice's dress, held out her hand with a dime resting in her palm, and proudly declared her daddy gave her money to paint a picture. Alice took a breath and led the little girl over to a wooden stool, handed her a brush, and let her pick out the colors she wanted to use for her picture.

"Ready?" Will asked.

I nodded.

"I think I passed a food vendor earlier on that had some sandwiches." We retraced his footsteps leading closer to the fair's exit, over by the parking lot.

"Everything going okay so far?" Will's hand brushed up against my elbow, keeping me close to his side as we weaved through the throngs of people coming and going on all sides.

"It's been fine," I said. "Not as many people have come to the booth today as yesterday, but that's okay. With fewer people at a time, it's less chaotic, and I can connect with them more."

"And it gives you more of a break, too," he said, not missing a beat. "I know this weekend has been hard on you physically."

"It's been worth it." The smile on my face was small but sincere. "If I allow my limitations to *limit* me, then I'll never do anything with my life. It's exhausting . . . but fulfilling."

"You're a brave soul, Josie Carter," he finally said, studying me. His words stuck like duct tape to that weary soul of mine, and they were like a healing balm to it. Never had Will called me by my full name—Josie Carter. Never had he called me brave. And I knew he said both because those words would get my attention, and he meant every one of them.

"Oh, there it is—*Sal's Baked Goods*. I'll order some sandwiches, and you find us a spot over by those benches?"

There were other people occupying most of the available benches. Parents sat on them while kids sprawled out on checkered picnic blankets on the grass and ate hot dogs with ketchup-stained fingers and ice cream with chocolate-stained teeth.

I spotted an empty bench shaded under a canopy of green trees, and Will found me there, handed me a tuna sandwich on rye bread in paper wrapping.

"Before I helped at the booth yesterday, I walked around the fairgrounds and saw all the booths and rides and games. There's a lot of fun stuff to do here." Mayonnaise rimmed his lips with its sticky white paste, but he didn't seem to notice. "Have you seen the line for the carousel ride? There must have been at least a hundred kids waiting in line."

"No." I swallowed a bite of my sandwich. "To be honest, I've been so busy with the booth I haven't had time to see much of anything here, except for the booths next to mine and the Ferris wheel—I can see it from the booth."

He brushed breadcrumbs off his black slack pants. "If you could pick one thing to do here right now, what would you choose?"

"I'd ride the Ferris wheel," I said, not needing time to think of an answer. "I've never been on one before. Sophie—my cousin—has before, and she told me about it on the phone. She loved it."

"Do you want to?" His question was an invitation to here, now, get on that Ferris wheel together.

I didn't want to miss this moment. "Yes, I would."

He grinned. "Then let's do it."

The two of us sat beside the other on either end of the passenger car. My left arm and Will's right arm hugged our sides of the wall, the barrier keeping us from tumbling out of the Ferris wheel.

Will nodded at me—*it's starting.*

I sucked in a breath of air like a hungry vacuum cleaner sucked crumbs off the dirty floor. And suddenly, though in reality, it wasn't sudden at all, the giant wheel started turning. We began our slow ascent into the sky in a counterclockwise motion, inching off the grassy ground and lifting into the air.

"You can breathe now, you know."

I let out a breath of air, mingled with embarrassed laughter. "I don't know why I was holding my breath." It sounded silly, holding my breath on a ride that went slower than the average person could walk or run.

"I did the same thing my first time on a Ferris wheel. My mom didn't notice I was holding my breath until my face turned blue, and I saw black spots." He laughed, and his shoulders bobbed up-down in a shrug, clearly exaggerating his childhood retelling. "I guess I just forgot to breathe until someone reminded me to."

We all needed someone like that—sometime to remind us we could breathe when we forgot how to.

The ground began disappearing under the feet of the passenger car. We were suspended in empty air, hanging in the space between the earth and clouds. And it was like a slow-motion invitation to see the world from a different perspective—a higher perspective that my five-foot-three-inch frame allowed.

Minutes ticked by as we crawled *up, up, up.*

"Jo, look over here." Will pointed out his side of the car, and I scooted across the foam cushion, closer to his side. I traced the line he drew with his finger through the air.

"There's your booth," he said.

"It looks so small from up here," I whispered.

"Everything looks smaller when you see it from a different perspective." Will's words caught me off guard as we reached the peak. Warm windy air blew strands of his copper hair over his forehead, and they poured down like a gentle waterfall, touching his eyelashes.

We reached the highest point the Ferris wheel dared to climb into the sky. When life tried to limit us, God gave us perspective, let us climb up on mountaintops or ride in Ferris wheel cars. Gave us ways to get higher, see things for what they were without emotions hurling smoke bombs in our eyes, blinding us to everything but the sting. Maybe life's problems always seemed too big, too daunting, too overwhelming because our perspective was too small.

The wind was stronger up here, like a mini-tornado causing our passenger car to sway to the rhythm of its swirling dance, but the sun warmed me and brought a series of goosebumps on my forearms. Looking down at everything below on Will's side of the car started to make me dizzy, and I instinctively slid back to my end of the car, but something stopped me, stubbornly resisted. The cuff of my plaid pants had caught on something, and each time I tried to pull myself free, tiny strings of material unthreaded themselves on whatever it was stuck on, wound around.

"Oh—it looks like a screw is sticking out a little bit."

Instinct told me Will was about to leave his seat and unfree my pant leg. "I'll get it," I said, panic accentuating my words.

I reached for Will's arm to keep him in place, but between the three seconds that had elapsed, I was too late. Will had already bent down, one hand unwinding while the other tugged on my pant leg.

"Done," he said, and with the final tug and freeing, my pant leg slipped up past my ankle. And as it did, flashes of something that shouldn't have been there were now exposed: leather and wood instead of skin and bones. My artificial legs beginning where the stub on my knees ended . . . something only my family, Sophie, and doctors had seen or known replaced what had been lost to infection and amputation.

My skin burned hotter than the August sun, and I wanted to hide. *No* . . .

I didn't want him to see me like this . . . to see *this*. I was the girl who wore ankle-length dresses on some days or full-length pants on most days. Not because I was ashamed that I wasn't what someone would deem a 'whole' person, but . . . because it was personal. Vulnerable. Something a passing stranger could readily judge and less easily understand. Something people could be so shallow about and make light of, make fun of. Something only to be shared with the few that were trustworthy and safe.

But he saw. He now knew.

Will was still half-bent, unmoved. And I was breathless again, forgetting how to breathe, drowning, and not knowing how to resurface. The legs he already knew I couldn't walk on now, he learned, weren't mine, too.

"*Jo*." He said my name so softly, like a whisper on the wind. He looked up at my eyes, and they were asking me something. I didn't understand what his silent question was, but when he momentarily broke eye contact, looked down at his hands, and then back up at me, wordlessly asking me to do the same, I understood. He wanted permission to do what his right hand was a breath away from doing: touching that part of me that was broken.

My head felt heavy, cement-stuck-in-place, and I barely managed to nod, to give him my silent answer to his silent question—a scared and vulnerable but trusting *yes*.

His broken fingers reached out and met my broken legs with a touch I couldn't feel physically, but, oh, felt in my soul. And his touch, gentle and brief, opened my eyes and my heart a little wider to the truth that the copper-haired boy—he didn't see me as less; he saw me as *whole*. A person with defined limits, but a soul like an untamed universe, where impossible turned into infinite possible. The galaxy sky where limits couldn't reach or hinder or influence.

A tear slipped down my face, stained my cheek as it dripped wet and salty. There were very few times, not even enough to count on one hand, that someone had seen me as whole, and I believed them for *myself*. It's hard, sometimes impossibly hard, to believe that when your body and your pain try and prove otherwise.

A warm presence was on my cheek: Will's hand wiping away my tear. Our eyes met for the briefest of moments, and my heart tried to leap out of my chest.

His hand left my face, but that memory would never leave my heart.

"I lost my legs ten years ago." The sound of my voice startled me because the thoughts and the torrent of memories I replayed in my head came out my mouth instead.

Will sat upright, stilled, listened.

"But before that, I was diagnosed with polio when I was five. I was at a park with my parents, and I drank water from a drinking fountain there. None of us knew that the sewer lines had burst in the city the night before and that the water I was drinking was contaminated with disease until it was too late."

"That's why you looked so afraid that time I offered you a drink from the fountain behind my house."

He saw that, too? I nodded. The warm wind had dried the residue from my tears on my face, crusted them on my cheeks, made my skin feel taut, glued in place.

"With polio . . . the damage can't be undone. And then when I was ten, my legs were amputated because of a life-threatening infection," I said. "I haven't walked on my own in a long, long time." Fifteen years felt like infinite years, time stretched beyond its capacity.

"Jo." His voice was soft, but his tone was earthquake-desperate to shake me, to get my attention. "Don't you know?"

I wanted to wildly shake my head *no,* tell him I didn't have the foggiest notion of what he was talking about, what I was supposed to have known. But his eyes anchored mine, and I couldn't look away.

"You don't need something to help you walk, Jo. You've been walking on your own all this time . . . even if you didn't know you were."

What I had lost all those years ago still hurt. But what I found today, up there in the sky with what seemed miles of distance between the passenger car and the ground and mere inches between two souls, helped heal more of that hurt. A boy with blue-green eyes gave me a perspective that I would never have found on my own. A perspective that didn't make me feel broken, but like a treasure set in a jar of clay—fragile but held together by two nail-scarred hands that were stronger than any pain, loss, disappointment, heartbreak, death . . . anything.

The copper-haired boy beside me and the God in heaven who held everything—they were the nearest things to me as the Ferris wheel went up, down, twice again.

# CHAPTER 52

**NOVEMBER 13, 1948**
**(18 Years Old)**

Sophie wasn't the same girl I'd spent three hours with talking on the phone a week ago, laughing and joking and sharing things with. Her smile was still there, but the light behind her eyes was dimmed, like starlight covered over by a veil of foggy night sky.

I wasn't the same girl, either. One week ago, I'd turned a year older—eighteen—and I had a head swollen with three-hundred-sixty-five more questions about my life and purpose. Growing up does that—makes you stop because you realize that all those times as a kid and you wondered what you would do and who you would be, you could always say that you'd figure it out when you were older. But I *was* older and . . . what now?

I didn't have a clue.

I broke the silence that was as thick as the clumps of hot cocoa sitting at the bottom of our matching kitchen mugs. "You okay, Soso?"

She shrugged and kept stirring her now-lukewarm cocoa, scraping a metal spoon against the edges of a metal mug, and it screeched all her *not* okayness. I waited. If I didn't give up and mistake Sophie's shrug for a refusal, she would tell me what was bothering her. She'd always done that . . . fought an invisible battle in the silence between holding back or letting me in, staying quiet or sharing her burdens.

Her breath hitched, the silence breaking. "Fred and I" —her voice cracked, even though she tried desperately hard not to let it— "we broke up on Friday."

I blinked.

Four days ago, my best friend's heart had been broken . . . and I didn't know how to begin putting it back together. Fred and Sophie —they'd known each other for years. Gone from enemies to friends to more than that and now . . . to nothing? They knew each other inside-out, finished each other's sentences, knew when the other was sad and when to help them get their perspective back or sit in the shadows with each other. They were happiest together, best together, *everything* together.

"What happened, Sophie?" I wouldn't push her to answer, but I desperately wanted to know if this breakup was just a bump in the road that would lead them back together or if it was a dead end. A bookmarked page and not an ending of a story.

"I don't know, Jo. Neither of us wanted to." Her voice was riddled with pain. "Fred called me Friday night and told me that he enrolled in university classes, and he was moving out of state to attend medical school. He—he wanted to know how I felt about '*us*' because he felt uncertain like I did. The next step would have been to . . . get engaged, but neither of us were ready for that." Words flew out of her mouth faster than any mad typist pounding the keys of a typewriter could keep up with. "We talked for *four* hours on the phone, Jo. And in the end . . . we both knew that we needed to let each other go. We ended on good terms, and I'm sure it was the right decision, but Jo—it hurt so much to say goodbye."

Sophie cried in front of me for the third time in her life. My brave, brave cousin sobbed into my arms as I held her in that kitchen room.

*God.* I whispered the only name that made sense when nothing else did. The hundreds of questions I had for myself were now aimed at Him: *Why?*

Why did He bring Fred into Sophie's life and let him be everything to Sophie that her dad had never been and then take him away? Why had He let years go by and allowed them to grow closer and closer until their lives were almost intertwined, only a ring away, and then tear them apart? Why did He give them so many *yeses* when the final answer was a shattering *no?* Why did He let my best friend cry hot tears into my sweater while the November-cold kitchen tiles numbed our bare feet?

Because He was God. But sometimes, in the thick of heartbreak and that Job-like wrestling and gut-wrenching pain, that answer wasn't enough. It just wasn't.

"I'm so sorry, Sophie." The words in my head couldn't reach the level of sorrow in my heart for her.

She wept, and I held on to her long past the numbness in my arms and the ache in my back. Long past the time she stopped crying, and my sleeve was soaked with her snot and tears. I couldn't fix this pain, but I could hold her and all the broken, sharp edges of her battered heart. And I would for as long as she needed me to.

# CHAPTER 53

**AUGUST 26, 1951**
**(Present Day)**

Dread—that's what I felt brewing like coffee in the pit of my stomach.

Will and I retraced our steps to the art booth, and Will's mom frantically paced back-forth in a line she'd worn thin with her footsteps.

"Mom?" Will ran ahead of me, reached his mom, steadied her with his hands on her shoulders. "What happened?" I could barely make the sound of his voice above every other noise on every side of me.

"Josie, I'm so sorry." Her words were directed to me, but her eyes were glued to her son's face. "About ten minutes ago, Alice's uncle showed up. He called home from the supermarket because apparently, he had forgotten his heart medication, and he needed Alice to bring it to him. But when she didn't answer the phone, he called where she babysits, and Mrs. Chambers told him she thought Alice was at the fair. He came here and . . . he knows everything. He took Alice home with him."

The world dizzied, and I teeter-tottered along with it.

*No.*

Alice had grown in so many ways since meeting with me every day—she'd become braver, more sure of herself, more alive when painting—and I knew she was able to have this confrontation with her uncle. But everything in me wished she didn't have to. That her uncle didn't have to find out she was going behind his back and feel the sting of betrayal because of the choice he had made to shelter Alice to the extreme.

Alice had taken a gamble when she'd asked me to teach her—and it was a price she was having to pay right now. Maybe the way she and I went about it wasn't the best way, but it was the only way we knew would work—even for a short time.

Wordless whispers of desperation filled my mind, wrote themselves against my barely parted lips: *Please, God. Please . . . be with her.*

My heart broke that I wasn't there to stand with Alice when the truth came to light. I'd been sharing my story with the copper-haired boy up in that blue sky while Alice was down here on the brown soil and green grass, facing down her uncle in an argument that he must have won because she wasn't here right now to tell me about it.

My mind's eye wandered to the parking lot, planned a mental route of how to get to Alice's house from here. Desperation had me making my way away from the booth without stopping to think through what I was doing. But the copper-haired boy jumped in front of me, stopped me in my tracks.

"Jo, you can't," Will said, blocking the path out of the booth. "Talking to Alice's uncle will only make things worse for Alice right now."

"Then what am I supposed to do?" My voice almost sounded angry to my own ears. Maybe because I was angry—angry at how unfair and maddening this whole thing was.

"Stay here in the booth and finish out today." His voice was so much softer than my words were. Maybe he sensed I needed that—for him not to shout back at me and get angry with me but to let kindness penetrate my stone-hard wall of anger.

"But—"

"Hey," he said, squeezing my shoulders, squeezing some logical sense into me. "You made a commitment to Catherine Davies to do this booth, Jo. You can't back out on the last day. The best thing you can do right now to help Alice is to see this through. Trust me on this. Don't let this booth be for nothing—not after how hard you've worked and how much Alice has helped you."

"We'll figure out how to help Alice tomorrow. I promise." His hands slipped off my shoulders.

A moment of trust. A moment of decision.

My answer was in my turned-around steps, taking me back to the booth. Logic hadn't won out. His dare to trust him was what had me staying grounded instead of plunging ahead.

I gave the rest of that day everything in me . . . for the honey-blonde girl.

# CHAPTER 54

**AUGUST 27, 1951**
**(Present Day)**

A promise to keep was what had the copper-haired boy and his mom ringing the front doorbell in the morning.

I poured them two cups of black coffee, something to combat the tiredness we all felt settle deep into our bones. Last night I had fallen asleep too late and awoken too early from a dreamless but restless slumber.

"What can I do to help Alice?" The question had been begging to come out. I needed an answer.

Will was the first to speak. "I don't know if there's anything you can do, Jo." If anyone but Will had said that to me, I wouldn't have listened. But this was *Will* . . . my friend and the only person who understood this situation with Alice as well as I did.

"There has to be something. I can't just do *nothing*." I couldn't sit there at the kitchen table and accept defeat. Not after how far Alice and I had come and how much she had learned in the weeks I taught her. I wrung my hands in my lap, hidden from view under the table. "Doesn't she have any other relatives she can stay with besides her uncle?"

"I don't know all the specifics of Alice's situation," Will's mom said. "But after Alice's parents died several years ago, her uncle was appointed as her legal guardian until she turns eighteen. He was the only relative Alice had that had a home and enough revenue to support her. After Alice turns eighteen, she's free to move out and live on her own. Until then, she has to stay where she is."

My mind churned as it traveled back into weeks-old memories, trying to remember if Alice had ever told me when her birthday was. She was seventeen, so the longest she would have to live with her uncle would be one more year. But if she didn't have a way to make her own income, to support herself, how was she ever supposed to leave and pursue her dreams?

"Maybe if I talk with her uncle again, I can—"

"Alice knew what she was doing when she asked you to teach her art, Jo. This is something she needs to work through with her uncle by herself." Will softened the hard but truthful blow of his words. "You can't fight every battle for her."

"If Alice did what she did yesterday on her own, she can do this, too." Will's mom's words had my eyebrows lift as my curiosity peaked.

"What did she do?"

"After you and Will left, that little girl Alice was helping paint asked Alice to tell her a story. She said that her mom always told her a story when she colored pictures at home. And Alice did—she made up a story right there on the spot about learning and growing and painting that that little girl could understand. By the time she finished, there was a small crowd of kids and their parents, too, listening to her." The small smile on her face reflected how the joy of that moment yesterday was greater than the disappointment we all felt today. "You should have seen the look on her face—she looked so happy with those kids, so natural at storytelling and art. She acted like she'd done it a hundred times before and not that yesterday was the first."

That chest of mine was robbed of breath and filled with pride because *that* was Alice—who she really was beneath the deep layers of fear and hesitancy. She was good with kids, good with art, good at teaching . . . good at everything she was *meant* to be good at, that God had designed her to do—to weave life-lessons into stories and paintings like Jesus did with parables.

I wished I could dump a cold bucket of truth over her uncle's head, brain-freeze his fears long enough for him to see the truth because only truth could set someone free.

The phone ringing in the kitchen startled me. Will and his mom took it as their cue to leave, to let me think and work through all my kitchen-table thoughts alone after I answered the phone.

I reached for the phone on its last ring.

*Me:* *"Hello?"*

*Catherine:* *"Hello, Miss Carter."*

*Me:* *"Hi, Miss Davies. What can I do for you?"*

*Catherine:* *"I wanted to thank you again for all the hard work you put into the art booth this weekend. I talked with some of the people there, and they spoke so highly of their experience with you. I knew you would do well. Well done, Miss Carter."*

*Me:* *"Thank you—that booth wouldn't have been possible without you."*

*Catherine:* *"You're most welcome. If you have time, there's something I wanted to talk to you about before I leave next week. I know it's short notice, but would we be able to meet tomorrow?"*

**Me:** *"Of course. For lunch at the diner?"*

**Catherine:** *"*Oui. *I'll see you then.* Au revoir. *"*

**Me:** *"Bye."*

# CHAPTER 55

"Need any help?"

My bedroom door creaked open, a trail of light filtering in from the yellow bulb in the hallway as Mom peeked her head in. She spotted the pile of clothes on my bed waiting to be folded and stuffed in my suitcase. I'd never been good at packing, never knew what to take and what to leave behind, how to make everything I needed fit inside the leather compartments. Mom knew that, and that's why her offer of help came from the doorway. And she knew —knew I needed to spend my last night at home with her. I think Mom needed that, too.

I nodded. "Thanks."

Mom stood on my left, took in the colored mess of clothes splayed across my white bedsheets and the small army of hangers on the floor. "Did you take everything out of your closet?"

"Basically," I said and laughed under my breath.

"First, let's sort out the clothes you have, and then we can decide what outfits to pack from there." Mom was good at that—helping me make sense of the mess and unorganized chaos and finding something complete within it. The mess on my bed transformed into three organized piles—tops, bottoms, and dresses.

A question birthed itself in the silence as we organized the piles and folded them into neat stacks. A question I had been thinking about for days and needed to ask, needed some kind of solace for my unsure mind. "Mom, are you sure you're okay with me leaving?"

Mom had kneeled in front of me and told me she loved me less than a handful of nights ago in the aftermath of my decision to leave for the summer. I knew she understood and that she was willing to let me go, but she hadn't breathed a word about the trip since that night, and I could tell when her mind was on it because she looked lost in thought with her brow wrinkled in worried lines. I couldn't spend a summer away with a *maybe* she was sure hanging over my head and weighing heavy on my heart. I needed to know for sure.

Mom's face was like a closed book as she studied mine, and I couldn't read the words within its pages, couldn't figure out what the thoughts in her head and emotions in her heart were saying.

"It's hard for me to let you go, Jo," Mom finally said. "The three of us—you, me, and your dad—have never been apart for more than a few days, much less a few months."

My heart felt like a balloon deprived of helium, slowly deflating, shrinking.

"*But*" —it was her *but* that arrested my attention, filled me with an inkling of hope— "I'm sure it's okay. It's not easy when life changes, but I'm proud of you for going, Josie Girl. It's okay to go— and if you feel so certain that this is what you're supposed to do, then there's a *reason* for you to not miss this opportunity."

"What if I'm wrong, Mom?" The blouse in my hand wrinkled in my anchor-secure grip on it. "What if I heard God wrong and He doesn't have something for me out there? What if this amounts to nothing? Do you think God will really ever use me to make a difference with my art, or will my dreams always be stuck in the attic?"

Those questions, those grapplings, had been festering deep into my soul for two years, and I spent every one of those days wondering, asking, searching, praying, and finding nothing.

Mom cupped both of my hands in hers, took the blouse out of my grasp before I wrinkled it beyond recognition with my white-knuckled fingers. "God's got something out there for you, Josie Girl. All you have to do is ask Him to help you find whatever it is and be patient enough for Him to show you *where* it is. Do that, and He'll take care of the rest. God doesn't give us dreams that we stuff up into an attic where they collect dust and fade away over time. Sometimes, dreams start there . . . but for those who are patient enough for God to do something with them? They never *stay* there."

Mom was like God's gentle whisper in my ear. Always trustworthy. Always loving. Always comforting. I felt like just how I had on the night when I was scared but determined to try and walk as a six-year-old girl in my bedroom, but I did it anyway . . . and I failed. I was scared to try again. Because on the flip side of every success is failure—and failing means falling, and falling means hurting, and hurting means breaking.

But at the bottom of every floor was a chance to get back up, to try again, to keep going and resist quitting.

I rested in the comfort of her words, that gentle whisper of God-sent truth, as we went back to packing. Mom laughed at the end result of my feeble attempt to fill my suitcase with folded clothes when they didn't come close to fitting inside their respective compartments. I laughed, too, and said if she could do better—and we both knew she could—then she should have at it. She was like an origami-whiz, folding everything into perfect shapes to allow for more room in my suitcase so that I could take more art supplies.

Our laughter together was the last thing I remembered before I collapsed in bed. How it carried louder and longer than the radio waves coming from the living room, broadcasting Dad's favorite baseball game played by the *New York Yankees'* Yogi Berra. How it brought me a measure of peace and made my fears of the future fade away.

Because the present was worth being *present* in.

# CHAPTER 56

Catherine sat across from me, told me she'd already ordered coffee, and the waitress would be back in a minute to take our lunch orders.

I smiled at her kindness, but the aching in my heart that awoke me before the sun scratched the surface of the sky returned. *Why had Catherine wanted to meet with me? How was Alice doing?* Today felt heavy with a great lack—there was no rush to step out of the diner doors and wait outside the church doors for the copper-haired boy to meet me there; there was no art class with the honey-blonde girl at one o'clock; no three bundles of energy and joy for Will to play with in the nursery until two o'clock.

Those days were an ending ... and that ending was a loss.

"How did teaching go today?" Catherine was generous with her money and her words, carving out time for our relationship to be centered on friendship and not just business.

"It went well," I said. "My students have learned so much over the past few months, especially Rose. She's very talented. Patricia, the youngest in the class, is definitely the most enthusiastic about painting—she can hardly sit still during the lesson until she can start painting."

Catherine laughed at that—the joy of a child about to burst from the excitement of doing something they loved was contagious. "I'm so glad to hear that. You're an excellent teacher."

The waitress with the bleached blonde hair and the sunflower-yellow apron found us at our table, took down our lunch orders, and told us she'd be back with our food soon in a thick New York accent.

"I know you're probably wondering why I asked to meet with you today, *non*?"

I nodded.

"I wanted to be honest with you," Catherine said. "The reason I asked you to have a booth at the fair wasn't just so that art would be represented there, but because I wanted to see if you were qualified."

My stomach was a cyclone of nervous butterflies. "Qualified . . . for what?"

"You're very talented at art. You're a good teacher and an organized leader. You have what it takes to go far in the art world, and I want to help you get there." Her face was completely serious, leaving no room for doubt or misinterpretation. "I want to offer you a scholarship to my art school in Paris."

I was too stunned to say anything, think anything but *what?* over and over again, wonder if this moment was real because how on earth could a lunch invitation at a diner booth turn into an offer for a scholarship in Paris?

"You'd have the chance to learn from some of the top art professionals. And once you graduate, it would be easier for you to get a job as an artist—if that's what you want to do as a career. Also, you'd be tutored in French classes, and dormitory housing would be provided. It wouldn't be an easy transition, but I'd help however I could."

All the noise in the diner—couples in neighboring booths chatting, cutlery clanking, and orders shouted to the cooks behind the kitchen door—drowned out in that moment. I stilled, and I could hear my heart pounding against my chest, loud and strong. *Wait . . . what?*

My mind couldn't wrap itself around Catherine's offer. This opportunity she handed to me—it was a chance some people were never given. The trajectory of my life could match the path I wanted my dreams of professional art to take me down.

And that could all happen with one word—*yes.*

"I don't know what to say." It was the cliché movie line I'd heard a handful of actors say in the movies. But maybe it wasn't so cliché because that was the only honest answer I had that would form into words when I was at a loss for them.

"I understand." She smiled at me. "Take a few days. Think it over and talk with your parents. And we can meet here again on Friday with your answer?"

I nodded again.

"The scholarship is there for the taking *if* you want it and yours to turn down if you're not interested." She leaned forward, and her gaze was steady, focused on mine, holding my attention. "When I first started out in my career, I had to make several decisions that would change my life. To accept an offer to study at one university over another. To decide if it was worth it for me to try and start my own business or to work for someone else. Dreams are costly, just as decisions are—and every person has a different road to take to get there. Only you can answer what path that is. Do what's best for you, *d'accord?*"

I nodded once more and left the diner with a stomach full of food and a head full of questions.

**Me:** "Hey, Sophie—it's Jo."

**Sophie:** "Jo, it's so good to hear your voice. I was thinking about you tonight and was going to call you tomorrow, but you beat me to it."

**Me:** "Oh, I forgot about the time difference—is it too late to talk?"

**Sophie:** "I need to be getting to bed soon, but until then, my time is yours. How are you, Jo? You don't sound very okay . . ."

*(A sigh slipped past my lips, burdened and heavy)*

**Me:** "A lot has happened the past few days. You remember I told you that Alice was going to help me at the fair?"

**Sophie:** "Yeah, of course."

**Me:** "Her uncle found out about it and showed up while she was there. I was gone at the time, so I didn't know until I got back, and Will's mom told me what happened."

**Sophie:** "Oh . . ."

**Me:** "And then this afternoon, I met with Catherine Davies for lunch, and she—"

*(I paused, taking a breath and formulating words to match my thoughts)*

*Me:* "She offered me a scholarship to her art school in Paris."

*Sophie:* "Oh my goodness, Jo. Wow. I don't even know what to say. Did you tell your parents about it?"

*Me:* "I called them about an hour ago and told them. They were so surprised, but they sounded so proud. They told me to do whatever I felt was the right thing for me. But I have no idea what that is. I don't even know what to do about Alice, and now I have to make a life-changing decision by Friday. I'm . . . so overwhelmed."

*(Sophie's end went silent for three seconds)*

*Sophie:* "Jo, what are you looking at?"

*Me:* "What do you mean?"

*Sophie:* "What are you looking at right now?"

*Me:* "The . . . floor."

*Sophie:* "Look up. When life overwhelms you, look up. That's where your help comes from."

*(I closed my eyes and remembered to breathe)*

*Me:* "I will."

*Sophie:* "I love you, Jo. You're never alone."

*Me:* "What would I do without you?"

*Sophie:* *"You don't have to wonder. Even if I'm not always here, I'll forever be there—in your heart, remember?"*

*Me:* *"I remember."*

*Sophie:* *"Good. Don't ever forget that. And if you want my advice, Jo, always do the next thing that's ahead of you. Don't worry about the next hundred steps you'll take. Just focus on the one that's in front of you. One decision at a time, right?"*

*Me:* *"Right. Thanks, Sophie."*

*Sophie:* *"The next decision you need to make soon is what you're going to eat for dinner."*

*(Sophie's unexpected comment made me laugh loud)*

*Me:* *"You sound like my mom."*

*Sophie:* *"Well, I am older than you."*

*Me:* *"Not even by a year and a half."*

*Sophie:* *"Which means I'm over a year wiser than you are."*

*Me:* *"Alright. Let's call it a truce."*

*Sophie:* *"Giving up?"*

*Me:* *"No. You need to get to bed."*

*Sophie:* *"Fair enough. Goodnight, dear Jo."*

**Me:** *"Goodnight."*

**Sophie:** *"Call me again soon?"*

**Me:** *"Always will."*

# CHAPTER 57

AUGUST 29, 1951
(Present Day)

The copper-haired boy walked home with me after class at the art gallery finished.

My feet were on the ground, but my head was lost in the clouds. Wondering what to do about Alice. About Paris. About everything. I hadn't missed the curious and almost worried look Will cast in my direction as he walked by my side.

"When are you going to tell me what's bothering you?" The sideways glances that he gave me for brief seconds turned into a stare that he didn't break. "You look dead tired. Jo, did you even sleep last night?"

Even I had noticed the circles that hung like dark moons under my eyes when I caught my reflection in the mirror this morning.

My one-shoulder shrug was answer enough for him: *no.*

"Jo, talk to me." He gently slowed me to a stop on the sidewalk two blocks from our homes. "What's going on?"

"Can we go somewhere to talk?" I wanted to tell Will what had happened yesterday at lunch with Catherine, but not on a street corner with cars driving down it every so often, washing out our words.

"Sure," Will said, squinting his eyes against the sun's noon glare. "Sandy Creek?"

In the short months I'd known him, he knew me well enough to know that I would rather be somewhere blanketed in peaceful stillness, talking in whispers rather than shouting over city noises just to be heard. I wasn't the kind of girl you'd find sitting at a drug store soda fountain. I was the kind of girl you'd find in the library-quiet stillness of an old attic, doing what I loved: painting.

I nodded, and we went to his house, climbed into his old car, and sped past nature and old trees and sticky summer air and down narrow streets and wide roads until we got there: Sandy Creek.

We reclaimed our spot on the same hollowed-out log our friendship had been rebuilt on. Nothing had changed about this place except for the leaves on the trees—their light green hue had morphed into a color that would soon leave the tips in the color of marigolds. Fall was almost here, and with the changing of the leaves, my life would change, too. In just a few weeks, Sophie and Aunt Carol would be on a plane, flying back here to Adams, and then I'd be on a train, heading back home to Philadelphia. And from there . . . I would either be home for a few months and then off to Paris or home for a long while.

I took a breath. "Catherine Davies asked to meet me for lunch yesterday. She had something she wanted to talk to me about."

"Oh?" Will prompted.

"She offered me a scholarship to her art school in Paris." The words felt fantastical as they slipped off my tongue. Like they were a far-off dream I could finger and not an up-close reality that was within my grasp, just a *yes* away from holding.

Will looked as shocked as I had sitting across from Catherine, expecting to hear anything but the words she had told me, and I now told him.

"Wow, Jo . . ." A trace of a smile took over his facial features but fell short when a smile was missing on my lips—a smile that should have been there after what all my hard work had accomplished: something I never dreamed anyone would give me. My face was like a blank slate—emotionless—and I think that confused him as much as it did me. "Have you decided if you'll accept it or not?"

"I haven't, but I have to give Catherine my decision on Friday." I saw it on his face, how he did the same mental calculation I did, realizing that today was Wednesday, and Friday was two short days away. "I called my parents, and they said they wanted me to do whatever was best for me. I talked with my cousin, Sophie, about it, too. She basically told me the same thing my parents did. I'll never get a chance like this again, Will, and I know that whatever decision I make . . . it's going to change my life."

"If you'll never get another chance like this" —he paused, and I knew he was searching for a way to word the rest of his sentence carefully, with gentle words that searched for the truth and not ones that might come across as attacking— "then why haven't you taken it?"

"I don't know." My hands found my face, rubbed the tired lines under my eyes. "For years, I've hoped and prayed that a door would open for me to pursue art on a professional level because I want to make a difference in people's lives with my art. But now . . . I'm so uncertain if *this* is the door I'm supposed to walk through. Something—I don't know—just doesn't feel right, but I don't know why or what it is."

So many questions, and each one of them heavier than the last. Piled up high enough to easily topple, easily crash down on me. This Paris offer was like a set of puzzle pieces on the floor, waiting to be put together and matched with the pieces it belonged with. But none of them were fitting together as they should. Some, close. Others, not at all. And only twisting and bending and reshaping the pieces could make them fit, but that felt wrong, like I was taking something that wasn't meant to be and forcing it to be. Like this open door in front of me that I could step through with a *yes* was open for me to walk through . . . but the doorway was only high enough for me to get through if I crawled. I could still do it—I could.

And there was the taunting question, the one with the endless question marks at the end of it, that kept me up last night: *Am I supposed to do it?*

"I'm sorry, Jo." Will's whispered sympathy brought me out of those puzzle pieces and back to this moment. "I know that's not easy . . . to have to make a decision like that so soon."

"It's different than when my aunt Carol asked me if I wanted to spend the summer here. When I read her letter, it was like I instantly knew that I needed to say yes and come. I felt peace about going." I looked out at the water flowing steadily in the creek in a steady direction, a clear flow, a sure path. "I wish the decision was as easy to make as it was last time."

"What's different?"

I thought about it. "I'm unsure. I don't have peace about saying yes *or* no. Both feel wrong."

"Take it from someone who spent six months deciding what university they wanted to attend and another six months figuring out what they wanted to get a degree in" —I didn't know if I was supposed to laugh at his indecisiveness or sympathize with how hard decision-making can be, but when his lips parted like the Red

Sea in a wide grin, I knew he was trying to get me to smile, so I did—
"I know it's hard to make *hard* decisions."

Will leaned forward to the right, and the backdrop of his
childhood treehouse came into view. I wondered for a moment if
maybe the year it took him to make a decision was because he
wrestled with the loss of his dad years later, wondered what his dad
would have wanted him to do and how he could make him proud,
tried to figure out what was best for *him* in the process. He'd found
out, and he didn't regret his decision to study business in Canada.
He'd told me that much himself. That gave me hope . . . that within
the short time frame I had, my searching for the right decision
would come to a conclusion; an answer I would be at peace with,
without regret.

"I don't know if this helps to hear," he said, his voice as calm as
stilled waters, "but sometimes peace doesn't come until after you
make your decision—a way of showing you that you made the right
one. It's a reminder on the days you wonder if you made the wrong
one. That's how it was for me, anyway." He shrugged his shoulders,
turning to look off in the distance.

"Thank you, Will." I meant that—more than I could express and
more than he knew.

I felt a pang of sadness hit me because things
were *already* changing. He would be leaving for Canada and
university at the end of the summer, and I could be leaving for Paris.
Our friendship—it felt like it could be coming to an end. But I
didn't want it to end. Whatever decision I made, there would be a
goodbye waiting for him and me in just a few weeks from now. The
absence of him in my life cut deep just imagining it. Would our
time together result in a farewell and memories that would fade and
distance themselves from our minds over decades of time?

I didn't want that—and the way Will looked ahead, lost in
thought with a vacant expression in his eyes, I guessed he was

thinking similar thoughts to me.

Goodbyes were coming; and neither of us were ready for them.

# CHAPTER 58

AUGUST 30, 1951
(Present Day)

I grabbed my paintbrushes and filled my palette with paint because I knew I needed to do this—to sit, to think, to process. When desperation clawed at my soul, I needed to do what brought a sense of clarity to my searching heart: take the thoughts stuck in my head and paint them on paper.

I called Mom again today. The struggle, the invisible tug-of-war that pulled and yanked—the *yes* or *no* decision—threatened to tear me apart completely. I needed to hear Mom's voice, sit with her over the phone, be as close to her as miles of distance allowed us to be.

*"Josie Girl,"* Mom had said in a voice that always comforted me since the womb, *"deep down, even though you're confused, I think you know what you're supposed to do. You just need to stay quiet long enough and listen to your heart. Be still."*

*Be still.*

I'd tried to be, but my mind was running marathon laps in my head that I couldn't keep up with.

*"How?"* I'd asked, desperate for straight answers.

*"Don't try and figure out what answer to give Catherine tomorrow. Just sit and breathe and . . . listen. You can't figure things out when it's loud. But when it's quiet enough, you'll be able to hear what your head and heart are telling you—one's telling you* yes, *and the other is saying* no. *You'll know which voice it is and which one to listen to."*

My thoughts were like blaring sirens, loud and deafening in my head. Could I turn down the volume, get them to be quiet long enough for me to sit and breathe and listen? That's what I was attempting to do by painting something abstract that didn't require detailed precision. It could just be . . . for what it was and what it became.

Two hours and a painting later, I was no closer to deciding than I had been.

My eyes shot open at two a.m., blinked in the shadows and darkness of my bedroom. I felt something as clearly as one would feel arms wrapped around them in a tight embrace—something I couldn't ignore and a presence I couldn't miss: *peace.*

The puzzle pieces finally fit together. I realized that this whole time, I was making this decision—this *yes* or *no*—about *me,* and peace had been slipping through my fingers like sand because it *wasn't* about me. This dream opportunity in Paris was given *to* me, but it wasn't intended *for* me. And God wasn't letting me say *yes* or no because that decision He intended for someone else to make, and He woke me up in the middle of the night when it was still and quiet enough for me to hear Him.

He gave me this chance so that I could . . . give it away.

Because it was meant for someone else.

# CHAPTER 59

*Alice.*

That was the name God dropped on my heart like a bombshell last night and the person I'd asked Catherine to give the scholarship to instead. The honey-blonde girl—she was the one who changed lives at the fair and painted and told stories that kids listened to and adults lingered to hear. She was the one with talent and ambitions, and she needed a place to plant her dreams and let them grow, flourish. She was the one who needed a way out when she turned eighteen, a chance to stand on her own two feet and not be held back by someone because of fear.

Catherine had looked surprised, but something else, too, that I couldn't put my finger on. She'd listened to everything I had to say, all the reasons why Alice qualified for this scholarship and all the ways she had helped make the booth at the fair a success, without saying a word. And when I'd finally closed my mouth after rambling until my throat hurt and I'd run out of words, I recognized the other emotion on Catherine's face: she was touched.

I'd held my breath, dared to hope that she understood how much I wanted my *no* to become Alice's *yes*.

"Alright, Miss Carter." That *alright* . . . it had changed everything in that moment. When Catherine gave me permission to give away what she had given to me, I didn't feel a sense of loss. I had gained something—a peace that went beyond human comprehension, was greater than any ache or disappointment.

Catherine wanted me to ask Alice and let her know what Alice decided. I said I would.

"I've never met anyone like you, Miss Carter. And I'm proud to know you," she'd said to me just before we shared one last lunch together and shook hands before saying goodbye—sealing our time together in the grasp of each other's hands.

And now, two hours after leaving the diner, it was a countdown— four hours and fifty-seven minutes—until I would call B.B. and ask him to pick me up, to drive me to Alice's, where I would make things right with her uncle.

The seconds it took for the door to open after I knocked felt like minutes stretched into unending, agonizing hours of time. My ears picked up the sound of the lock turning on the other side of the door just before it creaked open on old, rusty hinges. Alice's uncle stood there and stared at me through bloodshot eyes like I was a ghost on his doorstep.

"May I speak with you?"

He didn't invite me in, but he didn't tell me to leave. He just stood there and looked at me, his face unreadable. Whatever words I wanted to tell him, whatever this confession and apology and Paris offer for Alice looked like, I needed to do it here—a doorway keeping him inside and me outside.

"I wanted to apologize to you, Mr. Johnson. It was wrong of me to go behind your back and teach Alice." I paused, breathed in the night air. "I'm not sorry for helping her, but I am sorry for the way I went about it. I just . . . Alice is my friend, and I didn't know what else to do."

Nothing on his face changed after my apology, my confession of wrongdoing. He just looked at me . . . and maybe it was his silence that gave me the courage I needed to keep going.

"I've lived my whole life with a lot of disappointments, Mr. Johnson. One of the hardest was losing something I wanted more than anything—my ability to walk. And every day I live, it's a reminder that I'll never get that back. It's hard . . . harder than most people imagine it would be after living most of my life with handicaps."

I didn't know why I was sharing pieces of my story, the most fragile pieces, with a man who was just as much a stranger to me as I was to him. But something told me that he had been just as broken . . . and maybe was still just as broken.

It's easy to recognize pain in someone else when pain is so familiar to you.

"People die every single day, Mr. Johnson," I said. "From disease or old age or . . . car accidents. But we can't let our fear of losing keep us from living. That's what I've had to do. I've tried my best to live my life and chase after my dreams and grow my talents in spite of all I've lost and all I'm still afraid to lose. If we let fear win, then we've wasted the life we have and the time we've been given to live."

I shook my head and my hair teeter-tottered left, right. "That's not what God or anyone we've loved and lost would want us to do. That's not honoring their memory or living out their legacy . . . it's burying it. It's forgetting them. Alice can't live *for* her parents and do something great with her life if you're scared to even let her try."

That's what you do for someone you lost: you live your life *for* them and make the most of the time you've been given that they weren't. You leave behind a legacy where loss would have you make nothing of yourself. You mourn and grieve and then pick yourself back up and live every moment intentionally, never forgetting that yes, time is an hourglass, and the sand in it will run out sooner or later than you expected, but you *still* live the moments you have left. *Still* choose to live for the lost.

He shifted, his left leg bearing the brunt of his weight, and sighed. "Alice told me it was her idea for you to teach her and that she asked you to. Not the other way around." The words that traveled up through his throat and came out in a gravelly voice startled me because out of all the things I thought he might say to me—harsh words, cutting reprimands, demanding I get off his property and out of Alice's life—he told me his niece took responsibility for everything when she could have blamed me for all of it.

And that meant Alice had stood up to her uncle—stood up and fought for what was right, took responsibility for the choices she had made, said her peace and probably angry words and maybe even hurtful ones. I couldn't imagine what ugly arguments and cutting words these walls had contained and kept secret from neighbors overhearing and passing strangers from eavesdropping on.

"I—" I didn't know what to say.

"Why did you want to help Alice?" His eyes, even though exploding with a million little red veins, were sober and searching for truth.

"Because I care about her. Alice has a dream that's worth chasing after, and I want to help her reach it. I love her . . . just as you do."

This man's brokenness went deeper than the deepest tree roots. He swept a dirty hand across his face, closed his eyes. He could blame it on the dry air or the fact that he had scarcely blinked since I showed up at his doorstep, but I knew something had cracked in him, and the confusion and heartbreak he'd stuffed down now threatened to come out. The man who drank off his troubles to numb his emotions now struggled to hide them, to blink back tears under his closed lids.

"I don't know how to love her." His voice cracked. I had never expected to feel anything but unending frustration towards this man. But now, I fought back tears of my own. "But if you know how to help her . . . then do so. Alice deserves a better life than anything I can give her."

My eyes rapid-blinked away tears. He *wanted* me to help her? He *wanted* her to have this chance to live out her dreams and pursue art? Somehow after everything that had happened, I had earned his fragile trust, and I didn't know what to say with that gift.

I set my hand on his arm and softly nodded. I left him with the Paris offer for Alice and a slip of paper with Catherine's number on it. He left me with his word that he would tell Alice tonight and the decision would be hers to make, and with a goodbye.

# CHAPTER 60

**SEPTEMBER 03, 1951**
**(Present Day)**

The honey-blonde girl had slipped into the art gallery five minutes ago, stood in the back of the room while the rest of the class finished up their paintings for the day. I could hardly focus and kept selfishly glancing at the clock, waiting for the remaining minutes of class to pass because Alice—she was *here*. And she looked as happy and nervous to see me as I was to see her.

A few minutes later, it was just me and Alice in that gallery hushed with silence.

"Hi, Alice," I said. "It's so good to see you."

A lot had happened since we were last together . . . a lot had changed. I couldn't help but wonder what she thought of me right now—if she thought less of me because of everything that had happened. Because if I hadn't been here in New York, she wouldn't have been at the art gallery or at the fair, and I wouldn't have been at the house she babysat at, teaching her painting. There wouldn't have been secrets between her and me and her and her uncle.

There wouldn't have been a lot of things.

"It's good to see you, too." She sounded like she meant it. "I have to go soon to my babysitting job, but . . . could we talk for a minute?"

I nodded my head before the words *"Yes, of course,"* came out my mouth.

Alice pulled up a chair, sat across from me. "My uncle told me a few days ago about the art school and Paris and . . . I called Catherine Davies this morning. I'm accepting the scholarship, and I'll be leaving for Paris in a few months."

*Yes.* My heart felt like it could burst in my chest because the honey-blonde girl—she was *going.* This was right. This was meant to be. And it *would* be, soon. The closing of one chapter in my life was the beginning of a lifetime of stories for her.

I smiled so wide that my cheeks hurt, but I couldn't *not* smile right now.

"I was there—the night you came to see my uncle. I was in the kitchen and" —she paused— "I couldn't help but listen. I—I heard everything you told him, and he told you."

She reached out and grabbed my hand, and her touch startled me. Alice had always depended on words, never on physical touch, the months I had known her.

"I don't know why you've done all you have for me, or why you asked Catherine to give me a scholarship, or why you said everything you did to help my uncle. I don't know why, and I think if you told me I would never be able to understand . . . but all I can say is thank you." The skin around her eyes turned blotchy-red as she tried not to cry. "Thank you for changing my life."

Before I could say anything, she reached over and wrapped her arms around me, hugged me . . . for the first and last time. And that hug was everything we couldn't whisper into words without losing our resolve, breaking down, and crying hard in each other's embrace.

Our friendship.
Our memories.
Our goodbye.

"Jo?"

Will's voice was close behind where I stood, locking the front door to the art gallery. I jumped and nearly dropped the key from my hand. I didn't have to look at him to see that he was grinning, belly threatened with impending laughter, because it had been his intention to startle me, and he had succeeded.

I kept my back to him, didn't give him the satisfaction of seeing me fight back a smile of my own. "You have a bad habit of sneaking up behind me."

"What would be the fun in coming right up to you? I've got a record on you, you know—hiding, twice; startled, three times."

"This time doesn't count."

"And why not?"

"Because the only reason you startled me is that I didn't know you were out here."

"This time *does* count," he corrected, "because I told you I'd wait outside for you after class ended."

"Oh." That defeated *oh* of mine as I turned around to face Will had his grin growing wider by the second. "But your record's still off, you know—the only thing you have on me was being startled when you sneaked up behind me. I was never hiding."

"Right. Because sitting in secluded corners by yourself isn't hiding."

Oh, he was stubborn—and somewhat right. And we both knew it.

"Is that" —he gestured to the frown on my face— "your way of admitting defeat?"

"Maybe."

"Fair enough," he said, and this time, laughed, too. "I definitely prefer seeing you smile, though, so I'll do my best to try and not be right too often."

"You're impossible." The way he looked at me when I said that got me to laugh, too.

"I'm sorry to have kept you waiting, though," I said as we broke through the gravel pathway onto the sidewalk street. "I was . . . a bit distracted. You could have just gone home."

He ignored my last sentence and focused on the second one. "I noticed. I saw Alice come inside a few minutes before class ended. I was" —he searched for the right word— "surprised to see her here. Is everything okay?"

"Everything's great." I felt like I could breathe because of those words, like I could finally exhale because things *were* okay. Better than I hoped and prayed they would be. "Her uncle knew she was coming to see me. She . . . came to say goodbye."

"Goodbye?"

"She's leaving in a few months, and I'm leaving in a few weeks, so we probably won't see each other again while I'm here."

"Where's she going?"

I hesitated, knowing as soon as I told Will where Alice was going, he would put two-and-two together. "To Paris."

"Jo, wait a minute." He gently put his hand on my arm, pulled me to a stop. "You gave Alice your scholarship?"

"Yes."

"Why?"

"Because it was the right thing to do," I said. "And the only thing that gave me peace."

He looked . . . proud of me, looking at me with those soft but still intense eyes. For what I did and why I did it. And that was worth more to me than a scholarship ever could be. His hand reached out and touched my arm, squeezed it in a soft touch.

His touch made me lose my breath, and my heart *thump, thumped*, hard against my chest.

"Come on," I said, hoping that with each telephone ring that Sophie would pick up the phone, answer it, and we could talk. I wanted to tell her about the decision I made about the scholarship. I wanted her to know she was *part* of that decision, and I wanted her to share in the good that had come out of it. But either the line was busy, or Sophie wasn't around because neither she nor Aunt Carol answered.

I made a note to call again tomorrow afternoon.

# CHAPTER 61

**SEPTEMBER 04, 1951**
**(Present Day)**

"Mom?"

Ten seconds ago, the doorbell rang, and I answered it, not knowing who to expect on the other side. Maybe Will or his mom? But *my* mom was there—unexpected, unannounced . . . standing right in front of me.

"Mom?" I said again, heart pounding hard and painfully in my chest.

"Jo . . ." Mom's eyes met mine, and they were red and glassy, drowning in tears and pain.

Something was wrong—horribly wrong. This couldn't be Mom, showing up on a doorstep crying, her voice sounding so empty and wracked with grief. Mom was strong, always strong.

"Mom, what's wrong? What happened?" I almost didn't want to ask. Whatever news brought her here all the way from home was going to devastate me—break me inside.

Mom reached for me, pulled me into an embrace that almost knocked my crutches out from under me. Her hand on the bare skin on my arm made me startle, made a million little goosebumps of cold and prickling fear appear.

"Jo . . ." Mom's voice broke. The tears she held back in her eyes fell, dripping on my shoulder.

My breath felt foreign in anticipation—dread. Like all the air wanted to stay locked away in my lungs and never come out, and I just held my breath until I couldn't any longer.

"Sophie's dead."

Two words.

I screamed.

For more years of my life than not, I've known what it's like to be numb. To forget what it's like to have feeling in my legs, before the amputation, and now with my prosthetics. To not feel even the tiniest thing—prickling sensations, hot or cold, pain . . . anything.

I felt that again, but this time it wasn't just my legs. My whole body was numb, trapped in the deepest state of shock I'd ever known. If shock was a coma, I would never wake up from it. I'd forever be stuck in the lonely and horrible dark.

There were other people in the house, other voices in addition to Mom's. I'd heard those voices before. I recognized the sound of them like I did my own, but I couldn't remember whose they were. My eyes were open, but I wasn't seeing. I was listening, but I couldn't hear. I was beside someone, but I couldn't remember who they were. I didn't even know how much time had passed. Minutes? Hours?

All I knew was that Sophie was gone—dead. She was never coming back. *Never.* How could forever change in an instant, with two words, and become never? Sophie promised—promised she would be with me always, forever. But for reasons I didn't understand, ones she couldn't control, the promise was shattered. Now I was alone, forever.

Mom's words were just soundwaves bouncing off my ears, not making sense to me. Not penetrating the Jericho-thick wall of shock that wrapped around my mind. Not making anything okay. Words explaining to me and whoever else was in the room about the phone call she got last night. The one from Aunt Carol, who could barely talk on the phone because she was sobbing so hard. Mom had to piece together her words because they were choppy like ocean waves, hard to hear like static over the radio. She told Mom the real reason she and Sophie went to London this summer. It wasn't to vacation, to spend time together and see the sights like Sophie had told me. No. It was to find a doctor at *The Royal Marsden Hospital*—a cancer treatment hospital— that could help Sophie and find something, *anything*, to stop what had been slowly killing her since last November: cancer.

How could Sophie have kept that from me, lied to me, and made me think everything was okay? *Why, why, why?* A million questions and no answers to them.

Mom didn't even know about Sophie's cancer until yesterday, when it was too late. Why had Sophie sworn her cancer to secrecy and not told anyone about it except for her mom? Why?

Mom cried so heartbreakingly hard when she said that Sophie's funeral would be this weekend and that Dad was taking time off work and would be here tomorrow, and Aunt Carol would be here the following day. She had to make funeral arrangements . . . and ship Sophie's body back home. Sophie left with a suitcase in hand, and now she was coming home in a coffin.

I couldn't cry. All I could think about now was Sophie. How she had always been scared of the dark, of cramped places, of being alone. I wanted to rip the lid off Sophie's coffin that would be coming home on a New York-bound flight so that she wouldn't be stuck in the dark, trapped in a box. And I wanted Sophie to wake up, to open her eyes and grab on to me, and thank me for turning on the light, for waking her up, and not leaving her there in the dark, alone.

Someone whispered soft words to Mom—words I couldn't hear because I was too lost in shock, in grief, in pain that tore my heart out and almost made me wish it would stop beating all together because it hurt too much to stay alive.

Sophie had needed a miracle all those months, but God withheld it from her. And He had let death, with its ebony eyes and devouring touch, take Sophie far, far away from me. Sophie, the girl with so much life in her—a whole universe of it—and a life ahead of her wouldn't get a chance to live out the years that she should have, would have, if not for cancer.

I must have made some kind of sound, some indication that beneath the shock and grief, I was still alive—a shaky breath, a whimper, another guttural scream?—because the person sitting beside me that I'd forgotten was there stirred.

A hand reached for mine. Fingers broke through my stone-tight fist, wrapped themselves around mine, and held them.

I knew that hand, those bony fingers that were curled and bent in unnatural ways. A touch that was so safe and comforting to me. I'd felt it once before, on a day where a friendship was rebuilt beside a lake, and a boy and girl had an honest conversation, shared pieces of their brokenness for the first time. Even in the thick of grief and numbness, I hadn't forgotten that moment, that touch.

Will—his hand. He kept it there—in mine—for the longest time. Longer than the explanations, the questions without answers, the initial reeling and devastation went on for. Longer than all of those things.

I couldn't squeeze his hand, thank him for holding onto me when I needed it more than ever before. I was too numb to respond to the brain signals telling my fingers to bend and squeeze his fingers. But he didn't need anything from me to make him stay. Because hours later, after time that felt impossibly long had passed, and I opened my mouth, and all that came out was the sound of grief and loss, of loving and losing, of needing and never again getting, his hand was still there. Wet with my tears, but still there.

It didn't leave until the sun had set and night had fallen, and Mom knelt in front of me where I sat on the sofa and told me I needed to try and get some sleep. Only then, until he had held on until the very last moment that he could, did his hand leave mine.

# CHAPTER 62

**SEPTEMBER 08, 1951**
**(Present Day)**

Dirt.

That's what was being shoveled over Sophie's coffin, lowered several feet into the exposed roots and untreaded earth. That's how her life in this world, the shell that remained of her, was ending: in a box, under the ground. Out of reach, soon to be out of sight.

Those men who worked quietly and tirelessly with shovels—they could cover up a coffin with dirt, but they couldn't cover up a life. Sophie's life wasn't in there beneath the ground, but out here all around me. They could pile up a mound of dirt that went sky-high, but it would never hide Sophie. She was visible to me in that coffin that was see-through only to my eyes.

The wailing, the deepest kind of gut grief that came out in horrible sobs, came from Aunt Carol, standing three feet away from me. I wanted to clap my hands over my ears how thunder claps its invisible hands in the sky, but I couldn't unhear: shovels scraping the dirt, cries coming from a broken heart, words falling short of healing any of the pain spoken by a pastor conducting the outdoor funeral service.

Fifteen people attended the service, and half of them I didn't know. Dad, Mom, Aunt Carol, Will, and his mom, I knew them. But the woman with the black dress that fell just below her knees, aged and old, I didn't know. The young girl wearing the locket necklace, holding tight to the hand of a man that I could only guess was her father, I didn't know.

But I knew this: There should have been sixteen people standing here on this cemetery plot, not fifteen. Sophie's dad—he should have been here, standing beside Aunt Carol and my parents and me, mourning with us. But when Dad arrived the other day and called Sophie's dad—Uncle Jack to me—he answered the phone but not the call to come, to be here, to attend his daughter's funeral. Instead, he had made excuses, something about spending the weekend at a cabin with his wife and not wanting to cancel that two-day getaway. Family didn't matter to him, and he ended the call by saying that he needed to get ready for his trip and to leave a bouquet of flowers at Sophie's graveside.

Was that what his selfishness, his hardened heart, had reduced him to? A dad who asked someone to leave flowers at a graveyard for him instead of putting them there himself? A dad who didn't care that cancer had taken the life of his only daughter, a daughter who loved him for every day she had him in her life and hurt for every day she didn't? A dad who let strangers take his place and fill a spot on that cemetery plot, shoe prints sinking into the soggy earth wet from drops of rain starting to fall from the grey sky, that he should have filled?

Last night, I had called the medical school Fred Casey was attending, the only boy in the world that Sophie had trusted and loved. I told him about Sophie's death and her funeral. He told me on the phone with a voice that sounded as heavy as the phone felt in my hand that he would give anything—*anything*—to be there, but he had finals exams on Sunday. If he missed them, he wouldn't be able to retake them, and he would have to accept a zero on his test. He didn't have to tell me that that grade would affect his schooling now and his career later. We talked for an hour on the phone, cried more tears than we spoke words.

*That* was the difference between Sophie's dad and her former beau: the one who didn't have to come would have given everything to be here, and the one who should have come didn't want to give up anything to show up.

My eyes were like cement, stuck to the rip in the earth now stitched back together where Sophie's coffin was lowered. As the pastor read the last lines of a prayer and his words died away, the skies let loose. Like they had waited, choked back sobs of their own to hear the whispered words of the ordained minister, and then released a dam of tears. Relentless rain, unending tears. With the conclusion of his words and the introduction to rain, umbrellas burst open, and the small crowd broke apart while walking back to their cars, to their homes, to their loved ones.

The black dress I had slipped over my head with numb fingers this morning that fell below my ankles symbolized mourning. And it hung heavy on my shoulders as the rain began to soak it, weigh it down on my already heavy-laden frame. But I didn't care about the rain.

Time was running out, slipping like the rainwater that dripped through the cracks separating my fingers apart. Mom was taking Aunt Carol back to the car, and Dad had put his hand on my arm, silently coaxing me to follow after Mom. My feet were glued to where they were, shoes sinking in wet dirt, refusing to move. I didn't want to move, didn't want to leave Sophie behind, even though she was gone. Because that felt like accepting that she was never coming back, and I wasn't ready to let go of her.

"Let's go, Jo," Dad said.

I shook my head, rooting myself to the spot I had been in since arriving at the cemetery. The two-letter word refused to make its way past my envelope-sealed lips—*no*.

I couldn't go back to Aunt Carol's house, step onto that porch where I hugged Sophie just before she left for London, and know that it was the last time I would ever hug her again. I couldn't do it.

Dad raked a hand through his greying hair, damp with rain, not knowing what to do with me.

I shook my head again—*I can't go, Dad.*

"I can't leave you here standing in the rain alone," he said, refusing to leave me here while I refused to go. Dad and I were both like that—stubborn and refusing to change our minds like the sun refused to set until it had no choice but to surrender to night.

But Mom needed him, called after him right then, desperate and pleading for him to help her bear the heavy burden of her older sister's broken and bleeding heart.

"Go," I said, breaking the silence. Mom knew what she needed— she needed Dad beside her, helping with his hands and his words— but I didn't know what I needed.

Dad looked torn in two.

"Go," someone said behind him, echoing to Dad what I had said seconds ago. "I'll stay with her, Mr. Carter."

The copper-haired boy with the red umbrella took Dad's place beside me. He held the umbrella over both our heads. Because that's what he did: he was always there when I needed him the most.

And sometimes . . . being there looks like holding an umbrella over someone's head when they would have stood in the pouring rain alone. Sometimes it means being a hand to hold when theirs would go cold and numb without yours. Sometimes it means just being there in the thick of silence and not filling that space with empty words, but with their presence, their being *there*.

The sound of Aunt Carol's wailing was cut off as the car door shut, and Dad turned the steering wheel towards her home and drove away. Shallow breaths and heavy rain—those were the only two sounds I heard now.

"Why didn't I call her more? Why didn't I make sure she was okay?" I didn't know where those words came from. Somewhere deep inside of me that I didn't even know was struggling with those two questions, wrestling with guilt and regret.

Will looked at me, standing so close beside me to keep me under his umbrella that I could feel his warm breath on my face, but he didn't say a word. His silence was an invitation for me to unload my grief-filled questions and a promise that he would listen.

"Why didn't I tell her how much I love her and how much she means to me? Why didn't I tell her how she's changed my life and helped me get through things I never could have gone through without her? Why didn't I tell her how proud I am of her? She could do anything she set her mind to. Why did I take for granted that she was always there for me?"

My eyes begged Will—*please*—to say something, to help me sort through this pile of guilt on my shoulders, to help me understand what went beyond my own comprehension.

"She knew, Jo," he said with a quiet conviction. "You don't have to tell a person you love them every single day for them to know that you do. Love is fragile, but it doesn't break that easily. And if it does, then it's not love. She knew you loved her . . . she knew."

I wrestled with doubt and belief, and I was desperate for certainty. "How do you know for sure?"

A sadness rolled over his eyes, like storm clouds rolling over a blue sky. An aching, a losing, a breaking. "Because I never told my dad those things, either. Maybe I did in a birthday card or on a special day, but every day between? I didn't even think about it until he died . . . from cancer. I wondered for the longest time if he ever knew that I loved him and I needed him more than anything."

He knew.

He was, and had been for longer than I, carrying the weight of losing someone you love to cancer.

He knew, and he understood.

"It took time for me to believe that, but in the end, I did believe it for myself. My dad knew I loved him and needed him."

"How?" In the depth of all my sorrow, I couldn't fathom how Will had stood in the same shoes I did—ones that were laced with loss, soled with grief—and still known for certain what felt like the greatest uncertainty.

His eyes misted over with tears, but he blinked them away. "Because he was my dad . . . and I was his son."

That, out of all things and all reasons, was reason enough for him. A father and a son, and another Father and Son—a bond of unbreakable, undeniable love. One made by flesh and bone, but one strengthened through heart and soul.

*Because she was my cousin . . . and I was hers—and that was reason enough.*

I wanted to believe it for myself as Will had, to rest in the peace that comes with certainty, but in that moment, I couldn't. And all I could do was trust Will's words—that Sophie knew—truly knew— that I loved her and needed her.

Will set his arm around my shoulder, pulled me close. Something in me hesitated, wanted to pull back and unwrap myself from his secure embrace. The hurt inside me almost made it hurt to be touched on the outside. But I couldn't bear the weight of this on my own. Didn't even Jesus need help bearing the weight of His cross? This was too heavy, too laden with sorrow and grief.

I let the copper-haired boy hold me close against him, and I rested my head against his chest. I needed him to help me carry what I couldn't.

I leaned into him, closed my eyes when I felt his chin rest on the top of my head. I heard his heartbeat, steady, strong, a sign of the strength inside him that let him still breathe, still exist, even after such loss. His embrace didn't undo anything that had been done. Didn't untangle any of the wreckage in my heart that left me shipwrecked, but he held me. Held me and all of my heaviness. Didn't let go.

I was held close and not left alone.

# CHAPTER 63

**SEPTEMBER 09, 1951**
**(Present Day)**

Dad left last night, headed home for work the next day.

Not even death gives you a chance to grieve when the world demands you show up because otherwise, you'll be left behind without a job. Dad's absence hurt, and it was just me and Mom and Aunt Carol in that lonely house that needed Sophie in it.

I hadn't slept again. All night long, I'd listened to the pounding of heavy rain on the roof, watched the flashes of lightning light up the sky and peals of thunder make the windowpanes creak and groan. I cried as hard and long as the sky did that night—from dusk till dawn—and I could barely peel my swollen eyelids open enough to see through them.

Shafts of light were slowly creeping into the bedroom, illuminating the dark and lifting the shadows. But with the breaking of a new day, I was lost in the dark, freefalling into an abyss of grief. Every time I thought I reached the bottom, the bottom would fall out, and I'd fall harder, longer, deeper than before.

A new day meant another day without Sophie in it. Another day I lived and breathed while she lay still, unmoving, in that *Adams*

*Rural Cemetery* coffin. I felt hollow, laying there in a soft bed while Sophie lay in a splintered box buried under the earth.

I needed to get out of bed, out of this room, away from the haunting reminders of Sophie's death. Sitting in my wheelchair, I wheeled myself out of the room, down the hall past Aunt Carol's room and the guest bedroom Mom slept in. But as the hallway came closer to its end, I stopped.

At the end of the hall, just shy of the corner leading to the kitchen and the living room, was Sophie's bedroom. It had been her bedroom since she was three years old. It held nineteen years of memories and struggles and growing up and tears and love within its walls.

*God* . . . I knew He was the only person who could hear my wordless words, understand the depth of my sorrow. I'd passed Sophie's room a hundred times while she was gone in London, and I was here for months. But this time . . .

*God, I can't do this.*

I couldn't wheel myself past a room that would forever be empty. The room where the last memories Sophie and I had together, they were made in there—three feet and one door away. Why did I take that night for granted? The night before Sophie left for London, and we did a sleepover in her bedroom. Talked late into the night about anything and everything and reached for the stars together. I wished more than anything I'd have known that was our last night together. I would have stayed up all night and found a way to make time stop ticking onward and make that night last forever.

Something drew me close to Sophie's door, so close that my wheelchair butted up against its frame, reeled me in like a fish caught on one of Grandpa Joe's hooks. Shaking, I lifted my hand and touched the doorknob. I knew exactly what I would see if I opened it: Sophie's bed against the corner wall, an antique desk beside it, and a corkboard hanging on the wall above the desk.

A cold, hard shiver raced down my spine. I wasn't ready to see— to remember and hurt and break. Looking at all of Sophie's belongings, some she'd kept since she was a little girl and others that were new, holding them in my hands . . . it felt cruel. Cruel to only be able to hold an object, a possession, but not her.

A war waged between my heart and my fingers wrapped around that cold metal knob. In the thick of that battle, I heard something . . . a whisper. A whisper so quiet that I didn't miss it, because I was leaning in, straining hard to hear its voice: *come.*

Tears pricked my eyes again, but I didn't let them spill over as I answered that gentle whisper—*come.*

I opened the door.

With the turning and creaking of a doorknob came the undoing and the breaking of my heart. I heard it break there in my chest, just as I heard the rusty hinge creak as it surrendered to the weight of my hand on it, pushing it open wide.

When things break, even unhearable things, there's always a sound. Breaking is just as much a sound as it is a feeling. And the way my heart broke hard and irreparably as the door stood open and golden sunlight filtered through the windows, shone on the walls and floors, made the imagining of what Sophie's room would look like beyond its closed door now a reality staring at me as hard as I stared at it . . . my heart broke. I felt it shatter like a hundred glass shards covering the floor in sharp diamond-colored edges. I heard them fall, one by one, to the ground. Gently, I pushed my wheelchair beyond the doorframe.

The air was strangled tight with memories and grief. But yet . . . I knew God was in this place. It had happened more times than it didn't—me wondering where God was and how He could possibly be close to me when He felt so far away. After I lost my legs, I couldn't fathom how it was possible for God to be with me when my grief went beyond belief. But this time, I knew . . . He was here.

He saw the heartbreak. He listened to me—and He heard what shattered on the inside. He saw the invisible breaking of my heart that wouldn't show up on hospital scan machines like Sophie's cancer did. Broken hearts went deeper than the human eye or manmade inventions could go. But God saw and heard all. Every invisible breaking and unhearable sound, He was in it. He was there.

There were fifteen black-and-white photographs pinned to the corkboard—pictures of Sophie and me over the years. I pulled the pins out, set them on Sophie's desk, looked at those photos in my hands through a blurry, teary-eyed lens. My fingers trembled as I traced Sophie's face, her eyes, and her smile. Even in a photo that was void of color, Sophie was the radiant hue in it.

I wanted to take these photos home with me, hang them on the corkboard in my room, have the memories they captured on the wall above my head, where I could see them every day. Where I could remember and never forget. But after I emptied the board of photos, there was something still on there: pieces of paper, folded in half, pinned on the bottom left corner of the board.

A letter. Sophie's handwriting. A name written on the top line of the paper, visible when I unfolded the creased pages. *My* name. Hundreds of words penned for me that I never would have found if I hadn't been here, hadn't come into Sophie's room.

I lifted the pages, held them up to the morning light. And I read.

# CHAPTER 64

**JUNE 27, 1951**
**(Almost 11 Weeks Ago)**

*Dear Jo – I'm writing this letter to you the night before I leave, and I'm writing the date down because I know that dates, good ones or bad ones, matter to you. So here it is—June 27th, 1951.*

*You fell asleep so fast after we whispered goodnight to each other right here in this room a little after one in the morning. You're sound asleep right now as I'm writing by lamplight, sitting at my desk. You asked me before you drifted off to sleep if I was okay. I think you were too tired to notice how my breath hitched, and I hesitated for two-three seconds before I could answer. But the answer I left you with tonight is the honest truth: Yes, Jo, I'm okay.*

*If I know you (and after doing life together for so long, I can proudly say that I do), you haven't been in my room since Mom and I left. And now, you're back in here, reading this letter I pinned for you on the bulletin board, because I'm . . . gone. Mom would be upset with me if she read those words. She's hanging onto hope that this eight-week chemo treatment will help and that I'll start to recover. But I've made my peace with God . . . and He's given me peace, too. It sounds strange to be so certain of one's death, but I know I won't make it home by the end of the summer. Don't ask me how, but I just know. And you're probably wondering how it was possible for me to say that I was okay when I wrote this. (It's weird—using past tense like I'm gone already. But I know by the time you read this, I will be.)*

*I want to tell you why I'm okay, Jo. But first, I want to tell you how much I hate writing this letter. I hate to say goodbye; because goodbyes mean I'm gone, and you're still here. It means I have to leave you behind, and I'm not ready to. But I know if I don't get these words down on paper now, I won't ever get them down, and I can't leave you without leaving something behind—even if it's my scribbled words written at three a.m.*

*Jo, how do I even begin? How do I tell you about last fall when I got so sick and threw up more in a week than I had in my entire life put together, and Mom came home from work and found me on the floor, in a puddle of barf, crying because my stomach hurt worse than any pain I've ever felt? Really, really hurt. How do I tell you about the doctor and the test results that led to more scans and blood draws and tests? How do I take you to the room where I was given a medical diagnosis that made me feel so hollow, like everything in me had just died, when I was told that I had stage-four stomach cancer? How do I tell you what the doctor told Mom and me in that hospital room, after another round of chemotherapy, that my cancer had not gotten better, not even in the slightest, but it was worse—and I was slowly dying with no way to reverse that, no way to bring me back to life? How do I tell you that in a last desperate attempt, Mom decided to take me to London to get the best medical help we could find, even though we both knew the damage the cancer inside me had done to my body couldn't be fixed—not with chemo, not with medicine, not with shots or pills or with time or rest? How do I tell you how when I saw you at the train station, and I hugged you, I prayed that you wouldn't notice how sharp my bones were against my skin, and how fragile I'd become, and how the hair on my head wasn't mine anymore, but a wig to cover my bald scalp? Either God put a veil over your eyes like I begged Him to since Mom told me you accepted her invitation to stay here for the summer, or you knew something was wrong but decided it wasn't the right time to ask me about it. Jo—how do I tell you that I'm not on a summer vacation in London, relaxing and sightseeing, but I'm fighting for my life? How can I take you back even to tonight, where I begged God once again that you wouldn't notice how my baggy, oversized pajamas hung thin on me because of the ten pounds I'd lost, and how empty my closet was because I'm taking everything I want to have with me because I know I won't come home again? How can I take you back to five minutes ago, where I kept wanting to gently wake you up and tell you that this was the last night we would have together until we spend a lifetime of days and nights together in heaven?*

*I want to so badly that the only thing that's stopping me from waking you up is that—my desperation. If I told you right now about my cancer, you would have gone with me to London and stayed by my side through every last desperate attempt to heal my body. You would have given up your summer here without a second thought, because that's who you are, Jo. You're loyal and selfless and stubborn to the end.*

*I don't want you to miss this, Jo. Whatever this summer holds for you, I want you to live. Live for me. My life is coming to a close, but yours? It's just beginning, and I felt like God whispered to me to ask Mom to let you come here this summer without saying a word to you about me. There's a reason for it, Jo, I know it—and by the time you've read this letter, you know it, too. And if you don't yet, you will.*

*When you're close to dying, Jo, you think more about life than you ever did before. The life you lived, the life you'll never get to live. When I first got my cancer diagnosis, and I thought about my life, how I've only lived twenty-two chapters of my story when I should have had so many more, I wondered why God even gave me life because . . . it just didn't make sense that He would give it to me and take it back so soon. I've cursed at Him and questioned Him and doubted Him and wanted to walk away from Him.*

*Cancer and dying don't make sense. It's hard and devastating, and everything I can't put into words. But even though I'm scared to let go, part of me is tired of holding on. You know I'm stubborn, Jo, and I can be just as stubborn as you are, and I would never give up until my body gave up. But I'm tired . . . so tired. I think it's God's grace that He's taking me home soon. He knows I'm tired, and I need this fight with cancer to end; and if it can't end here, He'll heal me there.*

*When I was packing my bags a few days ago, I found a photo in the closet—a picture of Fred and me on the night we graduated high school. It's been three years since I've seen him, and I've missed him so much . . . and I found myself asking God why all over again. Why did He let Fred into my life for both of us to decide in the end that we were right for each other for a season, but not for a lifetime of them? It doesn't even make sense to say this—it sounds so backward, like it's going against the tide of logic—but again . . . I think that Fred and I breaking up was God's grace. Because God knew more than we did and He knew that I wouldn't be around for long. He didn't want Fred to lose me and know what it's like to be abandoned and left behind, even if the person doing the leaving doesn't have a choice in it.*

*Everything in life—it's a season. My dad and I, we were a season. Fred and I, we were a season. You and me, Jo? We're a season, too. And I think God gave me life because He knew I wouldn't want to miss any of the years I've had with you. I don't regret it—any of it. And if I could, I'd choose to live twenty-two years with you and have stage-four stomach cancer than have lived no life at all and not had you.*

*You, Josie Lou Carter, are the light in all this darkness. I know with you, even after I'm gone, I'll live on. You have the half of my heart I gave to you. Our halves still make a whole. And I know if I'm tucked safely in your heart, I'll always be with you, and you'll always have me, too. That helps me, Jo, more than you know. Everything you've said and done for me my whole life, it's been preparing me for this moment I never saw coming. You're helping me be okay with all this cancer and knowing time is running out.*

*How are you helping me? I know you're wondering that. You being here in the place I've called home for so long, painting and helping others and making new memories and growing in new ways, that's made me okay. That's helped me be brave enough to not wake you up tonight and ask you to come to London with me. If you can be brave enough to be here this summer on your own, living here for months without your parents for the first time, I can be brave, too. As much as I want you to come with me, I need you to stay here.*

*Please don't be angry at me for not telling you . . . or for having to leave you like this, Jo. I'm so very sorry—a million times over—that I don't have a choice. You know that summer where you took me to the attic, showed me your workspace, and shared your dreams with me? Dreams you had kept to yourself for a long while because they were a secret between you and God until the time was right to share it with others? That's how it is with me right now—God and me sharing this secret and bearing this heavy burden together until the time is right to tell someone else about it.*

*It's funny, everything I didn't know how to tell you in this letter, I guess I somehow did. Because I don't want to leave you behind wrestling with a hundred questions and no answers to them like my dad did to me. I want you to know everything: I love you. I'm proud of you. I'm not angry at you for not guessing something was wrong with me all these months. I'm okay—and you'll be okay again too, Jo.*

*I need to end this letter. My hands are tired, and I know my handwriting is getting harder to read as I go on. But I don't want it to end . . . because at the end of this letter means it'll be the last words from me you'll ever read. It means goodbye. Our whole lives, we've never said goodbye because goodbye is permanent. It's final, and it's an ending. We've always said 'see you soon.' So, I won't say goodbye to you now.*

*Keep me in your heart, please? I know with you, I'll never be lost.*

*I'll see you soon,*
*-Sophie (Soso)*

*P.S. Will you do something for me, Jo, after you go home? Paint—paint all the memories we've made together. For me. That's how you'll keep me alive even after I'm gone.*

# CHAPTER 65

**SEPTEMBER 10, 1951**
**(Present Day)**

Somehow that night passed, and the next day came. The sun bled red into the sky as dawn broke over the slumbering sky. Red. The color of loss, of death.

I didn't know how I'd managed to sleep last night, but I had fallen into a dreamless sleep, and my heart had stopped when I woke up, as it had every morning since the news of Sophie's death. She was gone. It wasn't a sickening nightmare; it was a sickening reality. And the more days that passed and the numbness of grief began to wear off a little, the more it hurt.

I held Sophie's letter, the last tangible thing I had of her, to my heart. Somehow it helped to hold it there, like a Band-Aid over a wound. It contained until what was hurting underneath was ready to heal on its own.

The smell of fresh coffee wafting under the doorway and china dishes clanking in the kitchen made me realize I wasn't the only one up at the cracking of dawn. Mom was awake, too.

I wheeled myself to the kitchen, found Mom sitting at the table, stirring cream into her coffee. Round and round the mug's brim she went, metal scraping against glass, countless times. I left my wheelchair as I slipped into the chair at the round table with its chipped white corners across from Mom. Dark circles hung under her eyes like the moon weighed down the night sky. She hadn't slept much, if any.

"I talked with Carol last night," Mom said, realizing I was there. "She just . . . needs some time right now, to grieve alone. I'm going to the train station later this morning to buy tickets for the day after tomorrow." She stopped stirring her coffee. "I wanted to give you enough time to wrap up your commitments here before we go home. Can you take care of that?"

Going home meant saying goodbye, leaving more people I had come to love and care for over the months behind. It meant another loss, another ache. But Sophie's *P.S.* at the bottom of her letter, where she asked me to paint the memories we made so that she wouldn't be forgotten, came rushing to my mind as fast as hurricane winds. I . . . needed to go home, even though it hurt to leave. I was just as certain of that as I had been about coming here; a silent confirmation that it was time. Time to go home. Time to paint in the attic.

"Yes." I thought of the copper-haired boy and his mom. How I'd have to tell the woman who had become like family to me that I'd have to cut my classes two weeks short, end them now, because life and God were taking me back to my roots, and I had to follow. How I'd have to tell the boy who had become my closest friend that I was packing my bags, leaving, saying goodbye.

I didn't know how I'd tell either of them, but somehow, the words came out in lengthy, run-on sentences, missing commas and periods and spaces between each word, and I told Will's mom everything. She came close to me and hugged me tight, and I closed my rambling mouth and stilled in her embrace.

Creaking floorboards and a lanky shadow spared me the second confession, the hardest of the two. Will, standing out of sight but close enough to listen, had heard every word. But he didn't move from where he stood, didn't pretend he hadn't heard and ask me to explain to him. He knew, he heard, and the words were too hard for him to hear to his face, too hard for me to repeat again.

But in the silence of his sadness, I heard his understanding, and that was enough.

# CHAPTER 66

**(Present Day)**

Maybe Sophie was right. Maybe life really was a series of seasons that came and went.

From the back seat of Aunt Carol's car, the one that crept over two miles of paved roads to reach the train station, I saw the trees out the window. How they were shedding their summer colors, and the tips of their leaves were turning the lightest shade of brown and red. With the ending of summer came the ending of this season of my life.

The street we were coming up on gave us a choice to either continue straight or turn right. My mouth opened, and I wanted to ask Mom while we were grounded at the stoplight blinking a red warning for us to stay put if she could turn, let me go to the cemetery one more time. But while my lips formed the words, I stopped myself.

There wasn't time.

Yesterday had been a whirlwind, like a tornado funnel of busyness doing laundry and folding and packing and getting out the door to get on a train. A whirlwind that didn't allow me to stop by the cemetery, to spend five more minutes saying goodbye to Sophie, to tell her that I was doing it—going home, going to paint, going to fulfill her last wish.

I whispered that final farewell as the light turned green, and we sped ahead. *See you soon, Sophie.*

Three minutes to the station and fifteen minutes until the train whistle blew; a faithful siren blaring on the dot, beckoning its passengers aboard. Will—he'd dropped by yesterday and rang the doorbell and asked my mom to tell me that they—he and his mom—would be there tomorrow. At the train station, to say goodbye. They wouldn't let me slip away quietly, and I didn't want them to.

"We're here," Mom said. And with that declaration, she and Aunt Carol stepped out of the car, unloaded the luggage, and hugged the other close. Mom's mouth moved, and I knew she was whispering words only for her older sister to hear, and then they parted.

Aunt Carol whispered goodbye to me as Mom helped me out. I reached for her hand and squeezed it. She was like a statue: cold and silent. She didn't return my squeeze, but she looked at me in the eyes, and her gaze said everything her despondent heart couldn't voice: her goodbye, her love, her thanks.

She took Mom's place behind the steering wheel and drove away. Mom and I stared after the car that was slowly blurring out from where we stood on the train platform, each praying silent prayers that she would be okay. Divorced and bereaved—those two things left more scars than anything.

Mom went ahead, put our bags in the train compartment above our assigned seats. The sound of taxicab and car doors opening and closing filled my ears, and I scanned each face until I found the two faces I was looking for. Will's mom reached me first and pulled me into a hug. With my arms under my crutches, it was the same as my hands being tied behind my back, and all I could do was stand in her embrace and let her hold me when I couldn't hold her, too.

"You'll always have a home here, Josie," she said, just before letting me go. Tears pricked my eyes like splinters pricked soft skin. She and Will . . . they were and always would be home to me. A safe place.

I had yet to meet Will's gaze. Saying goodbye to one's closest friend is never easy, never gets easier, was never meant to be easy. Because when you care for someone, there's always a price to that. A price that's worth paying, but it's costly.

Will moved towards me, and I paused, unmoving. I didn't want this to be the second time he hugged me, and I wasn't strong enough to hold on to him, too. He anchored me the first time in that cemetery, but we needed to anchor each other this second time on this train platform.

So I did what I hadn't dared to do in months and months and months: I let go of my crutches, of the one thing that was keeping me from crashing like china cups slipping off counter space and falling hard, surrendering to the laws of gravity, onto the floor. I leaned them against the wall behind my back.

Will's eyes widened, and he swallowed hard. He knew what I was doing and that I had never done this before, and why out of all the places and times in my life I'd lived, I chose now: for him. I teeter-tottered, felt weightless without my crutches and yet heavy at the same time. I stretched my arms out to balance myself like I was walking across a tightrope.

Will reached out and grabbed hold of my floundering arms and pulled me against him. He held me secure and just . . . held onto me for as long as he could. His breath was warm against my hair as he whispered four words that meant everything and hurt everything to hear: "I'll miss you, Jo."

I couldn't imagine each day without him being part of it. He'd always been there—holding an umbrella over my head, making me laugh, bringing out the best in me, and holding my hand when I cried. And after months of that, I wouldn't have that, have him, tomorrow. I'd be home, and he would be packing his bags for Canada and his fall semester at university.

Life and God and circumstances brought us together, and now those things were taking us apart.

"I'll miss you too, Will." The copper-haired boy was an ocean to me: wide and deep and endless. Sometimes unpredictable, but always trustworthy. I didn't want the tide to recede and separate the waves from the shore—me and him.

Mom came back seconds later, told me it was time to go. But before Will let me go completely, he slipped something into my open hand: an envelope with my name on it.

I looked up at him, trying to understand why he'd given me this.

He shrugged a little, smiled a little, too. He knew I'd wonder, and curiosity would be the feature that schooled my face. But then he got serious again; soft, but serious. "Please, Jo . . . don't read it until you're ready. Will you do that for me?"

I knew he hadn't said that to heighten my curiosity and make me want to rip through the envelope seal as soon as I got on the train. He said that because . . . he meant it. He wanted me to wait until I was ready. Ready to read his words after I had taken time—time to grieve and to process and to heal from losing Sophie. And for him, I would wait until I was ready, whether that was weeks or months.

No one can rush the healing process of a broken heart. It takes time, sometimes longer or shorter than one thinks, but rushing it only delays it. Just as a broken bone needs time to set and to heal— and trying to use it before it's ready only breaks it harder, makes things worse. I wouldn't push myself to heal faster so I could read his words, and he wasn't asking me to, either.

But whenever I was ready, his words would be there for the reading.

I gave him my word and my goodbye. "I promise, Will."

And I went home.

# CHAPTER 67

**DECEMBER 08, 1951**
**(Present Day)**

In the three months that had passed, I had learned three things. Thoughts that I needed time to think through. Memories I needed to resurface and remember and live again through colors on pages. Questions I needed to pray and cry over, wrestle and struggle with.

Three things that brought me to where I was: sitting in the attic with Will's unopened letter in my hands.

One: Life was hard. And at times, it was horribly unfair. Losing my legs, that was horribly unfair. Will losing his dad, that was horribly unfair. Aunt Carol losing a daughter and Mom and Dad losing a niece and me losing my best friend, that was horribly unfair. All of those things had left scars on our hearts that no amount of time could take away. Those things—the deepest wounds of all—are ones only God can heal in heaven. It's hard to trust God to heal when He allowed the hurt to happen. It's hard to have faith in a God who is in control of heaven and earth and is the one who can give and take away with a single word. It's hard to believe that God can heal what's broken when the repairing doesn't have a timetable, and it can take longer than I ever wanted it to. Life was hard—and I couldn't expect it to deal me a fair hand.

Two: Sophie—she had made more of an impact on my life than anyone else ever had. She was my cousin who lived every day intentionally. She was my best friend who was there for me through every high and low, even when she was dealing with her own highs and lows.

Sophie—she put others above herself, and she did so in a way that half the time, I forgot she was dealing with her own struggles because she made her pain invisible when we were together so that mine would be seen. Even when she was in London and fighting cancer and low on energy and life, she called me, talked with me on the phone, sat there and listened to my problems when the whole world was crashing down hard around her.

It seemed so cruel of God to take her from me in such a horrible way, but it was never cruel of Him to give Sophie life to live. Because she changed me, and God only knows how lost I would have been without her. I wanted to do that—live life like I was terminally ill, not taking today for granted or assuming there would be a tomorrow because then, I would be living my life intentionally. For me, living intentionally meant . . . painting.

Three: I missed Will. I missed the copper-haired boy so badly. Time was playing on the drawstrings of my heart, and the time I had with him and the time I had away from him birthed something in me that I didn't know was there, didn't think I'd ever find planting roots and growing deep in me: longing. Longing to see his smile and his hidden child-like side filled with wonder and faith. Longing to talk to him and take walks with him. Longing to hear whatever he wanted to tell me—something to make me laugh, something to sober me to find the good things in the bad ones, something to make me teary-eyed because I needed to hear those words—because I wanted to listen to him. Longing to be honest and open and share things with him that were hard and scary that I could trust with very few. Longing to have him in my life.

As weeks went by after being home, I began to see him differently. I'd picked up that painting I'd thrown down and never finished— the one of the ballroom at his aunt's home, where he hurt me with his words for the first time—and I sat down, finished it. He wasn't the first one to hurt me with angry words, but . . . something had changed between then and now. I saw him as less of a friend but as *more* than a friend. Will—he was the first one to ever be more than that to me, and it scared me. Not a day had gone by where I hadn't wondered if . . . maybe he saw me as more than a friend, too. With him, I felt seen and known and wanted and cared for. Aren't those things the ones that make love, love? Because love is more than an emotion; it goes so much deeper than that. The things we say and think and do for someone else, that's how we love. And if the sum of all my thoughts and actions and words for Will were added together, it equaled something that had taken having him and losing him to realize added up: longing.

It was those three things that brought me to this moment, finally ready to read the three-month-old words Will penned to me.

*Please, Jo . . . don't read it until you're ready. Will you do that for me?* His parting words were never far from my mind.

I lifted the envelope flap, and I held my breath, like I was being submerged into a pool of water, and pulled out a sheet of paper with typewriter-print words filling a white page. I knew this gift from him—it had cost him, typing hundreds of words with fingers riddled with pain. This letter was like holding part of his pain, holding a piece of him, and I held it with careful hands.

*Dear Jo:*

*I'm not good with letters—but here I am, attempting to write this for you. I'm just as bad with beginnings as I am with middles and endings, but again—here I am. I'm writing this on the morning you leave. I'll be honest: saying goodbye to you will be one of the hardest things I've had to do. I don't know how much time will have passed since you left and when you're reading this, but don't think I've forgotten about you. You're one of those people that comes into someone's life and makes such a difference . . . an unforgettable difference.*

*Do you remember the afternoon you came to see my mom and told her about your leaving? I know you knew I was there and that I'd heard what you said to her. I had been on the phone with one of my buddies, Gregg, from university, and I was just coming downstairs to tell my mom what he had told me. When I saw you there, I wanted to burst into the room and tell you both what I'm about to tell you now. But I saw you crying, Jo. And as much as I wanted to tell you then in person before you left, I knew I needed to wait. I couldn't spring good news onto your lap when you were stuck in so much bad . . . losing Sophie. So, I waited until now.*

*Gregg lives on the university campus like I do, and he told me that the college is adding an art museum onto the campus grounds. The school has already started construction, and it should be opening in the spring. Gregg said that they're hiring anyone who has experience with art to work there part-time year-round—and that a woman named Emma Perkins is handling the job applications. Jo, it's the same Emma that came to your art booth at the fair and asked about my dad's paintings. She found my mom and I later that same day at the booth and talked with us. Maybe it wasn't my place to do this, and you can be angry at me if it wasn't, but I asked Gregg if he could find out where Emma was staying so I could get in contact with her. He came through, and I called Emma. She remembered me, even though we only met once and talked for ten minutes. She remembered you, too, when I mentioned your name and your booth at the fair. I don't know what you said to her, Jo, but you made a huge impression on her —a really good one. I asked her if she would be willing to offer you a position at the museum. You should have heard her—I barely finished my sentence before she said, "Yes—absolutely yes." The job is yours, Jo, if you want it. Whether a week from now or a year, it's there for you.*

*I know moving to Canada and working at an art museum was probably something you never expected me to write you about. Believe me, until I talked with Gregg, I never expected it either. But all I know, Jo, is that life is a series of open doors; one closes, and another opens. And God gives us openings that we never saw coming, ones that seem so crazy or far-fetched or impossible that we doubt they're for us. But if He opens the door, it's for us to walk through.*

*I'm not assuming this is an open door for you, Jo. I want you to do what's best for you, what you feel like you're supposed to do. You know that. But I also want you to know that if you decide to go through this door, I'll walk through it with you if you'll let me. I'll be there to help however I can, and we could . . . do life together again. I'd give anything for that, Jo. But I would never ask you to give up your life at home with your parents if that's something you don't want. Sometimes God puts people in your life for them to stay and to be there through everything . . . and I can't help but wonder if that's why He brought you to New York and me to your art class and everything else. I've wondered about that a lot, Jo.*

*Either way, I'll be here for you, whatever that looks like. You have my word on that. And whenever you're ready . . . call me and tell me what you decided? I'll answer whenever you do.*

*And for every day until then, I miss you.*
*-Will*

*(P.S. My record still stands—hiding, twice; startled, three times.)*

# CHAPTER 68

DECEMBER 21, 1951
(Present Day)
*Telephone conversation*

*Will:* "Hello?"

*Me:* "Hi, Will. It's Jo."

*(Will sucked in a surprised but happy breath of laughter)*

*Will:* "Jo—hi! Wow, it's so good to hear from you."

*Me:* "Is now a good time to talk? I called the number you gave me for the university, but the receptionist said all the students were gone for Christmas break. I forgot you'd be home with your mom for the holidays."

*Will:* "Now is always a good time to talk with you. And yeah, I just got home a few days ago. Mom's out doing some last-minute grocery shopping for some apple pies she's planning on making. A few relatives are coming over tomorrow night for dinner, so Mom signed me up for *house cleaning duty. I've discovered I'm about as good at dusting and vacuuming as you are at painting walls."*

**Me:** *"So, you're pretty good then."*

**Will:** *"Something like that."*

*(His voice sobered with seriousness and care)*

**Will:** *"How have you been, Jo?"*

**Me:** *"I'm . . . okay. I'm getting there, at least."*

*(I paused, nodded my head as if to reassure myself that I would be okay again someday)*

**Me:** *"I read your letter a few weeks ago . . . and I've thought a lot about everything you said. You asked me to call you once I made a decision on the job offer."*

*(Will cleared his throat in anticipation and nervousness)*

**Me:** *"Yes."*

**Will:** *"Oh, Jo, I'm so happy. Are you sure you want to do this?"*

**Me:** *"I'm more than sure. I can hardly wait—I've missed you so much."*

**Will:** *"I've missed you, too. Spring can't come soon enough. Oh—and Jo?"*

*Me:* "Yes?"

*Will:* "You know I'm not one to beat around the bush—I say what I'm thinking, whether for good or bad. I know you've been on the receiving end of both sides of my bluntness. But I've needed to tell you something since you left . . . something I didn't write in the letter."

*Me:* "What is it?"

*Will:* "I think . . . I love you. If part of loving means hurting from missing someone so much, then I finally understand why part of me feels like it's been missing since you left. Because it has. You took part of my heart with you, Jo. And without you, I won't be complete again."

*Me:* "Will . . ."

*(My heart pounded hard against my chest, just as it had each time I was with him, close by him)*

*Me:* "I think I love you too."

# CHAPTER 69

**DECEMBER 23, 1952**
**(Present Day)**

*Dear Sophie – It's me, Jo. It's been a long time now since we last talked. I miss the sound of your voice. It's faded in my mind, like a distant echo, a blurry memory. I wish I could hear it again. But some things will never fade away with time—your smile, your life, your love. I hold those things close to my heart every day that I've missed you . . . which has been every day since you died.*

*So much has happened, Soso—and I want to tell you about it. Because even though you're not here on this earth anymore, you're still in my heart—where I promised to keep you, every day. And I want to include you in everything because I know you're sharing my joys and disappointments right alongside me in heaven.*

*I've been in Canada for the past nine months now, working at the art museum that opened on Will's school campus. It was a big adjustment at first—working a job, living in an apartment a few blocks away from the university, being so far away from Mom and Dad. In reality, I know it's not much different from what I did last summer—going to*

*New York, staying at your house by myself, and teaching art classes—
but it's different this time because I haven't just been gone for the
summer. And I don't think I'll ever be living at home again (except
for visits, of course). A lot of things changed two weeks ago. They
started changing a while back—but they've officially happened now.*

*My life since moving to Canada has been spent mainly with one
person each day: Will. While he's at his classes, I'm working at the art
museum, and we both finish up around the same time. Every day now,
for as long as I can remember, Will always does one of two things: he
either walks me home or takes me somewhere. Sometimes we go to the
library, and he studies for tests while I work on painting sketches, or
he takes me to see a movie. Other times, we just go on walks and talk
for hours. I think Will and I both realized after a certain point that
we love to do things together . . . we want to do life together, always.*

*A year ago, Will told me on the phone that he thought he loved me.
Six months ago, he told me while walking me home that he was pretty
sure he loved me. Two weeks ago, when we decided to visit his mom
over Christmas break, and the train pulled up to the Adams Train
Station, he told me he knew he loved me. Yesterday, he proposed—and
I was so happy, I cried before I could get out the answer I already
knew I would give him if he ever asked: yes.*

*I wish more than anything you were here, Sophie. I wanted to pick up
the phone and call you and tell you to start looking for a bridesmaid
dress—because there's no one else I want to stand by my side when
Will and I get married next summer. I miss you more than I could
ever put into words. Sitting in the cemetery plot you were buried in,
right next to your tombstone, penning these words—I feel your absence
as clearly as I did the day you were buried. And I wanted you to
know . . . I haven't forgotten you. I never will. The way you lived your*

*life showed me how to live mine—and that I could be brave and strong and fight for life.*

*I saw your mom a few days ago—it's the first time I've seen her since your funeral. We talked about you, laughed at the silliest memories of you we had and cried over the hardest ones. After you died, Aunt Carol shut herself away in her grief, and no one could reach her—not even my mom. But now . . . she's letting others into her grief, sharing it with them—and it's helping her heart to heal. Shutting out memories and forgetting them doesn't allow someone to heal from loss; sometimes, it's remembering them and talking about them that brings about healing.*

*I told your mom that I met with Emma Perkins—the one who offered me my job—and I asked Emma if she could arrange for me to send one of the paintings I've worked on to the hospital you went to in London for cancer treatments. I don't expect them to hang it in the hallways or in the waiting rooms, but I pray they do. I want others to see you and find hope—maybe not that things will turn out alright, but that no matter what happens, they'll be okay . . . just like you were. I've been thinking a lot about that lately—how things don't always turn out how I want them to, but that, in the end, I'll be alright. The Paris scholarship I was offered last year made me realize that I had the wrong perspective on a lot of things, especially painting. For the longest time, I thought I needed something—an opportunity, like the one Catherine offered me—for my life to have meaning and to truly make a difference. But I was wrong. God's not limited by the things I am, and He can work wonders into the smallest of things. If He could turn two fish and five loaves into a feast to feed thousands of people, He can do the same with my art. And He is—He's using me at the museum to make a difference in the lives of those I encounter each day at the university campus. He's using me to show others that, despite their limitations, they can still have dreams, and those dreams can still come true. Until coming to Canada, I hadn't pieced that together . . . but my time here has shown me that there's purpose in the here and now, not just in the 'what may come.' And whatever may come, I know I'll be okay . . . just as you were, my brave Soso.*

*It's starting to snow again, and Will's hounding me with an umbrella and telling me I need to get inside and warm up. He's always a little demanding when it comes to me taking care of myself, but I love him for it. And he's right—it's getting cold, and I should go for now. But before I do, I want to tell you one last thing.*

*You are loved—and I love you.*

*Love,*
*Jo*

*(P.S. One last thing—I did it: painted all the memories I can remember we've made together. Let's paint memories together in heaven when I get there someday. Wait for me, alright?)*

# AFTERWORD

The inspiration for *The Memories We Painted* started over three years ago when my younger sister received a diagnosis that only five other people have had in medical history. As I've walked through these past years with my sister, I've had my eyes opened to a world I was familiar with but not well-acquainted with: suffering.

I wanted to write a book that chronicled the same journey my sister has been on: a long one, a hard one, a life-altering one. My sister is the inspiration behind this book because her bravery to keep living life when each day is so challenging for her to get through has inspired me and challenged me never to give up.

This book is personal for me because so many of the life lessons the characters learn in the story are ones I've had to learn as well. The questions the characters grappled with are the same ones I have, too. So many pages of this book I've lived out in my own life, and while it's vulnerable for me to write this book, I want others to have a perspective I didn't have before watching my sister suffer and also walking through my own health struggles this past year.

My deepest desire is that this book will enable you to better know how to be there for suffering friends, how to persevere through trials, and how to hold on to God when everything in you wants to give up on Him. Those are three of the hardest but greatest lessons we can ever learn in this life.

# ACKNOWLEDGMENTS

For every person who has helped me on my writing journey and is reading these words right now: *thank you.*

For my family – Dad, thank you for helping me chase after my dreams and supporting me. Mom, thank you for letting me be your Catie Girl. Christian, thank you for the encouraging messages you've sent me about my writing. Grace, thank you for being the inspiration behind this story and the first to read the complete first draft. Lily, thank you for always shaking my hand after each chapter you read and 'grinning like a hyena,' as you put it, to show me how much you loved what you read.

For my grandparents, Aunt Jenny, and Granny – Gramma, thank you for reminding me on a hard day not to allow the things others do to me to harden my heart but to stay true to who I am. Grampa, thank you for calling me your Little Ninja and making me laugh with your unintentional puns and your great sense of humor. Aunt Jenny, when you told me years ago that I would write a book and become an author one day, you were right—and I couldn't be happier about that. Granny, thank you for keeping me motivated to work on my book because of your excitement to read it.

For my friends – Caiti, thank you for being my dearest friend and for all your support, prayers, and encouraging words. I love you so much, my favorite Miss Anderson. Gracelyn, thank you for cheering me on every step of the way and for reminding me every week to give myself grace on my writing journey. LiliAnna, thank you for celebrating each step of progress I made and for always putting a smile on my face. Frank, thank you for showing me that strength is shown in how you rebound—I'll never forget that text message and how it helped me get through a really tough day. Brennen, thank you for reminding me that it's okay to need help and ask others to come alongside me during my hardest seasons of life, and for always telling me you couldn't wait to read my book when it released. Eden, thank you for always checking in and asking me how my writing was going and for your genuine care and interest in my book —that meant the world to me. Bee, thank you for cheering me on, praying for me, and helping me write my book blurb—I'm so grateful for your support.

For my writer friends – Ellen McGinty, thank you from the bottom of my heart for reaching out to me and telling me about your editing services. This book wouldn't be what it is without you. Ashley Clark, thank you for taking the time to message with me and answer writing-related questions and for the notebook you sent me with these hand-written words on it that helped me to keep going: *Always hold on to your dreams.* Alissa Zavalianos, thank you for Zoom calling me and answering so many questions I had about the self-publishing world. Even though we've never met in person and live a world away, you are one of the kindest people I know. Thank you for endorsing my book—your words humbled and honored me, and I'm thankful beyond words for your friendship. To my amazing Instagram community, thank you for rallying around this writer girl in Japan and for all your encouraging words.

For my Savior – Thank you for being in the broken places with me. Thank you for showing me that even when you feel far away, you are ever close. Thank you for giving me the words to say when I ran out of my own. Thank you for giving me the strength to push through health challenges and keep writing every day. Without you, I never would have written this book. Thank you, always and forever.

# ABOUT AUTHOR

Caitlin Miller has long dreamed of spinning words into stories. She draws her storylines and characters from things most familiar to her: her relationship with God, her family and friends, and life lessons she's learned along the way. She is a part-time college student, part-time English teacher in Japan, and part-time author. When she's not writing, Caitlin loves to read books and post reviews on Instagram. Aesthetics, historical fiction, and green tea are just a few of her favorite things.

Made in the USA
Las Vegas, NV
09 March 2022

45257099R00203